K. J. SIMPSON

HVALDI

Twisted
Pencil

Edited by Nikki Busch Editing
Cover and Book Design by K. J. Simpson

ISBN: 978-1-7351896-0-4 (paperback)
ISBN: 978-1-7351896-1-1 (e-book)

Published by Twisted Pencil Books
www.kjsimpsonbooks.com

For Nelson.
Thank you for always believing in me more than I believe in myself.

CHAPTER ONE

All great societies fall. Those are the words my father often told me, but sometimes that wasn't true. In the years spent on archeological digs, I'd found that some cultures seemingly disappeared with barely a trace of evidence indicating where they went or what led to their demise. I often thought about these things during our long trips from one place to another. The rhythmic rocking of the wagon allowed my mind to drift off as I gazed out at the horizon.

With the sun high above and hardly a hill in sight, I could see for miles. In the distance, poking out above the treetops were the remnants of one of many giant decaying cities from the last great society of man. Some referred to that era as the Disposables or the Age of Destruction. Either was a fair description. Little of what they built was designed to withstand the test of time. In another few hundred years, I doubted much would be left of even their biggest, megalithic cities as nature took them back. I'd seen cities from cultures thousands of years older that were in far better condition.

Many believed they'd advanced beyond their means, which finally led to their demise. Most of their big cities were declared "no-go zones," thanks to a growing number of stories that claimed simply breathing the air could kill you if you ventured too close. It was hard to imagine what kind of technology could poison the air to the point that even centuries later, it was still unsafe. No one knew for sure what caused their ultimate downfall, only that it reduced the human population around the world to a fraction of what it had been. A person from that time would likely look at us as being quite primitive.

One thing was for sure—they populated the world much more than any who came before them. Cities from small to massively large could be found at every corner of the globe. Settlements were discovered even in the coldest, hardest-to-reach regions.

In the last decade, failed research about our last great society turned the profession of historian and archeologist, a once reputable title to hold, into a forbidden trade. Scientists' and researchers' attempts to redevelop machines and medicines from our past sadly ended in disaster, costing tens of thousands their lives.

Since then, digging into the past was declared illegal across the planet, punishable by lengthy jail time or, in some cases, death. But that didn't stop those who devoted their lives, literally, to uncovering our ancient past.

Even before I was born, my mother and father dedicated years to the study of ancient cultures that lived in northern Europe. Their favorite culture was known as the Norsemen or, more commonly, Vikings. The history, lore, and belief system of this culture so attracted my parents that they traveled thousands of miles, following the Vikings' migration through different countries.

After their profession was made illegal, my parents continued their research in secret, traveling under assumed names and titles for their own safety.

It wasn't until my thirteenth birthday that my father's focus changed while we were on a dig of a small Viking village in the far northern part of Europe once known as Norway. Earlier that year, we had lost my mother to an illness that nearly killed me as well. After some coaxing and flat-out begging on my part for him to continue his research as my mother would have wanted, he finally gave in. Less than a week into the project, I came across an artifact that wasn't Viking but from a culture far older.

2

From the time I could walk, I started helping with excavations. The uniqueness of each culture's writings fascinated me, and I soon became fluent in translating many of the writings we encountered, even learning to speak a few as well. I knew the moment I brushed the dirt off the small tablet that we were dealing with a different race of people.

For the first time since my mother's death, there was excitement in my father's eyes when I showed him the rare find. From that moment on, he was addicted to discovering the identity of these unknown people and where they went.

Due to the dangers of our profession, we never spent more than a few weeks to a couple of months at a single site to avoid attracting suspicion. We returned several times over the next two years until we learned the site had been found and destroyed. All that remained of the village's existence were a few artifacts we took with us and the notebooks we filled with translations of inscriptions we found on walls and statues.

Five years later, after traveling across six countries, we discovered three more small villages belonging to this ancient culture known as the Hvaldi. Unfortunately, they had been reduced to rubble long before we reached them. What little remained was not legible enough to help us learn more about the culture.

That is, until a couple of months ago when my father received a letter from his friend and colleague, Banks Rothmann. In it, he stated he may have found a city belonging to the Hvaldi in a land he called Idaho. At the bottom of the letter, Banks included a copy of an inscription his team had uncovered.

My father recognized the symbols and handed it to me to translate. Having been studying their writing relentlessly for years, I reviewed the symbols and wrote out what it said. Once satisfied I had it right, I read it aloud to him. *Bless the life and beauty of Balfjord; her fertile grounds and vast landscapes are unmatched. Never has it been seen, a realm with so many unique creatures and races of man. May they continue to grow and prosper for all time.*

After reading the passage, there was no doubt in our minds of what he had discovered. A chill ran up my spine as I read it to myself again. I found their choice of words strange and was curious about the place they called Balfjord. It only increased my excitement to learn more.

Before my dad could finish his letter accepting Banks's invite to join the dig, I had my bags packed and ready to go. He would always laugh and shake his head at my enthusiasm.

I'd spent all of my life researching the past and it was rare for me to be around kids my own age. Those I did encounter treated me like I was from another world because we had so little in common. Even having a simple conversation with them was difficult. What interested me I couldn't talk about, and what interested them seemed childish. It was no wonder I was ready to go so quickly.

With Banks's assistance, we made our travel plans and obtained forged paperwork so we could safely make the trip without any issues. My father's documents identified him as Professor Gunner Bastian, a botanical scientist on sabbatical to research the healing properties of pollen and sap from various species of pine. Traveling with him, his adorable intern, me, Semmi. Short for Gersemmi. Given to me by my mother, which she once told me was an ancient Norse name meaning *treasure*. This trip was just in time for my eighteenth birthday. I couldn't imagine a better present than finding more information about such an amazing race of people.

***

Shouting from ahead brought my mind back to reality as the wagons came to a stop on the dirt road. The tall grass on either side swayed with the breeze and the wind rustled the surrounding trees.

"What's going on?" my dad yelled up to the driver.

The man pointed toward a blanket of dark clouds in the distance. Before he could answer, a bright flash of lightning spiderwebbed over the clouds sending a bolt down to the ground followed by the growl of thunder.

"We're going to have to stop to allow the storm to pass," the driver shouted back as another crack of lightning lit up the dark clouds. "It's not safe to be out in a thunderstorm." The cool breeze picked up and the smell of dampness filled the air.

My dad nodded and waved to the man before leaning over to me. "Sorry, sweetie. We'll get there eventually."

"It's all right. Besides, I could use a break to stretch my legs." He gave me a hand as I jumped down out of the wagon. I had never been to this part of the world and found myself lost in the many ruins we passed, wondering what untold stories they may hold about the people who once lived there.

While the wagons were rounded up and horses secured, I took a moment to look again at the old city. In the distance were a big cluster of structures and a few jagged tops of tall buildings, which had partially collapsed centuries ago. It was hard to imagine how so many could live that close together.

"The driver said it was called Springfield," my father said from behind. Not having heard him walk up, I jumped at the sound of his voice, and he laughed at the gasp and quiet squeak I let out.

Shaking my head, I pulled my long brown hair up into a bun to keep the wind from blowing it in my face. "Springfield, huh." I crinkled my nose, a little surprised by the name.

When I thought of spring, I pictured a meadow full of flowers and butterflies, not a cluttered mess of buildings and roads where there was probably no room for a flower to grow.

"Is it safe to be this close?" The stories of the poisonous air came to mind.

"Yes. I was told this city is. I guess there's a bigger city to the north called, um"—snapping his fingers, he tried to remember—"Chicago. That's it. That's the one we have to stay clear of. I heard some of the others saying that if you can see it, you're too close."

"Good to know," I said, raising my eyebrows. "I can't wait to get far away from any of these big cities." That's what I loved about researching ancient sites—they were usually located off the beaten path, away from the larger, dangerous cities.

"Me too." He smiled and gave my shoulder a squeeze. "Come on. Let's get inside a tent before the rain hits."

Another crack of thunder boomed nearby as we hurried to our tent, barely making it before the sky opened up and it began to pour. The heavy drops beat against the side of our canvas tent, but we were nice and dry inside. Two cots were set on either side and our bags were placed at the foot. My dad lit a lamp as I organized my things and got some clothes out for tomorrow. When I turned around, there was a small tin box sitting on my cot.

"What's this?"

"Your birthday present." He sat down across from me as I placed the box in my lap and gently opened the lid. "It was your mother's. She found the box on one of our first trips together and kept little things she liked inside."

I smiled at the items it contained. On top was a lock of my hair, the barrette she always wore, and a bracelet I remember my father giving her for her birthday the year before she died. My eyes became glossy as I lightly ran my fingers over the items.

"I know it's not much, but..." my dad started to say.

"No," I interrupted, wiping a tear off my cheek. "It's perfect. I love it."

He stood up and moved to sit next to me, wrapping an arm around my shoulder and kissing the side of my head. "I miss her too. I know she would have wanted you to have this."

With his help, I took the remaining items out, which my father said she found during their travels. There was a card that had a picture of a beach on one side with the words, *Aloha from Hawaii,* and on the other someone had written, *Soaking up the sun on the beach. Wish you were here. Love, Mom.* I knew someone else's mother had written it, but it was something she would have said. I could picture her walking along the beach letting the water splash over her feet as she turned her face to the sun and let the wind blow through her long hair.

Underneath the card was a picture of a strangely dressed woman leaning against a big shiny, red machine. In her hand, she held a small object, which she was looking at while laughing.

"Why did Mom keep this?" Not knowing much about our most recent *ancient* society, outside of the horror stories about the dangers of the big cities and my dad's ranting about all the garbage they left behind, I was often confused when I saw pictures of their everyday objects.

"Because it made her laugh." He reached up and tucked a loose lock of hair behind my ear. "I know you haven't heard many stories about this era besides the doomsday theories I go on about. Your mother and I were more interested in cultures older than this one. But the things they had!" He opened his eyes wide and let out a breath, then pointed to the big red object the woman was leaning against. "This was called a car. It was an amazing machine that people could sit inside, and it moved without the use of horses or other animals. It's how they traveled."

"No way." My mouth gaped open. "What kind of machine could do that?"

"One we haven't figured out how to recreate yet. Supposedly, they were pretty fast too. Much faster than a horse." Upon hearing of such a contraption, I could only imagine the look on my face, but it made him laugh.

"That's crazy. I think I'd be too scared to move that fast."

"You think that's crazy…" He leaned closer with a half smile. "This object here in her hand was called a phone. I saw one in a museum once. They said there were numbers on the front and if you pressed a combination of them, it would connect to another one of these devices. Then you could talk into it and a person thousands of miles away with another phone could hear you and talk back."

"What?" I gasped, thinking he was spinning a tall tale, but he swore it was true. I couldn't imagine such a device.

"Pretty strange, huh?" He laughed. "Every phone had a number, so you could contact people. I find it amazing that by pressing a few numbers, you could bridge two of these together and have a conversation with someone far away like they were standing right next to you. They had all sorts of inventions. We've recreated a few of the less complicated ones but haven't come close to any of these. So many of their inventions ran off an electrical power source we hardly understand."

"Maybe it's better we don't," I suggested. "I think I'll be perfectly happy traveling by horse and writing a letter if I need to communicate with someone."

"You're just like your mother." He chuckled. "You look like her too."

"But I got your eyes," I replied, looking up at him and batting my eyes. "Mom always loved your dark brown eyes."

"Thank goodness you didn't get my hair." He snorted, taking off his hat to show off his bald head. Standing, he moved over to his cot to lie down.

"Yes, I don't think I could pull off the bald look as well as you."

"Hey, I used to have nice golden-blond hair," he said, rubbing the top of his head. "I think putting up with you and your mother's stubbornness scared it away." He gave me a wink and lay back against his pillow.

"Key words being 'used to,' and we're not that bad," I said, only making him laugh more. My dad was in his mid-forties and was a stout man with broad shoulders. What hair he lacked on his head he made up for on his face. Most of the places we went had little in the way of washrooms, so he always had somewhat of a scruffy beard but kept it trimmed short as much as possible.

Before moving on to the next item in the box, I noticed a date in the bottom corner of the picture of the woman: September 27, 2046. It was taken not long before the time when it was believed their society began to decline. Now, over four hundred years later, the cities that they

8

inhabited were still so polluted it could take another four hundred years before they were safe enough for researchers to discover the truth. That is, if the laws about digging into the past ever changed.

Next in the tin box was a black-and-white photo of my parents when they were younger. My dad, with a head full of hair and dressed in a similar outfit to the one he wore now, stood behind my mom. He sported long trousers with a long-sleeved shirt and a dark vest. His sleeves were rolled up and you could still see dirt on his pants and hands. My mom, on the other hand, was as beautiful as I remembered her. Her long hair was draped over her shoulder and she wore a long dark skirt with a simple white blouse.

"I didn't know you and Mom had a picture taken," I said, getting my father's attention. He opened his eyes and sat up to look.

"I didn't know she still had that." He crinkled his brow in disbelief and took the picture from me. "It's not often you find a place that has a photographer. We got lucky." He told me the story of how he and my mother came across a man whose wagon had a broken wheel. My father helped him fix it, and as a way of thanking him, the man took a picture of them. "It's the only picture we ever had taken. Your mother wanted to get a picture of you when you were little, but by that time, it was so expensive to get one, we couldn't afford it." His voice trailed off and I could tell it was something that saddened him.

Tapping his leg to get his attention, I said, "Maybe when we get to Idaho, we can find a place to get our picture taken."

"Absolutely." He smiled and nodded. "We will. No matter the price. I would like that."

He leaned over and kissed the top of my head. I stared at the picture for a few minutes longer before setting it down next to me, so I could remove the last item from the box: a thin, flat piece of stone wrapped in a cloth. Taking it out, I held it under the lamp to get a better look. It was a portion of a small, broken tablet containing the last few symbols of what looked like four lines of text.

"Dad, where did Mom get this?" As I stared at the unique stone, my heart began to race.

He lifted his head and looked over at the stone I was holding. "Oh, she had that for years." He sat up again and took it from me to look at it more closely. "She told me she found it when she was on an excavation site with the university. They're Viking runes—you should know that."

"Actually, they're not," I corrected him as a smile spread across my face. "I know the runes, Dad. These are similar, but they're not Viking. They're Hvaldi." I was so excited as I explained that these were the runes they used for rituals, blessings, and to decorate statues or artifacts. "They're almost identical to the Vikings' runes with the exception of these." I pointed to faint dots and notches around each symbol and bounced a little on the edge of my cot while my dad examined the stone.

"Are you sure?" he asked, putting on his glasses.

"Very sure." Having studied the Hvaldi language for years now, I could tell the differences.

"I always thought they were Viking, but the randomness of these few symbols here didn't make any sense. I thought it was a different dialect maybe." He handed the stone back to me. "Do you know what it says?"

"Not without the rest of the tablet." I shook my head and bit my lip. "It's strange though. The Hvaldi didn't use these for writing. This is the first time I've seen more than a couple symbols together. Usually it's only two or three. Here, each of the four lines has six symbols and the bottom one has seven. You can tell that there were probably more on the missing piece, wherever it is. I don't know why they would place so many in one line."

"You'd know better than I would," he grunted as he pulled his boots off. "I've never seen anyone excel like you do with learning different languages, written or otherwise. How many do you know now? Eight? Nine?"

"Fluently?" I smiled. "About a dozen or so written but only seven spoken."

"That definitely beats my four."

We both laughed, and he told me about how my mom had gone back to look for the rest of the tablet many times but never found it. He said for some reason, she thought it was important somehow and refused to let it go. I had to admit that the tablet was unique. The stone was smooth and thin but remarkably hard. I couldn't recall where I had ever seen another tablet like it.

I placed all the items back inside the tin box and tucked it away in my bag. Morning would be upon us soon, and we planned to set out again before the sunrise. Blowing out the lamp, I said good night and lay down.

CHAPTER TWO

The rest of the trip took longer than expected. Several late spring thunderstorms made passage over the mountains slow, but I didn't mind. As we moved west, the land changed so much I stared at it wide-eyed as it morphed from miles of flat open plains to tall mountains and beautiful forests. I saw animals I had never seen before. Some of the wagon drivers laughed at my amazement, but I appreciated their helpful insight on which ones to stay away from. Who would've thought such a horrible smell could come from such an adorable little creature? The name suited it well: skunk.

Even though I was eager to see the dig site, I was glad for the delays, so I could take in the sights of this new land and the few small towns we stopped in, especially when we entered the area they called Idaho. The townspeople were friendly and I made simple conversation but knew better than to say too much. I kept with our cover and people seemed surprised that we had come from so far. A couple of women in one shop giggled when I talked, but I wasn't sure why and didn't have the opportunity to ask, figuring it was because I was foreign and acted differently from them.

As we traveled north, we came across a canyon with a meandering river at its base and the most magnificent waterfalls. One of the wagon train hands told me there was an even bigger canyon far to the south. I could only imagine how beautiful it must be. Although the trip felt as though it was taking forever, the closer we got to our destination, the faster time seemed to pass.

My dad's friend was waiting when the wagons rolled into the little town nestled at the base of the foothills. We passed an old wooden sign carved with the name Eagle Valley right before the wagon came to a stop. It was much smaller than the other towns we passed through. Fewer than a dozen structures lined the main road with signs indicating what business they were used for.

Banks waved at my dad and called him by his assumed title so as to keep with our cover story. He wasn't a very tall man and his round belly jiggled as he hurried over to us, nearly losing the glasses that were perched on the end of his nose. His brown suit appeared old and well used, and when he removed his round hat, it was clear he shared my dad's same haircut.

"Professor Bastian, sir," Banks said and shook my dad's hand. "It's good to see you. This must be your intern Semmi. Good to finally meet you both." He smiled and gave me a wink as a way of acknowledging this was just for show.

"Dr. Rothmann." My dad nodded and turned to help me down. "Sorry for the delay. We had some unexpected storms. I hope you didn't have to wait too long."

"No need to apologize." He waved his hand in the air. "This time of year, the weather is unpredictable."

Our bags were transferred to a wagon Banks had waiting nearby. He offered us the opportunity to stay a night in town, but we were both eager to leave, with the exception of one thing we had to take care of.

As promised, before heading out we found a photographer to take our picture. When I saw the cost was more than a new pair of shoes, I tried to object, but my dad insisted, saying it was important to him.

It didn't take long, and I liked how the photo captured us as we were. Nothing fancy. Like the picture of him and my mother, I sat in a chair next to him wearing my normal traveling clothes: a pair of brown trousers and a simple cotton shirt. I quickly braided my hair since that was my dad's favorite.

I placed the picture in my box next to the one with him and my mom, then loaded up in Banks's wagon to leave. Once we were a good distance outside of town, my dad seemed more comfortable asking questions.

"Gunner, the inscription I copied in my letter is only the tip of the iceberg." Banks grinned. "We've uncovered dozens of structures and are finding more every day. The city is huge, and it's been incredibly preserved. If it is the Hvaldi, there are enough inscriptions to hopefully keep Semmi busy for months."

"Oh, it is," I blurted before my dad could say a word. "Sorry, Dad."

"You're sure?" Banks stared at me with wide eyes, his mouth gaping open.

I looked at my dad who nodded for me to continue. "The inscription you wrote in your letter, it's without a doubt their language," I explained. Pulling the letter from his pocket, my dad handed it to me to read.

Banks shook his head and smiled as I finished. "I can't believe it." His voice was low. "For a while, when you told me about the Hvaldi, I thought maybe you misidentified a Viking settlement. I'm sorry I doubted you, my friend."

"Don't worry about it. I doubted myself. It was Semmi who kept me from giving up. She insisted that I was right." He smiled and squeezed my shoulders. "And she also discovered recently that a broken tablet my wife carried around for years had Hvaldi runes carved on it, not Viking."

"Really? What did it say?"

"Unfortunately, without the rest, it's hard to say," I admitted. "The Hvaldi had two forms of writing: their standard one for recording information and another runic style for spiritual purposes."

"What's the difference?"

"Their standard form is structured similar to ours." I explained how each mark was like our letters and a group of marks made up a word.

"The other form is very different. Each symbol, like the Viking runes, has a specific meaning. Some have more than one meaning depending on what it's used for. I assume, like the Vikings, they probably have a name or sound too, but without ever hearing their language, I don't know." I pulled the tin out of my bag and removed the stone for Banks to see.

I babbled on for what felt like hours explaining the meaning of the various runes, but why they put so many in one line still baffled me. It didn't make any sense when all other carvings containing runes were limited to only a few characters. Banks tried to give me some reassurance that maybe the runic symbols he'd seen would give me some insight.

We spent the rest of the day going back and forth about all the information we'd discovered. Banks asked my dad to tell him about the European village even though he'd heard it before, years ago, so he could tell us about the similarities in the structures, and I explained what I knew about their people and culture.

The farther north we traveled into the mountains, the more magnificent the forest became. In areas where the trees left enough space for sunlight to touch the ground, green grass and brightly colored wildflowers grew. If this land looked as amazing during the time of the Hvaldi, their decision to live there was understandable.

It took nearly a day to reach Banks's base camp. It had been set up in a small clearing in the forest and consisted of a large tent in the center, which doubled as a mess hall and meeting area. On the east side, over a dozen tents were designated as sleeping quarters for the team, although most were empty. And on the west side of camp, two tents about three times the size of the living quarter tents were set up as labs. Each was filled with microscopes, chemicals, test tubes, and plant samples to complete the deception.

"I can see how you've been able to keep this place a secret for so long," my dad said, looking around wide-eyed at Banks's attention to detail. Everything looked well used yet was neat and organized.

"Yep. It hasn't been easy. People are nosy, and we get visitors every few weeks. We have a smaller camp at the dig site. We'll head there tomorrow morning." He further explained how they regularly rotated staff between sites and kept the lab stocked with new samples.

By the way he showed us around camp, you could tell he was proud of how he and his team worked to put all this together. He smiled and took delight in showing off the authenticity of the labs. I had yet to ever see a science lab and took his word for it without asking too many questions. A few of the tools were similar to ones I'd used when cleaning or examining artifacts, so that was a relief in case I needed to look like I knew what I was doing.

He showed us to a tent where we could clean up and get a good night's rest. All the sleeping tents were made of heavy canvas with see-through mesh screens and a wooden floor. Because of the rain and cool weather, they were raised about two feet above the ground on short stilts. Inside, there were two small cots with blankets and pillows already made up as if someone was living there, along with a desk in the corner. Banks explained that because some of their regular visitors liked to walk through camp, they did their best to make sure everything looked as if it was being used.

Within ten minutes of setting our stuff down, my dad was snoring away, but I was too excited to sleep. Thoughts of what we might discover raced through my head: more information on the day-to-day lives of the Hvaldi, their spiritual beliefs, and maybe, what happened to them. Most ancient cultures, if you dug deep enough, left behind little clues that would allow you to speculate on where they went or what led to their downfall. But not the Hvaldi. It was as if they'd disappeared.

The village my dad and I studied in northern Europe showed no signs of war, famine, or disease. No human remains were found either. All that they left were the numerous stone inscriptions and a few artifacts. It was like they packed up and moved without leaving a forwarding address.

With my mind filled with questions that I couldn't yet answer, I laid my notebooks out on the small desk to get in some further studying, but first I decided to wash up. It had been a few days since I had been able to do a thorough cleaning, and I could feel the dirt on my skin. There were a couple of buckets of water by the tent door, so I grabbed one and some clean clothes.

Around back there was a wooden platform with a curtain, which Banks said we could use for washing. It wasn't much, but it was better than trying to clean up on the road. Within a few minutes, I was finished and threw on my clean clothes. I wrapped my wet hair up in a bun and headed back inside.

My dad was still snoring away, so I sat down at the desk, and for what felt like the thousandth time or so, I reviewed the inscriptions I copied from the village to make sure I was ready. What we found wasn't a lot, but it was enough to decipher their two writing forms and to learn a little about their culture.

The next thing I knew my dad was shaking my shoulder. "Semmi, wake up." I had fallen asleep with my head on my arm across the desk.

"I'm awake," I muttered, lifting my head and trying to focus.

"You know you should've tried the cot. It's pretty comfortable."

"Oh, ha ha." I laughed and rolled my eyes at his sarcasm. It wouldn't be the first time I'd fallen asleep studying and I'm sure it wouldn't be the last. I gathered up my loose notes and notebooks and returned them to one of my bags. "How soon until we leave?"

"I don't know." He peered out through one of the screens to see if anyone was moving about. "I haven't seen Banks yet, but I'm sure he'll be by soon. We had better be ready."

It only took a few minutes to pack our things and set them by the door. I pulled on my boots and checked my hair. It was still a little damp from last night, and I plaited it up into a neat braid to keep it out of my face. The morning air was a bit nippy but was refreshing and smelled of pine. As I threw on my favorite gray jacket, Banks hurried toward our tent. His hands were full of books, papers, and branches, along with a sack dangling from one of his arms.

"Gunner! Semmi! Are you up?" he yelled between breaths.

My dad opened the flap door and helped grab a few of the items before he dropped them. "What's going on?"

"We have some unexpected visitors." The worried look on Banks's face told us that they weren't the friendly type. "Your arrival must have spurred some curiosity. Semmi, spread these books and samples out on the desk." I followed his instructions as he tossed a couple of papers on each cot, then asked us to lay out a few clothing items so the tent looked lived in.

Once he was satisfied, we followed him over to one of the lab tents. He gave quick directions on how to look busy and left us to meet the visitors. We were no strangers to putting on a show for whatever cover we were playing, but botany was a first for us.

My dad handed me a notepad and pencil from one of the tables and told me to act like I was taking notes for him. He grabbed a collection of tree samples on slides and headed over to the microscope. Had I not seen a doctor use one to look at blood samples when he came to examine my mother and me, I wouldn't have known what it was. "Where did you learn to use one of those?" I asked quietly in case our guests were near.

"Your mother." There wasn't time for him to tell the story with our guests nearby. From the sound of Banks's voice, he and the guests were moving closer.

When they arrived, we were ready to go. My dad was peering through the scope and I was next to him reading the notes already written on the pad and holding up a vial containing some golden sap.

"Professor Bastian," Dr. Rothmann said loudly and walked over to us. "Gentlemen, may I introduce Professor Bastian. He traveled all the way here from Europe to work with us, and this is one of his brightest pupils, Semmi."

My dad set down the slides to shake both men's hands and made a few comments about the beautiful landscape. There was a short, awkward silence as the two visitors looked around the room before the taller of the two stopped and looked down at me.

"Semmi, did you say? That's an interesting name." His voice was nasal, and he glared down his pointed nose. He was a slender gentleman with a long gray jacket over a matching suit.

"It's short for Gersemmi, sir." I tried to sound cheerful only to see him raise an eyebrow and let out a long breath. "It's a family name," I lied. Given his behavior, I doubted he cared.

"I see." The man's expression didn't change as he continued to look me over. "And what is your last name, Ms. *Semmi?*" Hearing the way he drew out the *S* in my name made my skin crawl.

"Foster," I answered quickly and forced a smile, hoping he wouldn't ask any more questions. For a brief moment, there was concern in my dad's eyes. We had only gone over my forged last name before we left Europe. Thank goodness I noticed the man was holding our travel paperwork in his hands with our names written at the top where I could see them.

"Mm-hmm." He rolled his eyes but finally looked away and scanned the room. The way he eyed everything was like he knew this was all a hoax but couldn't prove it. I only hoped it stayed that way.

"And how are you getting along with your studies, Professor Bastian?" another gentleman asked, sounding much more joyful and somewhat interested in what we were doing. He was a shorter, round man with rosy cheeks and a matching gray suit.

"Ah," my dad stuttered and cleared his throat. "Well, we've barely gotten started." He hated talking to people he didn't know, and it often made him nervous, but to my surprise, he answered the man's question and didn't trip over his words too much. "We arrived last night. I plan on looking through what's here first before heading out to collect our own samples."

"And what exactly are you looking for?" the rosy-cheeked man inquired.

When my father didn't immediately answer, I jumped in, handing the man the vial I was holding. "The possible healing properties contained in the sap of different species of pines," I rattled out our cover story, trying to sound excited.

"All I know about sap is that it's very sticky," the man joked as he looked at the vial.

"That it is." I giggled, holding up my hands, which had a few spots of sap on them from laying out the samples in our tent. I often found my bubbly personality helpful when talking to people who were obviously trying to interrogate us. "But there are some good qualities to it too that we believe can help with certain skin conditions. We're hoping to be able to refine it, so we can hang on to the good stuff and remove all the sticky stuff for easier use."

"Excellent, excellent." Clapping his hands, he gave me a wink. "We'll leave you to your work. It was wonderful to meet you both." He shook both our hands again, giving me another smile, then tipped his hat before turning to leave. "Thank you, Dr. Rothmann. As usual, you keep a tidy camp. We'll see you again. Come, Mr. Forbes," he called to the tall man.

"Mr. Walker, sir," Mr. Forbes said, trying to stop the cheery man from leaving. His hesitation to leave made me nervous and it was clear to see he wasn't nearly as satisfied with the conversation as the other man. He crinkled his nose and looked us both up and down.

"I said we're leaving," Mr. Walker repeated himself more sternly, then left the tent. The tall man, Mr. Forbes, huffed before following Mr. Walker out.

"I don't think Mr. Forbes was too convinced," I whispered to my dad.

"Yeah, well let's hope Mr. Walker's opinion is the only one that matters." He let out a breath and relaxed his shoulders now that the two men were gone. "At least he seemed satisfied. You did great by the way. You are much better at talking to people than I am."

"Why thank you, Professor Bastian." I teased, trying to mimic how Banks pronounced his name.

We continued poking around the lab looking busy in case they came back for a second look. Some of the open books and pamphlets had interesting information about trees that I'd never known. After about ten minutes, Banks returned with a couple of muffins in his hands.

"I'm so sorry about that," he said, handing us each one of the muffins. Sweat was beaded up on his forehead giving away the nervousness he must have felt with our guests' untimely arrival. "I wasn't expecting them for a few more days and had hoped to be gone before they came."

"No worries, my friend," my dad answered. "We're used to it. I'm guessing they're regular visitors?"

"Every week," Banks groaned and rolled his eyes. "A few of the others and I have actually had to start studying botany to keep up our cover. The big guy, Mr. Walker, seems happy with everything going on and doesn't ask too many questions, but not Mr. Forbes. He began coming up here a few weeks ago and is beginning to make me uncomfortable."

"Is it safe to still be here?" I could hear the concern in my dad's voice. In our experience, a person like Mr. Forbes would be our cue that it was time to move on.

"As long as Mr. Walker is in charge and happy, we're good," he assured us.

"I'll keep my fingers crossed," I said. Now that we were this close to learning more, I didn't want to be forced to leave. From what I had heard already, this would be the find of a lifetime.

"Well, at least they're gone and we can get moving." Banks's excited smiled returned as he smacked my dad on the shoulder. "I don't know about you, but I can't wait to hear your interpretation of the city we've uncovered. And I can only imagine what Semmi is going to be able to tell us after she's had a chance to look at everything. This is going to be fantastic!" He hurried out of the tent shouting for us to meet him with our bags at the northern edge of camp.

***

It didn't take long for us to grab our things and meet up with Dr. Rothmann. He was waiting with five horses saddled and ready. There was a horse for each of us to ride and two packed with supplies to take out to the dig site.

A couple of his team members helped tie our bags to the saddles and gave me a hand up. It had been a while since I rode a horse but was assured the gelding they assigned to me was a great trail horse and didn't spook easy. He was all brown with white socks and had been given the name Poko for his mellow disposition.

We headed north following a well-worn trail. Banks explained to keep with their cover as botanists, they set up several collection areas along the trail with tables, wagons, and tools. We passed two before reaching a fork in the trail.

Banks told us there were collection areas down each of the three forks. He made it clear that with Walker and Forbes's increased visits, they had to be careful. More than once the two men had asked to see the collection sites, but luckily, they hadn't desired to travel farther than the second area.

Taking the trail to the left, we continued on. I tried to pry more information from Banks about the city, but he became tightlipped, insisting that I wait until we get there.

"Then," he added, holding up a finger and pointing it at me, "you can tell *me* about the city we found."

CHAPTER THREE

By early afternoon, there was finally a break in the thick forest. Through the trees, I could see piles of dirt and what appeared to be a stone wall. My heart raced, and I kicked Poko to go faster.

Reaching the tree line, I stopped to take in the sight before me. The entire area along the southern side of a narrow river valley had been dug up to reveal dozens of stone buildings. Excavation had recently begun on the northern side. This city was far better preserved than the village my dad and I had uncovered and was more than three times its size.

"What do you think?" Banks asked when he and my dad caught up. "Is it Hvaldi?"

"Without a doubt." I took a couple of deep breaths and even pinched myself to make sure I wasn't dreaming before speaking again. "See the inscription carved in the large stone at the entrance?"

"Yes."

"It reads *Peace and welcome to all those who pass through these gates,* and the round symbol below it there"—I pointed to an engraving with three dots and what looked like a bird with outstretched wings inside a circle—"that's the symbol of the Hvaldi. The same symbol was carved at the entrance to the village we found in Europe."

"Incredible," my dad whispered as he stared across the open meadow.

Banks allowed us both to take in the sight before guiding us over to the camp along the southern edge of the city where we could leave the horses while he showed us around. An older gentleman named Cooper hurried over to help and assured us he would have all our things placed in one of the tents they had prepared for us. I grabbed one of my notebooks and chased after Banks and my dad who had already headed toward a nearby stone path leading into the city.

Most of the dig team was at the far end of the city clearing the dirt from some newly discovered structures. Only a few wandered here and there, logging artifacts and recording inscriptions for translation. We were introduced to Tessa, one of the individuals gathering artifacts. She was around my father's age with curly blond hair and a long blue dress. She gave her map of the city to Banks and let me look at the notes she had taken of an inscription located on one of the buildings she was cataloging.

Her notes were thorough, and all the symbols were well drawn, making it easy for me to quickly translate.

"I hope I wrote everything clearly enough," Tessa said, peeking over my shoulder as I read her notes. "I tried to copy it down exactly as it was inscribed."

"It's perfect. Much better than my handwriting."

She smiled at my compliment and giggled a little. "I've seen this same inscription in several other buildings. I think they were homes."

"I would say you're correct. This is a blessing on the home and the people in it for health and happiness." Again, Tessa giggled after I spoke. "Did I say something wrong?" I remembered the way the women in one of the towns we passed through had chuckled and I knew it couldn't be a coincidence.

"I'm sorry," she said. "It's your accent. It's adorable. I'm not as well traveled and it's not often I get to meet someone foreign."

I smiled, a bit embarrassed. Being from Europe, my dad and I pronounced words a little differently, but I hadn't thought much about it. Having traveled so much, I was used to hearing all the crazy ways people enunciated their words, and being a lover of language, I found it fascinating. Although, it never occurred to me that we were the ones with the accent.

"And what a beautiful accent you have, my dear," Banks chimed in, giving Tessa a wink that made her cheeks turn rosy. He unrolled the map of the city. "Gunner, with your help and Semmi's translations, I think we can improve our map."

"Absolutely." Taking out his glasses, my dad examined the map Banks and his team had put together. Written next to each structure was what they believed each building was used for and the overall size and relation to the other buildings around them.

"Do you have a place where you've organized the artifacts?" I asked.

Tessa's face lit up. "Yes," she blurted with a big smile. "We have six large tents." She pointed to a row of tents past the camp near the city's outer wall. "All artifacts and copies of inscriptions are separated by their location. There are also larger maps posted in each tent."

My dad smiled and complimented Banks and Tessa on the detail taken to organize everything. He gave instructions for Tessa to show me to the tents while Banks led him through the rest of the city, so we could get started right away.

As much as I wanted to finish my tour, I was far more eager to examine the items and writings found. I would have plenty of time to see everything later and would most likely wander out to each building during my studies.

Tessa wasn't a tall woman, but her joyful personality made me even more excited to be here. She showed me from tent to tent as she told me all about how they first discovered the site. As she explained earlier, all items from each building were set together with detailed drawings of where they were found. She provided me with a stack of blank paper, a can filled with pencils, and a hard board for me to write on.

"Is there anything else I can get you?"

"Um, some water would be wonderful."

"I'll have someone bring you over a pitcher and some food. I'm sure you're starving after the long ride. I'll come back and check on you in a little while." Before leaving, she expressed how excited she was that we had finally arrived and how Banks hadn't been able to stop talking about us since he received word that we agreed to come. I only hoped we could live up to her expectations.

***

In less than two weeks, I had every inch of the city memorized. Between my dad and me, we accurately identified each building and its function. Their living quarters were grouped in clusters surrounding the central city, which consisted of a park or gathering area, monuments, and what was probably once a beautiful temple.

The only portion of the buildings that had degraded away were the roofs. My dad speculated they must have been made from wood, which would have rotted away a long time ago, but anything made of stone, including the roads, walls, and statues were well preserved. Most recently, we discovered evidence of farming areas along the outskirts of the main town.

While my dad took charge of the team uncovering new areas, Tessa and I managed the collection and cataloging of all new artifacts. From sunup to sundown, I spent all my time racing between the tents and the buildings, taking notes and translating everything as fast as I could write it down. I learned more in the first two weeks than I did on all the trips to the European village. It was difficult to know where to start when asked questions about what the Hvaldi were like.

Banks spent most of his time between the dig site and the research camp to maintain the team's cover story. I was asked to return on one trip and had the pleasure of seeing Mr. Walker and Mr. Forbes again.

Fortunately, Banks had brought in new sap samples and had them displayed in the lab making it easy for me to look busy. I put on my best smile for Mr. Walker who seemed overjoyed at the portrayed progress we were making. Mr. Forbes, on the other hand, still looked at me like he was trying to analyze my every word, but he didn't pry and even laughed at a few of my jokes.

Thank goodness their visit was short, and to our collective surprise, they didn't even show up the second week, which we took as a sign that they were starting to relax with our presence. My dad encouraged Banks not to let his guard down. From past experience, we knew better than to get too comfortable.

"What do you think I should do?" Banks asked my dad during our weekly meeting.

"If they don't come next week, I would suggest going into town," my dad said. I had seen him do things like this before. He liked to call it recon work and explained that it would provide an opportunity to gather information about what people felt about our *research* up here. "Put together a fake package of samples to send back to Europe for further analysis and while you're there, stop by their office. Make up an excuse or something."

"All right, I'll make the arrangements," he agreed and changed the subject, looking to Tessa and me for his weekly fill of the Hvaldi. "Ladies, what new things have you uncovered?" Clapping his hands together, he gave us his full attention.

"Where do we start?" I boasted, holding up a stack of notes I'd brought to the meeting.

I let Tessa go first. Since our arrival, I had been working with her to better understand the Hvaldi writing. She grew excited when she was able to share with Dr. Rothmann what she'd discovered on her own. I could tell by their shy flirting that she liked him, and it made her feel good to impress him with what we found.

"For their time, they were a very advanced race with extensive knowledge of nature and the movement of the planets and stars. They even had a rudimentary calendar that followed the seasons and cycles of the moon." Tessa scooted closer to Banks to show him a drawing of the calendar we discovered. "From their carvings and what few inscriptions that actually describe them physically, we believe they were a tall race with very fair skin and either blond or possibly white hair."

As Banks leaned closer, Tessa's cheeks turned a rosy red and she started to stumble over her words, which was my cue to jump in. "As for their belief system"—I said, getting a silent thank-you from her for the quick recovery, so no one noticed her nervousness—"we know they were spiritual and have found many inscriptions offering blessings to the land, their people, and animals. No specific names to gods or goddesses. But," I paused and looked at Tessa who could barely stay in her chair, "we don't think they're human or at least not from here on Earth."

"What?" my dad and Banks gasped in unison.

"Hear me out before you start thinking anything weird," I said, holding up my hands for them to save their questions till I finished.

"Too late," my dad muttered, rubbing his hand across his face.

"Dad."

"Sorry, sweetheart." He waved his hand for me to continue. "Please explain because I'm confused. Why would you think they're not from here? From their statues and the description you gave, they seem human."

"In appearance, yes." I explained that like the Vikings, the Hvaldi believed in the existence of different realms. I mentioned how I first suspected this when I read the passage Banks wrote in his letter to us.

I shuffled through the papers in my lap until I found my notes from the temple describing the four realms they believed in: Norranheim, home of the great forests; Lothenbrow, described as being covered in ice and snow; Polarious, which the Hvaldi called their home; and Balfjord, the realm of man.

"So, this is Polarious?" Banks questioned, indicating the city.

"No, this is Balfjord," Tessa corrected him and tried to further explain some of the inscriptions from the temple at the city center. "They came here to observe and learn about man. Us."

"Wow, that's remarkable," he murmured, eyes wide. "Um…so is…ah…is this city, is it older than the village you found?"

"No," my dad quickly answered. He was the master when it came to the construction of ancient city structures. Before our trade was outlawed, many archeologists sought out his expertise to confirm the age and society associated with a site they had discovered. "If I had to speculate, they were built pretty close to the same time. This one may be slightly newer."

He explained the similarities in the building styles, but that this city showed a few advanced building techniques. He went on to tell how the Hvaldi were far more innovative builders than any other society that existed at the time and even many that existed thousands of years after they vanished.

"And speaking of advanced structures"—my dad sat up straight, holding his hands—"we uncovered another housing sector across the river to the west of the valley just inside the tree line." This was incredibly interesting and would be the first set of structures found outside of the main city.

"I wonder why they built housing all the way over there when everyone else either stayed within the city walls or right outside of them by the farming areas," I commented.

"I was hoping you could tell me once we've cleared enough dirt away for you to get in and start examining."

We agreed that my dad would take a team to clear the area and plans were made for me to set up a temporary collection tent near the new buildings. Tessa asked about bringing in more help, but given our recent arrival, they believed it would be too dangerous. Things were finally starting to calm down at the research camp and the fewer visitors who came, the better. For now, we would have to make do with the people we had.

***

That night was the first time since our arrival my dad and I made it to our tent before one or the other was already asleep. It was nice to have a chance to talk to each other without everyone else around. Before coming here, I always looked forward to our evening conversations. It was when we made the most progress piecing together all the information we'd found.

Our tent was identical to the one we stayed in at the research camp. When my dad walked in, I was sitting on my cot with pages of notes scattered all around me. He picked up a couple of sheets that had fallen on the floor and handed them to me.

"Thank you." I smiled, my eyes droopy.

"You look exhausted," he said.

"I am." I yawned. "But this is the only time I have to review my notes."

"Okay, I won't bother you."

"No, please," I said, reaching out and grabbing his hand before he moved away. "I've missed talking with you."

"Me too." He squeezed my hand and sat down across from me. "I've been thinking about the Hvaldi's belief in different realms. Banks thinks that maybe they thought of realms as different continents, but I'm not so sure."

"And I agree." A wave of energy came over me. "In some of their inscriptions, they talk about the different realms and the beings that live there. We haven't been anywhere or seen anything like them."

Digging through my scattered notes, I found one that described the creatures of the different realms. "Here." I handed the translation to him. "It says the beings in Lothenbrow are beast-like in appearance with long horns and gray or white fur, but they are gentle beings possessing great knowledge of building with ice and stone. Here." I gave him another page. "It talks about the beings in the great forests of Norranheim and mentions that while everything else there is huge, they are rather small, not quite the height of a man, with dark gray or brown skin and light hair. They're called Norranians and have vast knowledge of plants and animals."

I paused for a moment to take a breath, not realizing how fast I was talking. In my excitement, I forgot my dad couldn't read their writing and I had yet to write down the translations of my latest inscriptions.

He stared blankly at the pages I had handed to him. "Um, sweetie, I know a little but not enough to read this."

I laughed and apologized. "All I'm trying to say is I know we haven't been everywhere in the world, but I've read about a lot of places and I'm sure the Hvaldi are *not* talking about anywhere on Earth."

"Have you found any mention of how they traveled from one *realm* to another?"

"No." Slumping my shoulders, I set my notes aside. "I feel like I'm on information overload. Normally I read through my notes four or five times or more. Here, we're finding so much every day, I don't even have time to write a translation down."

"You don't have to solve it all this week. Take your time," he said, trying to help me think positively. "Maybe this new area will have some answers."

We talked for another hour sharing what we'd found lately, going back and forth, from the buildings and their construction methods to the artifacts and inscriptions left behind. Our conversation helped to build a better picture of their society in my mind. I made more progress that evening in understanding the Hvaldi culture than I did all week. We agreed to sit down together every night before going to sleep to discuss our day. Even my dad said he learned a lot from our talks.

"Thank you, Semmi," he said and blew out the lamp hanging overhead.

"For what?"

"If it wasn't for your encouragement to get back out here after your mother died, we wouldn't be here." He smiled. "You're going to find all the answers. I can feel it."

"I love you too, Dad." I lay back and looked up at the top of the tent, still thinking about our conversation. "Dad?"

"Hmm?"

"Do you think maybe they simply went back to their realm?"

"Anything's possible. Good night, sweetheart."

CHAPTER FOUR

Unburying the outlying housing site was a painstaking chore for everyone. Roots had grown through the stone walls making some of them highly unstable. The team had to take extra precautions to prevent getting hurt by falling rocks. In other areas, large boulders had damaged structures when they tumbled down the mountain hundreds of years ago.

There was one thing that still didn't make sense to me. Why hadn't we found a cemetery? Or *any* remains for that matter? Even if the Hvaldi left, as we speculated, you would think a city this size would have a sacred place commemorating their dead. Yet I found nothing that mentioned how they honored their lost loved ones.

Even more interesting about this section of housing was the number of artifacts we found. In the main town, only a few of the houses contained items, such as jewelry, weapons, or degraded pottery. The majority were empty. Most of the beautiful statues were found in the temples and shops. But this area was filled with all sorts of items from everyday life: tools, bits of fabric, and an abundance of pottery, some of which were completely intact. It was as if they left this area in a hurry and only had time to grab what they needed.

"Semmi!" I heard my dad shouting. "Semmi!" I stepped out of the collection tent and found him running toward me nearly out of breath. "Come on, you have to see this." He waved for me to follow.

"What is it?" I asked, chasing after him down the path to the far side, near a steep cliff.

He didn't explain, only encouraged me again to hurry. The smile on his face told me he must have found something big. We rounded the corner and came upon a small tunnel leading into the side of the mountain. One of the team members was holding a lantern and handed it to my dad. "This opened up when we removed some of the stones." He ducked his head and led me down the tunnel. "You're not going to believe this."

After a dozen feet or so, he stepped aside and handed me the lantern. Up ahead, there was an opening and I hurried forward. As the lantern lit up the room, I froze. It was like a time capsule that had been sealed for thousands of years inside the mountain. Everything was in perfect condition as if it was recently placed in there.

"Oh my goodness." Covering my chest, I struggled to breathe. The sight before me was unbelievable.

On the far side was a wooden bed with a reed mattress still covered in exquisitely stitched blankets. A doll in a pretty blue dress lay upon the pillow, and a couple of pairs of female shoes were set neatly on the floor at the foot. Shelves were chipped into the stone and filled with all sorts of trinkets. Several rings, a bracelet, and a necklace with a round pendant hung on a tree branch and a clay bowl was filled with gemstones and a few coins. In the opposite corner was a desk, and when I saw what was sitting on top, I almost passed out.

"Is that what I think it is?" I murmured, still unable to move.

"I haven't opened it, so I don't know if it's a book or journal. Either way, it's an incredible find."

Finally, I walked over to the desk, taking care to step around the woven rug on the floor even though it looked brand new. The colors were beautiful greens, blues, and yellows. When I reached the desk, I touched the front cover of the leather-bound book, halfway expecting it to disintegrate. To my surprise, the leather cover was soft and pliable. Being sealed in this room with little to no airflow had slowed deterioration of the items inside. Most everything seemed the same as it was when the entrance became blocked off.

"Which is it?" he asked, looking over my shoulder as I carefully opened the front cover.

The writing on the first page was a message to the owner. "It's a journal." I translated the dedication and read it aloud. "*To our beautiful daughter Jorunn. May your life be filled with more adventures than can fill the pages of this book. Love, Mom and Dad.* This is incredible."

"I know." He squeezed my shoulder as I picked up the book.

I carefully thumbed through the pages. Jorunn had filled nearly each one with the experiences from her everyday life. This was, without a doubt, the most valuable find ever. To actually hold the written words of a Hvaldi in my hands was an extraordinary gift. I turned and looked at my dad nearly in tears.

"I know," he said again, giving me a hug. "I can't wait to hear what Jorunn wrote about her life here."

***

That evening, during our nightly discussion, I translated and read aloud the first entry in Jorunn's journal. Not knowing how their calendar related to ours, the date she wrote in the corner didn't tell me much about how long ago it was written.

> *Father had hoped to celebrate my birthday at our new home, but the wind and poor weather made our travels west to this new land take longer than expected. I myself am thankful to finally be on land rather than the sea. It's still winter and snow covers the ground, but it won't be long before it starts to melt. I'll miss our old home in the mountains by the sea. I loved to watch the colors dance through the night sky. Father has promised that there will be mountains at our new home and a river instead of the sea.*
>
> *Our time here is coming to an end, and within a few more cycles of the stars, it will be time to leave. I can't*

say I'm looking forward to leaving. This realm is the only one I've ever known in the eighteen cycles of my life. Mother has told me stories of the other realms and can't wait to return. I hope it's as beautiful as she describes.

The people of man in this new land are very interesting and friendly. They all have dark hair and eyes and wear animal skins for clothing. A young girl named Anooka said she was told it was my birthday and gave me her doll as a gift. In return, I gave her one of my bracelets. She showed me how to weave my hair like theirs. I'll always remember her smile when I look at the doll.

"I wonder if the home she's traveling from was the village we found. It was near the sea," I said, remembering how I enjoyed lying outside at night to watch the Northern Lights.

"It seems possible. It's amazing to think this was written when they landed on this continent and met the native people living here during that time. We could've traveled across some of the same places she did on her way here."

"I know." I closed my eyes and pictured the mountains and plains we traveled through and wondered if my experience was anything like hers. The ruined cities from the last era of man wouldn't have existed yet and I tried to imagine how magnificent this land would be without them. "I can't even describe how amazing it is to read this."

"Especially since she's your age," he added. "Is that the necklace from Jorunn's room?" He pointed to the necklace I was wearing.

"Yes." Touching my fingers to the pendant, I added, "I thought it was pretty. I can put it back if you like."

"No." He smiled. "It looks beautiful on you." He leaned forward and took a closer look at the two runes on the front. "What do these mean?"

"That's a good question." I took it off to show him. The first symbol looked like an oddly shaped *C* with three dots down the back. The second was an *M* shape with notches at the bottom of each leg of the *M* and a dot centered between arches. "Together they would mean something like *look within,* but separately, the first one means mystery or something hidden and the second is the self. So…" I shrugged.

"Hmm. Interesting. Maybe it's a spiritual thing."

"Maybe."

Because my dad was as interested in hearing her entries as I was, we both agreed to read one each evening during our nightly discussions. I couldn't wait until tomorrow. Reading her first entry, we learned that she may have once lived in the small village we first discovered in northern Europe. I was also eager to hear more about the other realms and why their time here was coming to an end.

My dad had many of the same questions. He read my mind when he said that if the realms weren't different landmasses as Banks thought, but completely different worlds, how did they travel to them? *How indeed?* I only hoped that maybe the answer to that question was somewhere in the pages of Jorunn's journal.

***

Over the next few weeks, business continued as usual: uncovering, cataloging, and translating. By now, from watching me translate, my dad had become more familiar with the Hvaldi writing. This helped to speed things up. He was able to let me know which inscriptions I could skip over and others I needed to work on. "We make a good team," I heard him say on more than one occasion.

As promised, we sat together every night to talk about our day and read one of Jorunn's entries. With every entry, we learned something new and it enriched our discussions.

To hear about the life of a woman my age, in her own words, who lived thousands of years ago was eye-opening. It was like getting to know a new friend whose everyday frustrations were often those I could relate to. My dad liked the way she described the landscape as she traveled west, recognizing a few land formations she mentioned in passing.

We learned that the city was already being constructed when she arrived with her family and the others from her village. Those from her village chose to build their homes outside of the main city to have more space to graze the sheep they brought with them and grow crops the way they were used to from their previous home.

Jorunn wrote that she fell in love with this place. The mountains, trees, rivers, and meadows she mentioned were nearly identical to the way they looked now. If we had existed at the same time, I wondered if we would have been friends. Very seldom were there kids my age on a dig site, and when I went to an actual school, I struggled to get along with the others. I couldn't remember the last time I had a friend who wasn't old enough to be my parent.

Visiting the native people in the area was one of Jorunn's favorite things to do. She explained that the Hvaldi were the first to discover the existence of the four realms and set out to visit each one to learn of the cultures there. According to her, this wasn't the first time her people had come to our realm. The first few times, the native cultures were still too primitive, and their stay was short. This time, they spent over three hundred years traveling across vast distances to see how people living in different lands progressed.

Jorunn wasn't the only Hvaldi born here. There were many who had never seen the realm her people called home. In more than one entry, she expressed her nervousness about having to leave. When I was young, I shared those very same feelings every time my dad told me it was time to move. After a while, I got used to it. I wished I had a permanent place to call home and couldn't remember the last time I had my own room or wasn't living out of a suitcase.

"Dad?" I asked after finishing another of Jorunn's entries. "Did you and Mom ever have a home?"

Leaning back against his pillow, he let out a long breath. "A long time ago. You were only a baby." By the look on his face, I could tell the memory saddened him, but he continued. "Before our profession was declared illegal, we would often stay several years studying an area. Then, for a time, it felt like we were running for our lives, barely able to stay two or three days in one spot before things finally calmed down." He described the small home they had made of stone and mortar. I was too young to remember but was able to picture it in my mind and it was charming.

He looked over at me and for the first time, I think he realized that I didn't know what it was like to have a home. His shoulders dropped, and he looked down at his feet for a moment before looking back. "I'm sorry, sweetheart," he said. "I thought you enjoyed this."

"I do." It wasn't my intent to upset him or make him feel that I didn't love the research. "I only meant that it would be nice if we didn't have to move so much. I really like it here."

"Maybe someday we won't have to."

I hoped he was right. For as long as I could remember, we were always on the move, never staying more than a few weeks in one place. We had been here for more than a month now and our small group felt like a family. I found comfort in not constantly having to be on alert for suspicious people. With the addition of an awning and a couple of chairs my dad made for us to sit outside together, our little tent had started to feel more like a home, and I dreaded the day we would have to leave.

CHAPTER FIVE

The next day, Banks arrived from the research camp with some devastating news. Their cheery visitor Mr. Walker had passed away and Mr. Forbes had taken his place. He explained during his visit Mr. Forbes was even more unfriendly than usual and insisted on walking through every tent in camp. Before leaving, he threatened to bring an entire crew up to the camp to thoroughly investigate what was going on up there, promising to tear apart everything if he had to.

Plans were immediately put in place to vacate the area. Now, instead of digging, people worked frantically around the clock to cover the site. All the artifacts and information we had collected were loaded into wagons. Within two days, the first group left heading west; another left the next day heading north.

By the end of the week, the third group made their departure leaving only Tessa, Banks, my dad, and me. There was no way to cover everything, but we made sure to seal Jorunn's room feeling that it was the most important find of all. Hopefully someday we would be able to return to continue our research.

During our desperate attempt to save what we could and take as much as possible, my dad pushed me to read as much as I could of Jorunn's journal. With every free moment, I read, not even bothering to write any translation. I prayed that somewhere she left a clue about another Hvaldi village that we could head toward.

When I reached the end of her journal, my heart sank. I'd found nothing about any other cities or villages. The last entry she wrote was about it being time to leave and that even though she would miss her home here, she was looking forward to this new realm—her people's home.

"What? No!" I snapped at the journal. "I know you, Jorunn. You wouldn't have left this behind for someone to find unless you had a reason." Throughout her journal, she had written detailed information about her people beyond her daily activities, obviously in the hopes that someday it would be found.

I flipped through the last few empty pages looking for something that would help us. On the very last page, a long series of runes were written along the inside edge of the page. I turned the journal sideways to read it. That's when I noticed the binding on the back cover was missing some of its stitching. Gently, I lifted the loose edge to reveal a folded piece of parchment tucked inside.

Slipping it out, I laid it open. A letter.

"Are you all ready?" my dad asked, walking up to me with his pack over one shoulder.

I was sitting on the wagon while we waited for Banks and Tessa to return from the research camp. They were bringing the last of the horses to hook up and we planned to head farther west in hopes of finding a place to lay low while we decided where to go from there.

"Uh-huh," I mumbled, tapping my bag next to me. "You gotta see this." I waved to him, unable to take my eyes off the letter.

"What is it?" he asked, looking down at the parchment in my lap.

"It's a letter from Jorunn. Listen." I took a deep breath and began reading.

> *To whomever finds this,*
> *Honestly, I don't know why I'm doing this. Even if*
> *it gets found, you may not be able to read it, but I hope*

41

with all my heart that you can. If you don't know already, I am a Hvaldi. We're not gods. Nor are we responsible for your race's creation. I could no more tell you about your origins than I can tell you about mine.

We are simply people like you, only a little more advanced. Or at least we were. By now, we may be very much alike. Only we came from another place. A realm called Polarious. I'd describe it to you, but I've never been there. I grew up here. With your people.

What I can tell you is that we were the first to discover the existence of the four realms and traveled to them to learn about their inhabitants. If you've read my journal then you know about them already. What I haven't told you is that the realms are closer than you may think. We didn't fly through the stars to get here or have some divine machine. We walked.

The realms aren't different worlds, at least not exactly. They are worlds but on a different plane of existence, which means they are all right here. Traveling from one to another is easy if you know what to look for and how to open the door. Once you know, going from one to another is as easy as walking across a bridge.

You've seen these places before. A strange growing tree, a unique land formation, or maybe a cave where one shouldn't be. Places where the borders are close together, the land develops in strange ways. You simply need to open the door and walk through.

You have my journal and if you're reading this, then you have what you need to come to Polarious. Find us so we can grow together once again.

"Did I miss something?" my dad asked. "Where did she say how to travel between realms?"

"She didn't exactly." I turned the letter over to see if anything was written on the back then reread the last few paragraphs to make sure I didn't overlook or mistranslate anything, but I hadn't. "I don't understand. She told us how to find locations where the doors are but not how to bridge them together."

"Maybe—" A gunshot rang out through the forest before he could say another word. I followed his eyes across the open river valley when movement caught my attention. Banks came running out of the trees.

"Gunner! Semmi!" he yelled and waved his arms. "Run! They're coming."

Another gunshot overpowered his shouts. Banks slowly stopped, and his shirt turned red as he fell to the ground. I froze at the sight. He was dead, and all I could do was stare at him lying there.

"Semmi, hurry!" my dad yelled, but I couldn't move or respond. "Semmi!" He grabbed my arm and pulled me off the wagon. His eyes reflected his fear.

"Is he dead?" My voice shook.

"We gotta go, Semmi," he ordered, not answering my question. Quickly, he grabbed our bags out of the wagon and shoved mine into my arms.

Looking back at Banks, I saw more movement in the forest. A dozen or so men came out, some walking, others on horses. They looked around and spotted us on the other side of the river.

"Over there." One of them pointed in our direction. I knew there was no time. I tucked the letter in Jorunn's journal and slung my bag over my shoulder.

"Come on," my dad yelled and grabbed my arm, pulling me after him as we headed into the forest. "It'll take them a few minutes to cross the river. We can get ahead of them."

"Where are we going?"

"Anywhere that'll get us away from them. If we get far enough away, we can hide until they leave."

His voice was tight, and his breathing harsh. I always knew how dangerous it was to do what we did, but in the past, we'd paid closer attention to everyone we came across. My dad was good at reading people and made sure we left long before a situation turned into one of panic. Whenever people started asking too many questions or paying closer attention than they should, we knew we had worn out our welcome. But we had become so comfortable here, and with Banks running the research station to maintain everyone's cover, we had no idea it had gotten to this level.

We headed upriver staying inside the tree line to conceal ourselves as much as possible. We needed to put as much distance as we could between them and us while we had the chance. As we ran as fast as we could, my dad only stopped briefly to look back and see where the men were. Their shouts were farther away than before. My dad kept telling me not to look back and pushed me ahead of him.

"Are they still chasing us?" I asked when we stopped for a moment to catch our breath. My hands were shaking as I clutched Jorunn's journal to my chest.

"Yes, but I don't know if they know where we are." He breathed heavily as he looked through the trees. "We need to get to higher ground." We set off again heading away from the river and into the mountains. Climbing up was slow, but the tall trees and rocks would better conceal our trail, making it harder for them to track us.

My legs burned with fatigue, but the fear of what might happen if we got caught kept me from stopping. I pushed through the pain of my aching muscles. The image of Banks falling to the ground spurred me to keep running.

After we climbed over a ridge, my father told me to stop so he could watch for a moment. It was difficult to hear anything over the beating of my heart. Putting a hand on my knee, I tried to control my breathing, but my lungs burned. I closed my eyes and thought about Jorunn's letter to help calm my mind. Her words about bridging two realms so you could walk from one to the other kept repeating in my mind.

When I opened my eyes, a huge oak tree growing out of a small ledge up the hillside on the far side of the ridge caught my attention. Its roots draped over the side of the little ledge like a curtain. *An oak tree in the middle of a forest of pines. Very strange.*

"Something unique where it shouldn't be," I whispered, still staring at the tree. "How do you bridge two places together?"

"What did you say?" my dad asked, hearing me talking to myself as he scanned the forest behind us.

The sound of his voice reminded me of the night he gave me my mother's tin box for my birthday. The picture of the woman holding the phone popped into my mind and I remembered my dad telling me about how pressing a number combination into the phone would connect it to another phone. "A phone number, that's it," I blurted.

"What?"

"Come on." I pulled on his arm to follow me over to the oak tree and stopped in front of the curtain of roots. Opening Jorunn's journal, I flipped to the back page where she had written the series of runic symbols.

"Semmi, we have to get moving before they catch up to us." I could hear the urgency in his voice and knew there was no time, but something told me I was right about this.

"Let me see your knife." I held out my hand.

"Semmi!" He glared at me and shook his head but finally handed me the knife. "Make it fast. We don't have time for this."

"Remember in her letter she said the doors were located where you found a unique land formation where it shouldn't be?" I pointed to the tree.

"Yes, but she didn't say how to open the door." He looked back over his shoulder again.

"I think she did. I think that's what this is." I pointed at the series of runes along the inside edge of the back page. "I wouldn't have found the letter if I hadn't seen these." Kneeling in front of the roots, I used his knife to carve the runes in the dirt exactly as Jorunn had written them.

The moment I finished the last symbol the ground beneath it vibrated and I scooted away, holding the journal to my chest. I looked back but my dad wasn't watching, he was still looking behind us for signs that our position had been discovered. Voices carried through the trees, growing louder as the men came closer to our location.

"We need to go, Semmi." My dad grabbed my arm but didn't pull.

When I looked up at his face, his eyes were fixed on the tree. I turned my head and saw the roots pull apart revealing an opening in the mountain. Through the opening, instead of darkness, I could see the sky and clouds.

"It worked!"

I nearly forgot we were running for our lives until my dad gripped my arm and yanked me up to my feet. We ran toward the opening as a shot rang out, hitting the mountain nearby. I looked back as we passed the roots and saw the opening begin to close behind us.

For a moment, I felt weightless and could see my world getting smaller. My father's hand still firmly held my arm and I turned to look ahead, but before my eyes could focus, I stumbled forward into the sunlight. Still holding on to the journal, I hit the ground and tumbled over my backpack. I looked back at the tree to see the last glimpse of our world disappear before the giant trunk twisted back together.

"You did it, Semmi!"

"It worked. Dad, we're in Polarious. We're in another realm."

CHAPTER SIX

My father helped me to my feet and for the next few minutes we didn't speak, only stood there looking around at this new world. The tree we traveled through was once three different trees that had grown together. The bark was a blend of smooth tan intertwined with dark brown. The different-colored branches extended out in all directions, with a combination of large bright green leaves and a mesh of orange and red smaller leaves. It was the most beautiful tree I had ever seen, and it was the only one like it in the area.

On the ground in front of the tree was a flat stone with an inscription carved in the top. The line closest to the tree was written upside down, to be read as you entered this realm and it simply said, *Welcome Home.* The other inscription was meant to be read before leaving and it read, *Open your heart and mind to those you will encounter during your travels.*

Green grass covered the ground with little bunches of blue and red mushrooms growing here and there. Ferns with dark green and yellow leaves grew around numerous trees and rocks, their vibrant purple and blue flowers dangling in bunches.

The other trees in the area were unlike any I had seen in all my travels. The color of their bark ranged from dark brown to nearly white. Some had brightly colored flowers in pink, purple, blue, and yellow, while others had leaves in all shades and sizes. The air even had the scent of spices like cinnamon, ginger, and cloves.

As the minutes ticked by, the forest got used to our presence. Birds began chirping and moving about. Bugs played a little tune and what looked like dragonflies fluttered through the air. One pure white butterfly with a yellow body flew up to our position and circled us a few times as if trying to figure out who we were.

"Semmi, do you see anything that might tell us which direction we should go from here?" My dad's voice was nearly a whisper as he looked around us.

"So far, the stone in front of the tree is the only thing with writing on it." I walked around the magnificent tree, searching the vicinity for any other inscriptions or markings.

"Well, let's spread out a little to see if we can find something and meet back here in a few minutes," he said. "But don't go out of voice range. We don't want to lose each other in a place we're unfamiliar with."

I nodded and tucked Jorunn's journal inside my pack. My dad went to the east and I took the west, or at least what we thought was east and west according to their sun. The sky was blue with white clouds like our home. Polarious, though, had two moons visible above the horizon: a smaller one that looked similar to our moon back home and another larger one with a blue hue and two rings around it.

"Amazing," I whispered in awe at this incredible place. From reading Jorunn's journal, I had tried to imagine what Polarious would look like, but this was beyond anything I pictured.

I wandered a short distance from the tree, looking for evidence of a road or trail and checking the stones I came across for any markings. As I walked about, I stopped to look at all the brightly colored bugs crawling on the leaves or flying around. Most were similar to ones I had seen in my world, but their size and colors were different.

A bird flew by—at first glance, it was the same shape as an eagle or hawk but was only the size of a hummingbird. Its body was pure white with bright blue and pink tail feathers, and its legs and beak were orange.

"Semmi!" My dad's shout carried through the trees. "Over here. I found something."

Following the sound of his voice, I found him some distance away. He had located an overgrown cobblestone road heading in a north-south direction and standing next to it was a tall stone. On its face were carvings of what he believed were possible city names with arrows pointing in opposite directions.

"Do you know what it says? I didn't recognize the symbols."

"I think you're correct that they're city names." Names were always the most challenging for me to translate from Hvaldi because they were unique to their language, but these didn't appear too complicated. "This one would be something like Storm Wood or Storm Forest maybe, and that one Thorn Valley." I pointed at each word. "What do you think?" Unfortunately, there were no numbers to tell us which was closer, making it a difficult decision.

My dad pulled a coin from his pocket and held it out to me. "Heads, Storm Wood and tails, Thorn Valley."

I smiled and took the coin. Before flipping it into the air, I said a little prayer that it landed on the closest one and that someone would be there. The coin landed on the ground and we both looked down at it.

"Heads it is," my dad stated. "To Storm Wood."

The stone road looked like it hadn't been used in centuries or longer. Tree roots and bushes grew over and through the stones, pushing them up in awkward directions. In a few places, it was so deteriorated that it took time to determine which way to go. When reaching the top of a nearby ridge, we caught a glimpse of the city in a small valley, several miles from where we started.

After everything we had been through, I found myself looking behind us and through the trees every few minutes thinking that at any moment, I'd hear another gunshot or see someone chasing after us. I couldn't shake the feeling of being watched. The image of Banks falling to the ground flashed through my mind over and over. I could see the red blood on his shirt as if he was standing right in front of me. My heart beat faster every time I replayed it. I looked down at my hands and they were shaking.

When we first arrived, the sight of this new place took my mind off our recent events but now, after walking for hours, it resurfaced. The closer we got to the city gates, the more nervous I became until I told my dad we needed to stop for a moment and I sat down on a nearby log. Clenching my fist, I closed my eyes.

"Semmi, are you all right?" He knelt in front of me, turning my face up toward him.

"I need a moment." I inhaled deeply. "Everything seems to be catching up to me and I…" I took another shaky breath and my eyes started to water. He wrapped his arms around me and held me tight.

"It's going to be all right," he said as I rested my head against his chest. "I know this is a lot to take in, but I'm here. Okay?"

I nodded. "I'm sorry. I keep seeing Banks fall after they shot him, and I wonder what happened to Tessa. Do you think they killed her too?"

"I don't know. I hope not." Looking into his eyes I could tell he was doubtful of her survival. Mr. Forbes didn't seem like someone who would take prisoners. I prayed that the others who left before us would share what they found so what we discovered would not become lost.

"I keep feeling like we're being watched, and I'm scared something's going to happen."

"We're going to be okay," he told me again and squeezed my shoulders. "You're in shock and need time to calm down. When we get to this city, we'll find a nice spot to set up camp for the night. Okay?"

"Okay."

***

At the entrance to the city, a large black stone was set on the side of the road, the city's name engraved on its surface. While I had hoped someone would be there, it looked like my prayers wouldn't be answered yet. The town was abandoned and looked as though it hadn't been lived in for hundreds of years. The walls of the various structures were primarily made of a very light gray stone with other vividly colored blocks randomly set in, adding a bright flare to the city. The layout was similar to the village we found in Europe resembling a wagon wheel grid pattern, with all the main roads leading to the city center.

We located an area of the city that my dad identified as housing and found a building we could use to make camp. I helped gather some wood for a fire and my dad set a couple of snares to hopefully catch some dinner.

While it was still light, I looked around at a few of the statues and carvings. There were some inscriptions but nothing relevant to where we should go from here. The city center had a beautiful statue of a woman riding a horse like creature with a long shaggy coat and thick horns that twisted out of its head. Below her was an inscription that I read aloud: *"Your past doesn't define you. It's what prepares you for the future that has yet to come. Make each day better than your last."*

Again, it felt as though we were being watched. The hairs on the back of my neck stood up. Several times I heard the crunch of rocks, but when I scanned the area, I didn't see anyone and all I heard was the wind and the chirping of bugs. Nothing out of the ordinary caught my eye— if you could call any of this ordinary.

Maybe my father was right, and I needed some time to calm down to allow these feelings to pass. The door to this realm was closed and the men chasing us had no way of reopening it without the runic code. We were safe for now. At least I hoped we were.

Returning to our camp, I went to work gathering wood to get a fire going. After neatly organizing the smaller sticks and dry twigs, I retrieved a knife and flint stick from my bag. With a few strikes, I had a small flame started. By the time my dad came back, the fire was ready for cooking. In his hand was a small tan, white-and-black-striped creature.

"What is it?" I asked, staring at the strange-looking animal.

"Um, well." He cocked his head to one side and held it up for me to see. "It's a bunny-eared raccoon that barks like a dog and hops."

51

"Wow, that's interesting."

"I hope it's edible." He sounded a little uncertain. "Without knowing these creatures, I have no idea what's good to eat and what's not."

"I guess we'll find out." I took the animal from him and skinned it to put on the fire.

That evening was quieter than our usual evenings together. My dad hardly said a word, and after our meal, he sat for a long time staring down at the flicker of flames that danced over the coals. Clearly he was feeling the loss of his friend and nervous about the unfamiliar world we were exploring. It wasn't until I said I was going to lie down that he finally spoke again.

"Tomorrow, we'll look through the city to see if we can find anything that can give us some direction," he said in a low voice. "If we find something, we'll head where it says, and if not, we'll keep following the road to the next town."

"It doesn't make sense, Dad."

"What doesn't?"

"Jorunn's journal said they came here"—I shook my head—"but this city doesn't look any newer than the one we were at."

"From what I've seen, it may be older," he commented, looking around at the stone walls that made up the house we were in. "Keep your hopes up. Our world, or realm," he corrected himself, "is very big. We haven't gone that far yet. This may be an ancient city like we have back home. We'll find someone eventually."

He bid me good night and gave me his coat to keep warm. At first, I couldn't get my mind off the men who were chasing us and wondered what happened to Tessa. Again, the feeling of being watched swept over me and I pulled my dad's coat tighter around me. *Stop thinking about it, Semmi.*

I stared at the hot coals, watching the fire swirl inside them. It seemed like I had barely drifted off to sleep when I heard Banks yell for us to run in my dreams. I awoke with a start and my dad quickly clamped his hand over my mouth and held me still.

"Shh," he whispered in my ear. "There are people here and they look like soldiers." He slowly removed his hand and listened to their movements.

The thud of marching soldiers and horse hooves echoed off the stone walls. They made no effort to hide their approach.

"How many?" I asked.

"I don't know. A dozen. Maybe more from the sound of it."

"Come on out!" a man shouted. "We know you're in here. There's no sense in hiding."

My dad threw on his coat and handed me our packs. Pointing to a small opening created by a nearby collapsed wall, he told me to crawl inside and stacked up some branches and pulled a few vines off a nearby wall to conceal the entrance.

"Stay quiet and don't come out no matter what you hear until I come back for you."

"But Dad—"

"No arguing, Semmi." He held his hand up for me to stay put. "We don't know these people, and I want to make sure it's safe first. You are more important to me than anything. I love you."

"I love you too." I watched him walk away and sat, listening as best I could.

After a few moments, I heard my dad announce himself to the soldiers.

"I'm coming out!" he said loudly. "I'm unarmed, and I mean you no harm."

"Who are you and what are you doing here?" asked the man who shouted earlier.

"My name is Gunner," he answered. "I got lost and was trying to find someone to help me."

"Well, Mr. Gunner," the man hissed, "you have trespassed on sacred ground."

"I'm very sorry, sir," he responded. "As I said, I got lost in the dark and didn't know where I was."

"Lies," the man growled. "Everyone knows this is sacred ground and there is a punishment for trespassing."

"I'm from far away. I didn't know. I'm very sorry. I'll be happy to leave if I could get pointed in the right direction." I could hear the desperation in my dad's voice as he pleaded with the soldier, but it didn't seem to have any effect on the man.

"Oh, you'll be leaving all right. Seize him."

I covered my mouth to keep from screaming as I listened to the scuffle and heard my dad apologize and beg for them not to take him.

"The law is the law," the man snapped. "Is anyone else with you?"

"No."

My stomach turned and my heart pounded. Keeping my hand tight over my mouth even though I was gasping for air, I wanted to scream but knew I had to keep quiet or they would know he lied and we would both be taken prisoner.

Several men shouted in compliance with the man's orders and the sounds of horses and footsteps muffled other voices. I heard my dad yell but couldn't make out what he was saying in the commotion. Tears trickled down my face and I bit into my hand until I tasted blood. My body shook as I tucked back farther away from the opening. Soon everything was quiet again. I waited, trembling with fear as to what to do. I closed my eyes and prayed quietly for help.

My thoughts were interrupted by the faint sound of footsteps coming toward my position. I gasped as I heard the crunch of rocks and pulled my knees to my chest. *Stay quiet*, I heard my dad's voice in my head. One set of steps was all I could make out, and they were getting closer. Peering through the branches and vines, I finally spotted someone walking around.

A man wearing all black with a long black cloak came into view as he stepped around our camp. He was tall with short dark hair and looked not much older than me. A bow and quiver were slung across his body, and a long sword hung from his belt. He kicked at the smoldering coals in our fire a couple of times and looked around.

"You can come out now," he said loudly. "I know you're here. The others are gone."

Unsure if he actually knew where I was, I stayed quiet and watched. Was he trying to coax me out, so he could drag me off to wherever they took my dad? Still, he didn't move, only stood there waiting and looking around.

"What was it your father called you? Semmi was it?" he asked. I almost gasped when I heard him say my name. If he knew my name, then he had been watching us. I wondered for how long. "Please, I won't hurt you or turn you over to the authorities, if that's what you're worried about."

I waited a few more moments, watching the man. Finally, I decided that if he hadn't told the soldiers about me already, there was some other reason he was watching us. I pushed the branches and vines aside and crawled out. He turned toward me and looked me up and down before speaking again.

"Did I pronounce your name correctly?" he asked. "Semmi." His voice was deep and authoritative but had a kind tone.

"Yes." I nodded. He looked at me for a long moment as I stood there in silence holding our packs.

"Where are you from?" he asked. "And don't say faraway like your father did. I've traveled all over and have never met anyone with your accent or someone who didn't know this area is sacred. Where are you really from?"

His face showed no emotion when he spoke, no smirk or frown, but his eyes seemed kind and unthreatening. He didn't move toward me or make me feel as if he was going to pull his weapon on me, so there was no sense lying to him.

"Ear…" I started to say but realized if he knew anything about the realms, he wouldn't recognize the word *Earth*. I quickly corrected myself and answered his question hoping he would know the name of my realm as given by the Hvaldi. "B-Balfjord."

"What did you say?" he asked slowly, turning his head to one side almost as if he was surprised by my answer, but his expression never changed. Only his eyes narrowed slightly.

"Balfjord," I said again. "We came from Balfjord. Is this Polarious?"

"It is."

"Are you...are you a Hvaldi?" From the brief description I had of a Hvaldi, I was certain he wasn't, but the writings said that this was their realm and they made no mention of *the race of man,* as they called us, living here.

"No," he shook his head. "I'm human. As are you, yes?"

I nodded. He began asking more questions as he walked around as if trying to analyze me and determine if I was telling the truth. I answered the first few but then turned my gaze to the ground. All I could think about was my dad and what would happen to me now that I was alone in a strange land. The man raised his voice when I didn't answer him.

"I don't care about your questions," I snapped, crinkling my brow at him and gritting my teeth. "Where did they take my dad?"

"He will be taken to Yorkshire and held until his trial," he answered with a straight face. "If found guilty for trespassing, they will send him to the prison colony on Ra'Tone Island." He seemed unfazed by my emotions as I dropped to my knees and burst into tears.

"Please no," I pleaded to the strange man. "We didn't know. I swear." I covered my face with my hands. "Please, he's all I have."

The thought of never seeing him again was more than I could bear. I began to shake, and my stomach twisted into knots. Overwhelmed, I didn't notice the man kneel in front of me until I felt his hand on my shoulder gently pushing me up to look at him.

"We may be able to stop it, but I need your help," he said, looking into my eyes. He had the darkest eyes of anyone I had ever seen—nearly as black as his hair.

"Yes. Of course, I'll do anything to save him."

"I need to know how you got here and how you know of the Hvaldi," he said.

"Can I ask you something first?"

He nodded and helped me to my feet. I requested to know his name and how the soldiers had come to find us here. If these were sacred lands, why were they here?

"My name is Davik, but you can call me Dav." He hesitated for a moment before answering my next question. "They came because I alerted them to your presence."

"What?" I growled, taking a step away from him and pulling out my knife from my belt, even though I was sure if he wanted to hurt me there was nothing I could do to stop him. "I thought you wanted to help me. What do you actually want? To get information to use against him so you can lock us up side by side?"

"No." He shook his head and held up his hands. "Semmi, please understand, I thought you and Gunner were part of the Order of Calvar. They send people in here to destroy the ruins. It wasn't until I heard you translate the writing below the statue that I realized you weren't, but it was too late. I'm sorry." His apology sounded sincere, though I wasn't ready to let my guard down.

"How long have you been watching us?" I hissed at him, still pointing my knife at him and making sure to stay out of his reach, ready to run if I had the chance.

"Since I saw you on the abandoned road." This explained the uneasiness I kept feeling on the way here. "Semmi, I am sorry. I didn't know," he said again. "Please give me the chance to correct my mistake by trying to free your father, but I'll need your help."

Dav stood and waited for my response. His emotionless expression hadn't changed, but his words and the look in his eyes seemed genuine, and he made no attempt to harm me. Slowly, I lowered my knife and nodded.

"Thank you," he said, bowing his head.

I didn't trust him nor was I going to let my guard down knowing he was the one who turned us in to the authorities. But if there was any chance of getting my dad back, I would do whatever I could.

"What do you need me to do?" I asked.

CHAPTER SEVEN

Dav took one of my packs and instructed me to follow him. As we headed through the forest, he told me about the history of the humans in Polarious. Before asking me any further questions, he explained that it was once believed that they were brought here from another realm, Balfjord, by an ancient race. The Hvaldi.

They were taught by the Hvaldi about the different realms and told stories of Lothenbrow and Norranheim, but they were never permitted to travel out of Polarious. Then, for reasons unknown, the Hvaldi disappeared. No stories were passed down about what happened or where they went. Now, thousands of years later, all the old stories had been reduced to myths and a new belief about how his people came to be had replaced the old thinking.

He described how all books containing the old beliefs were destroyed and to speak of them was considered a crime in many areas. Because of this and the constant push of the new beliefs, most people in Polarious now widely believed that all people began here. And that the Hvaldi were merely a fictitious race of people or ancient gods made up by their ancestors.

"If they believe the Hvaldi aren't real, then who do they think built that city we were in?" I asked, baffled that anyone could deny their existence when the evidence was staring them right in the face.

"They believe our ancestors built them," Dav answered but added that there were still those with open minds who wanted to know the truth.

This was why the Hvaldi cities were considered sacred lands. He explained that they were heavily guarded and trespassing into these lands was dealt with swiftly and sternly in order to protect them. Those found trying to destroy them were put to death. Although, he said that most of the soldiers that I saw, known as the People's Army, were made up of Calvar supporters.

"Who is this Order of Calvar you thought my dad and I were part of?" I asked. The fact that Dav allowed and answered my questions eased my suspicions about whether or not I was his prisoner. My lack of knowledge about his world didn't seem to bother him, though it was hard to tell with his constant straight-faced demeanor. Still, I kept my knife close in case I was wrong. My dad was so much better at reading people than I was. I cursed myself for not learning better from him. I never thought I would have to be without him, at least not until I was much older.

"The Order of Calvar is a growing group of extremists that has been around for over a thousand years," he answered. The Calvar began the push of these new beliefs, he explained, along with the idea that *they* were the descendants of the ancients who built the Hvaldi cities.

"They've used this to push themselves into power," he continued. "Yet they're the ones who work to destroy the ancient cities and want to erase everything in our past that mentions the Hvaldi to keep the people from knowing the truth."

He told me the city where he found me was only one of many in the sacred lands. Yet dozens of the old cities were damaged beyond recognition by the Calvar. The number of people they caught inside its borders grew each year.

"Why are they so afraid to know the truth?" I asked, confused as to why people wouldn't want to know how they came to be in this realm.

"The laws that surround this new belief identify the Order of Calvar as some sort of pure race, and to defy them is a crime," he answered. "They have many devout followers who obey without question for fear of what might happen to them or their families if they don't. They believe that if they submit to the rule of the Calvar, they will be rewarded in this life or the next."

I could tell by the way he spoke he didn't follow the beliefs of this Order of Calvar. His choice of words told me he felt strongly about the way they manipulated people to maintain power, and he despised them, yet his expression remained unchanged. I continued to listen as I followed him through the forest.

"If people found out what they believed was a lie, then those in power who pushed those beliefs would lose control over them," he said. "I don't know about your realm but ours is very divided. There are those who believe that people should have the free will to live their lives as they please and others who feel we should be strictly governed as if we lack the ability to make our own decisions."

"Wow," I said quietly, raising my eyebrow. How could some people be so scared of knowing the truth while others were willing to do everything they could to find it? "Balfjord isn't like that," I told him. "For the most part, you can live your life freely, but research into the past has been deemed illegal all over the world."

"Why?"

I told him about the last great society of man and their amazing technology, some of which resulted in the near extinction of humans. I explained the tragedies that occurred when scientists tried to recreate some of those machines and medicines that inevitably led to the passing of laws forbidding the research of all past societies.

"Yet you and your father still chose to continue despite the risks," Dav stated, raising an eyebrow and looking back at me.

"We weren't trying to recreate anything," I explained. "My dad has always believed it was important to know where we came from. That if you lose your past, you're doomed to repeat it. Like learning from your mistakes."

As soon as I said it, I knew I'd hit a sore spot. Dav dropped his head and looked away. He had already apologized several times for what happened and now that I knew a little about his people's history, I could see why he did it. Still, I wasn't ready to forgive him. He had yet to explain where we were going and how I could help to free my dad. Until then, I wouldn't let my guard down.

We walked in silence and I looked around at all the colorful trees, bushes, and animals scurrying about as I thought of his people. It seemed so strange that they could be this divided with the proof right in front of their faces.

"Dav?"

"Yes."

"If your people wanted to know the truth, why didn't they translate the inscriptions in the ancient cities?" I asked. "I don't know about the other cities, but in Storm Wood, there were several inscriptions on the walls and statues that told about the Hvaldi and mentioned them by name. I'm sure they left something somewhere that would answer a lot of what your people are divided over."

"That would be a solution." He stopped and turned back. "However, until now, no one has ever been able to read their writing, which makes you a very valuable person."

"Dead or alive?" I said under my breath. If these Order of Calvar people found out, they would probably want my head on a spike somewhere.

Dav must have heard me because when I looked back at him, he was staring at me. "Let's hope it doesn't come to that. For your safety, if anyone asks, you're from the farmlands outside of Perth in the Great Valley to the south. Understand?"

"Perth, Great Valley, got it," I repeated, becoming a little nervous.

"And Semmi"—he reached out to touch my arm—"I promise I'll do my best to protect you."

***

That night, we made camp in some ruins that concealed us from anyone wandering around in the woods. The stone walls and buildings were in a dilapidated state and had been almost completely overgrown by the forest. As the night crept over the forest, I was shocked at how much light the two moons cast down. Many of the brightly colored bugs and night-blooming flowers appeared almost luminescent in the moonlight.

After we ate, Dav started with his questions, but this time he asked politely instead of making me feel like I was being interrogated. I told him about how my dad and I first discovered the Hvaldi in Europe and the years it took me to finally decipher their two writing forms. He confirmed seeing both writing styles in the various cities and villages belonging to the ancient race. To better explain how we found our way here, I showed him Jorunn's journal and even translated a few of the entries, as well as the letter in the back.

When I described how the doorway between our two realms opened, I got a little carried away, as usual, waving my arms around and babbling on. Describing how it felt traveling between the two realms helped me calm down and allowed my stress to ease. I looked over to see him staring at me with his same emotionless look.

Under different circumstances, I would have been excited and enjoyed having this conversation with someone close to my age. Most of the people I met were my father's age or older, and I couldn't remember the last time I had a friend, but my mind kept drifting elsewhere. I was worried about my dad and wondered where he was right now or if he was hurt. This was the first time in my life I felt alone.

"Semmi?"

"Huh?" Snapping my head up at hearing Dav say my name, I didn't realize I'd stopped talking in midsentence. "I'm sorry."

"It's all right," he replied kindly, closing the journal and passing it back to me. "You've had a rough couple of days. We can talk about this more tomorrow if you'd like."

63

"Thank you." Returning the book to my bag, I sat quietly with my knees pulled to my chest, looking at the little fire. Even though I was tired, I knew my mind wouldn't let me sleep. Every time I thought about my dad, my stomach started to hurt, and a lump built in my throat. "Can you talk to me, please?" I asked softly. I needed to hear something to keep my mind occupied.

"What do you want to know?"

"I don't know," I confessed. Anything would have worked. "What do you do that had you wandering out in the forest by yourself?"

"It's my job."

"Your job?"

"Only the most elite and advanced trained warriors scout the sacred lands for trespassers," he said. "When we find someone, we notify the closest squadron. Often the groups coming in are larger and if they attempt to destroy anything, it's our responsibility to stop them."

"So, you're like a one-man army."

"Basically."

"Am I allowed to know where you're taking me?" I finally asked the question that was burning in my mind. I had hoped he would tell me the plan to save my dad, but so far, the only thing I assumed was that it had to do with my ability to translate the Hvaldi writing.

"Semmi, you're not my prisoner," Dav clarified. "I'm taking you to see Master Orin Laudren. He sits on the High Council and will be one of the people who will oversee your father's trial." He must have noticed the look I shot him and further explained why it was important to go there. "He also holds one of the highest seats for the Warriors of Baleloch."

"Who are they?"

"It's a secret society of warriors that goes back nearly a thousand years, dedicated to the preservation and protection of our true history," he answered. "It was established not long after the Order of Calvar began gaining power as they pushed the spread of this new belief system that threatened to destroy our past. We've been trying to decipher the

64

ancient writing for as long as I can remember with no success. You have no idea how long we've waited for someone like you."

"You belong to these Warriors of Baleloch?" I asked, noticing his use of the word *we.*

He confirmed he did but said there were only a few within the People's Army, and they were secretive about their positions. With the Order of Calvar infiltrating all levels of his people's hierarchy, they had to be careful or risk being imprisoned or executed. Dav said he believed that Master Orin would be able to help by possibly postponing the trial or finding a way to keep my dad from being sent to the prison colony.

"I'm hoping that with your translations, we can finally confirm the truth of the old stories about where we came from," Dav said. "If your father knows as much as you do, both of you could help us learn who we are."

"He knows more." My eyes became glossy and I smiled as a thousand memories of watching my dad work flashed through my mind. I prayed they wouldn't be the last memories I had of him. "His expertise is in the construction of ancient cities. He can look at a city and tell you who built it and how. It's amazing."

"And you're the translator," Dav stated, to which I nodded my head. "How did you learn their language?"

"I can read over a dozen different languages, and I speak seven." I explained how knowing other ancient writings helped me to decipher theirs by finding similarities.

"So, you taught yourself?"

"Yes."

Dav nodded and confessed he'd never heard another language besides his own. I admitted that I could only read the Hvaldi writing. To hear it spoken aloud would be a dream come true. I had often imagined what it might sound like. Something majestic and foreign maybe. I was sure it would be beautiful.

Our conversation helped calm my emotions, and I hoped with all my heart that this Master Orin could help as Dav claimed. Before lying down and closing my eyes, I prayed I would get to see my dad again.

CHAPTER EIGHT

When I first woke, Dav was asleep nearby with his head against my dad's pack. I quietly sat up and looked around. The forest was quiet, and the sun wasn't yet above the horizon. Looking down at my clothes, I noticed how dirty I was from running through the forest and sleeping on the ground the last two nights. Doing my best to be as silent as possible, I opened my pack and looked to see what I had to change into.

Unfortunately, it wasn't much. Most of my clothes were on the wagon in Idaho. At least I had an extra shirt. My once blue, now mostly brown pants would have to do until I could procure a new outfit. From my pack, I removed the shirt and grabbed my brush knowing my hair was probably a mess.

I glanced over at Dav again who still lay with his eyes closed. Getting to my feet, I saw some bushes not far away where I could change, but before I could take two steps, I heard Dav's voice.

"Where are you going?" When I turned back, he still had his eyes closed but then slowly opened them and looked at me and at the items I was holding.

"I was going to change my shirt."

"Hmm." He looked again at the shirt I was holding. "Do you have anything different to put on?"

"No, I don't." I dropped my head, a little embarrassed that he didn't approve of my clothes. "This is all I have. I'm sorry."

Dav got to his feet and walked over to me. He took the shirt I was holding and held it up. "It's not that it's not a nice shirt, it's just not like what we wear," he explained. "Once we leave the sacred lands and get into town, you'll need to blend in."

He removed his cloak and instructed me to put it on over my clothes after I changed and said he would see that I got new clothes once we reached Master Orin's. It didn't take me long to slip out of my dirty shirt and fix my hair. I went with a braid as opposed to my traditional messy bun.

For as light as his cloak felt, it was surprisingly warm and soft to the touch. Dav nodded his approval of my outfit and offered to carry my heavy coat with him. Securing my pack over my shoulders, we set out again. Dav said we still had a long walk ahead of us, but if we moved quickly we could make it before the next morning.

By midday, we reached the border of the sacred lands. I could see now why the soldier who spoke with my dad didn't believe that he had mistakenly trespassed. There was no mistaking this boundary. Large rectangular stones were placed every twenty feet or so and engraved with the symbol of the Hvaldi. Dav knew what it meant but said most associated it with the dangers that would befall them if found inside.

The difference in the landscape was quite dramatic. The Hvaldi built their cities in the mountains, but the land beyond the stone border was mostly open farmland. The only trees were those left to mark the boundary between fields. It reminded me of the numerous farmlands I saw during my trip to Idaho. Most of the open valley was covered in tall green grass that swayed with the cool breeze. The fields were filled with a variety of different plants, some of which I had never seen before, and I was curious about what the vegetables looked like.

Farther to the south was another forest along the edge of a river. Dav told me that Perth, the city I was to say I was from, was beyond the forest in a valley larger than this one. In the distance was a dirt road heading west as far as I could see.

I asked for a moment to rest and sat down on one of the stones while Dav looked around. He walked much faster than I was used to, and my feet ached. I was sure several of the blisters I felt forming had already burst and the raw skin underneath was starting to burn. Not wanting to seem weak, I pushed through the pain even when Dav asked if I was okay. Taking only a couple of minutes, I was back on my feet, ready to keep going.

"We're making good time," he said when I walked up next to him. "If we keep this pace, we'll be there tonight."

"Great." I let out a breath between clenched teeth, feeling another blister stinging on my foot.

"Are you sure you're good?" His expressions were so hard to read. He didn't smile or frown, but the way he looked at me was like he was trying to read my mind. I noticed he frequently looked back at me during our walk and it seemed too often to simply be checking to make sure I was still there.

"Yes," I replied, and we set out again toward the dirt road.

It was well after dark when we finally reached a small village. Few people were out and most paid no attention as we walked past. All the buildings in town were made of dark wood logs and tan mortar. With the two moons constantly overhead, there was no need for torches or lamps to light the way.

I was looking forward to being able to sit down and rest my throbbing feet, but after turning down three streets, we headed north out of town and I realized my hopefulness was a little premature. It was another hour before we came to a small farm at the edge of a forest. The house was made of the same wood and mortar material as those I had seen in the village. Dav knocked on the door and waited.

"I hope someone's awake," I whispered.

"They'll answer," he said and knocked again.

Within a few minutes, I heard the sound of someone walking through the house and at last, the door opened. A tall man wearing a deep red robe stood in the doorway. His gray hair stuck out in all directions as he held a lamp up to better see us.

"Do you have any idea what hour it is?" the man grumbled and covered his mouth to hide a yawn.

"We're here to see Master Orin," Dav told him.

"Who is it, Lath?" came an old man's voice from inside the house. The tall man stepped aside to let the old man with a cane shuffle to the door. "Dav, my boy. What brings you here at this hour?" His hair was completely white as it stuck out from beneath his green nightcap, which matched the color of his robe.

"Master Orin." Dav bowed his head and covered his heart with his fist. "I've brought some important information and I need your help. May we come inside?"

"Yes, yes of course," Master Orin replied. "Lath, make some tea and bring some food for our guests."

The old man waved us in. Dav stepped aside and let me go first, lightly placing his hand on my back to coax me forward. Strangely, I expected his touch to be as emotionless as his face, but I found it gentle and, in a way, comforting as if it was his way of letting me know I would be okay.

We followed Orin into what looked like a sitting room of some sort. Several padded chairs surrounded a short table not far from a stone fireplace where a few hot coals were still burning. Dav introduced me to Master Orin as we dropped our bags. They waited for me to be seated before taking their place around the table.

"I'm sorry for coming so late, but what I have can't wait," Dav said.

"Ah." The old man waved off his apology with a smile. "My door is always open to you and our warriors. What have you brought, and I'm assuming this beautiful young lady is part of it? Semmi was it?"

"Yes, sir."

"That's an interesting name." His voice was a little raspy, but his kind smile and shiny blue eyes made me feel welcome.

"It's short for Gersemmi," I explained. "It means..."

"Treasure," Master Orin said before I could finish my sentence. I was shocked that he was familiar with the origins of my name. "I've heard this name before. It's a very old name. Ancient in fact."

"Yes, it is." I lightly smiled. "My mom gave it to me."

"It's a beautiful name and your accent..." He tilted his head slightly as if trying to figure out where I came from. "I don't think I've heard it before. You must be from far away."

Not sure if I should answer his question, I looked to Dav who nodded and asked for Jorunn's journal. I took it out of my pack for him, and Dav handed it to the old man. Orin opened it and turned a few pages. His eyes widened and he gently traced his fingers over the writing.

"Where did you find this?" Orin asked, looking to Dav, who turned to me and motioned for me to tell him.

"My dad found it in a Hvaldi city. In a room built in the side of a mountain that had been sealed and perfectly preserved."

"How did you not get caught by the guards?" He looked at Dav then back to me with a crinkled brow.

"Um, we weren't in the sacred lands," I replied slowly.

"She's from Balfjord," Dav clarified.

Master Orin was silent for a long moment. His mouth gaped opened as he stared at me in disbelief. Dav took the journal from him and laid it open on the table, taking out the letter in the back. When I'd read it to him the night before, I hadn't realized how closely Dav was listening to me until he recited it nearly word for word.

"How do you know what this says?" Orin asked and followed Dav's eyes as he turned and looked at me.

"She knows their language."

"Is this true?" I nodded and Orin leaned back in his chair. "Who else knows?" His voice quivered with concern as he spoke.

"I'm not sure," Dav replied and went on to explain everything that had happened, and that he hoped my dad hadn't said anything about where he was from. He admitted to Master Orin his mistake in prematurely sending for the guards before he knew our intentions and asked for the old man's assistance.

"With Semmi's help we could finally bring the truth to our people about the Hvaldi and where we come from," Dav said. "But I was hoping there was something you could do to keep her father, Gunner, from being sent to the prison colony while we're gathering the evidence we need."

"Hmm," Orin mumbled and rubbed his chin before turning to me. "Does your father have any useful skills? And like you, can he translate this?" He touched the journal.

"He can translate some of it," I answered. "His expertise is in ancient structures. He knows all about how many of Balfjord's ancient cultures built their cities. For a while after my mom died, he worked as a master mason and used many of the same techniques the ancients did to build anything out of stone."

"Excellent." Master Orin clapped his hands together and called for Lath.

Within minutes, Lath arrived carrying a tray filled with tea, several plates of what looked like some kind of biscuit or cookie, and a few pieces of fruit. Orin gave him quick instructions that he would be leaving at first light for Yorkshire and to send a message that the prisoner was not to be questioned until he arrived. He assured me that if he could get there in time, he was positive he could have my dad's sentence changed to life as a servant, which would keep him from being shipped to the prison colony.

"With the new cathedral being built, I could easily have him assigned to one of the crews," Orin explained. "Lord Atwood is in charge and is part of our warriors. I'll speak to him."

"Thank you, Master Orin." I breathed a sigh of relief knowing my dad wouldn't be sent away and that there was hope of freeing him if Dav and I could accomplish the task he presented.

"You're very welcome." The old man smiled as he reached out and took my hand. "Hopefully the two of you will bring proof of our true beginnings. Then we can do more. You truly are a treasure, Ms. Semmi."

"May I ask a question?" I requested of Master Orin.

He chuckled and told me I didn't need permission, and that he was happy to answer any questions I had. Knowing very little about their culture or spiritual belief outside of what Dav told me, I was nervous asking questions, but I still failed to understand how what we were doing would change anything.

"I'm a little confused," I said, looking at Master Orin then at Dav. "You said the current belief is that your people originated here in Polarious."

"That's correct," Dav confirmed.

"Why does it matter so much if your people originated here or in Balfjord?" I asked. "Where I'm from, different cultures from different places all have their own ancient stories about how man came to be. Most understand that the stories may not be entirely accurate, and science has even proven many to be completely implausible, but it doesn't change what they believe. No one knows for sure. Not even the Hvaldi know how they truly came to be."

"You are absolutely right," the old man replied with a wink. "It's not about proving or disproving where we originated from. It's about stopping those who use it to control our people through fear. To free us from their corruption."

"The Order of Calvar," I said, remembering my conversation with Dav.

"Correct." Dav nodded.

Orin went on to explain how the Calvar used this new belief to push the idea of an ancient bloodline meant to rule over the people. "As they've gathered more and more followers, they've been able to force themselves into positions of power in the council."

"Believers in the old ways are becoming fewer in number," Dav said. "Mostly because the Calvar have been able to persuade them, or they have mysteriously died and a Calvar was appointed as the replacement." I could tell his emphasis on *persuade* meant that the sudden change of heart to trade their old beliefs for new was most likely done out of duress.

"Proving the existence of the Hvaldi and bringing back their teachings of freedom, prosperity, and happiness could unite the common people to finally bring down the Calvar," Master Orin added. "If we don't stop them, we'll never be free."

"They've pushed themselves into every facet of our society, insisting that it's for the greater good, but all it does is give them more power and leaves the rest of us picking at the scraps." Dav's eyes narrowed as he spoke, and the muscles in his jaw tightened. These Calvar reminded me of the men who chased after us, and I wondered if they too were willing to stop at nothing to achieve their goals. From the look in Dav's eyes, I knew the answer.

Master Orin called for Lath again and requested him to wake Ms. Button, his maid, to have her draw me a bath and bring me some new clothes, which he called leathers. Orin also asked him to have the guest room prepared for us. While we waited, he asked me questions about Balfjord and my journey here. His eyes lit up as I described my realm and the process of uncovering the Hvaldi city where we found the journal.

"Is the journal the only thing you brought with you?" he inquired.

"No." I dug out the broken tablet from my mother's box and showed him the necklace I was wearing that belonged to Jorunn.

Master Orin held the necklace up to the light and Dav leaned over as well to see it.

"I've seen a necklace like this before," the old man said, raising an eyebrow. "Do you remember it, Dav? You used to play with it as a boy."

"Nan's necklace," he answered. I swore he almost smiled as he held out his hand for Orin to give it to him. "But if it's like the one Nan wore, it's not a necklace. It's a key."

Even the old man looked at him curiously, unaware that the piece of jewelry held its own secret. Dav grasped the pendant between his fingers, pressing on the two runes, and turned it. A dozen small teeth in different shapes rotated out from the sides of the pendant and he handed it back to me.

"I had no idea." I lightly ran my fingers over the little teeth. "What does it open?"

"I don't know," Dav replied. "I remember playing with it once when I was a boy and it opened."

"Amazing," Master Orin whispered.

"What happened to the one you played with?" I asked.

"I'm not sure," he replied, looking over at the old man.

Master Orin confessed he wasn't sure either. "It's possible Nan was buried with it. I never gave it much thought. It was a gift from her mother." He encouraged us to get some rest and said he would see us in the morning. Stiffly he stood up and left the room.

***

Soon, Ms. Button, an older woman with short curly hair and a long dress, shuffled into the room to show me where I could clean up. The thought of a warm bath sounded wonderful to soak my aching muscles and clean off the dirt I was covered in, but when I stood up, the pressure on my already hurting feet sent a shock of pain up my legs. I would have fallen had Dav not caught me by the arm and helped me steady myself.

"Are you all right?" There was concern in his voice, but I did not want to admit that I was hurt.

"Yes," I lied. "Just a little stiff from the long walk. I'll be fine."

He held my arm a moment longer, looking me in the eyes before letting go. It was so difficult to read him. His eyes seemed to say so much, but I couldn't tell what and I didn't know enough about him to understand his silent and seemingly blank expressions.

Swallowing my pain, I followed Ms. Button down the hall to a small room with a large stone bathtub. Steam drifted off the top of the water. Next to the tub was a small table with a bowl of cream, which I was told was for cleaning myself. A wooden bench along the wall had a towel and a long purple gown set on top.

"This gown is for you to sleep in," she explained. "When you're done, your room is across the hall. I placed the clean leathers Master Orin requested on one of the beds for you."

"Thank you, Ms. Button." She smiled and left the room.

I hung Dav's cloak up on the back of the door and sat on the end of the bench to take off my boots. I winced as I pulled them off and tears filled my eyes. Blood stained my socks where the blisters had split. Taking a couple of deep breaths, I removed my socks and the rest of my clothes before stepping into the tub.

It felt like my feet had been lit on fire as I stepped into the hot water. I could barely hold back from screaming and I was glad no one was there to see me cry. Soaking my tired legs was out of the question. Quickly, I washed up and climbed out, praying the burning pain would soon stop.

The gown was a little big but felt comfortable. Having never worn a nightgown before, I looked at myself in the mirror on the wall for a few moments, turning one way then the other. To myself, I looked strange and a little silly. I was never one to wear dresses unless it was a special occasion, but I appreciated not having to put my dirty clothes back on. Knowing it was late, I gathered my things and walked across the hall.

When I entered the room, Dav was sitting on the edge of the bed closest to the door. He looked me up and down, stopping when he saw my bare feet. There was no hiding the redness and blood that had beaded up on my heels and toes.

"Why didn't you tell me your feet were hurting?" Clearly irritated, he clenched his jaw and took a breath through his nose.

"I didn't want to slow us down."

"I could've at least wrapped them for you."

I apologized, and he instructed me to sit on the bed across from him. The table between the beds had a pitcher of water with two glasses. He filled one of the glasses then grabbed a box from off the shelf below.

Inside were a half dozen little jars, rolled strips of fabric, and a small saucer. He sprinkled a few dashes of powder from two of the jars into the glass of water and handed it to me, saying that it would help with the pain and infection.

Using the saucer, he mixed powders from two other jars together. Gently he lifted each foot and lightly sprinkled the mixed powder over each of the blisters. His hands were warm and he was careful not to press too hard on any of my sores. As he set my foot down, his fingers lightly drifted over my ankle sending a tingle through my body and making my breath catch in my throat. Thankfully he didn't notice.

"I find your connection to your father strange," he said as he wrapped my feet. "Are all children from your realm this attached to their parents?" His voice showed a tinge of sarcasm as he finished tying the wraps.

"I'm not a child," I snapped and pulled my foot away. "I'm eighteen. How old are you, nineteen?"

"Twenty." He lowered his head and looked at the floor. "I didn't mean that you acted like a child but that you are your father's child. By your age, most women here are married with a family."

"Well, I wouldn't know." I scooted back on the bed against the wall and pulled my knees to my chest. "I've spent my entire life on dig sites, studying the past or traveling from one place to another. It wasn't often anyone my age was there. My toys were artifacts and scrolls. My parents have been the only friends I've ever had." When I glanced up from staring at the edge of the bed, Dav was looking at me with his same emotionless expression. I wished he would smile, frown, or even lift an eyebrow so I would have some idea of what he was thinking when he looked at me. "What about you? What's your family like?"

"Master Orin is my family," he answered. "I never knew my parents. Orin found me when I was a baby, left on the side of a road wrapped in a blanket. He and his wife Nan raised me. I started training to be a warrior ever since I was strong enough to hold a sword." Dav put away the box and sat back on his bed. "I didn't mean to offend you, Semmi. I'm not very good at talking to people."

"You do just fine." I let my legs relax and apologized for snapping at him. I knew it wasn't his fault and honestly didn't know where I'd be right now without him. "A lot has happened the last few days and I'm having a hard time. First, Banks gets shot. Then we're running for our lives. And now, my dad's been taken prisoner in another world, and I don't know if I'll ever see him again. I've never been alone."

"You're not alone. I give you my word—I'll do everything I can to get him back for you."

His words were sincere, and they eased the pain in my heart. We talked a few more minutes but soon my eyelids became heavy. Dav advised me to get some rest while we had a bed, stating that we had a long journey ahead of us.

When I wished him sweet dreams he looked at me like he had never been told such a thing. I smiled, and he bowed his head and stuttered a bit over his words as he bid me good night. For the first time, his expression changed. His eyes looked a little softer and I could see a faint smile. We still didn't know each other well, but he was the closest thing I'd ever had to a friend.

CHAPTER NINE

That night's sleep was anything but restful. My dreams were filled with visions of me running through a forest, chasing after my dad. I kept trying to run faster, but no matter how fast I ran, I couldn't catch up to him, always seeing the back of his coat as he ducked around another tree. Then he was gone. In my dream, I yelled for him, but there was no answer.

Sitting straight up in my bed, I yelled for him before I realized where I was. To my relief, Dav's bed was empty and he hadn't heard me. He was so much stronger than I was, and I wanted to do my best not to look weak. Yet in his world, I felt helpless. I drew my strength from my dad and without him, I was lost. A lot more than my dad's life depended on the success of our mission, but he was the only family I had left.

I could hear Dav's voice in my mind reminding me that I wasn't alone. Strangely, I found the sound of his voice comforting. We hadn't known each other long, but I hoped the journey would give us the opportunity to become friends. I needed his friendship now more than ever.

Taking a moment to collect my thoughts, I got out of bed and put on the leathers Ms. Button had set out for me. They were similar to the ones Dav wore, but instead of all black, my long-sleeved jacket was dark blue. It was a bit longer than his jacket, going down to the tops of my thighs and included a black belt. There was a matching blue cloak and long black leggings.

Looking over at my boots, I dreaded having to put them back on. My feet felt much better than they did last night, but they were still a little tender. As I pressed my fingers against the wraps to test their soreness, there was a knock at the door.

"It's me," I heard Dav's voice. "Are you awake?"

"Yes."

Dav slowly opened the door and looked in. "Good, you're dressed." He walked in carrying a bowl of water and a towel. "How do your feet feel?"

"Much better."

He knelt in front of me and removed my bandages. The redness from last night was reduced to a healthy pink. The skin under the torn blisters was still tender to the touch as Dav carefully rinsed my feet in the bowl of water. He added more of the same powder from last night and wrapped them with clean cloth.

"Thank you," I said, and he bowed his head. "How soon until we leave?"

"Not long," he replied. "Master Orin will be heading out shortly. Can you wear your boots for a little while longer?"

I let out the breath I was holding in, not really wanting to put them on, but said I could.

"Good. We are going to go back to the village for a few supplies," he explained. "While we're there, we can get you a suitable pair." Instructing me to leave my old clothes behind, Dav handed me another pack from the closet made of thick black leather. "Take only what you need to do your examination of the cities."

"Dav?" I asked as he headed for the door. He stopped and looked back. "Does Master Orin have an empty journal, so I can record inscriptions I find?"

"I'm sure he does. I'll get one for you and meet you outside." He nodded and closed the door behind him.

Following his instructions, I left my clothes and those from my father's bag on the bed. Into the new pack I transferred all other items I thought I would need, including my father's cleaning kit filled with small brushes and picks, Jorunn's journal with my bag of pencils, and the fire-starting kit. The only weapons I had were the knives and sling I used for hunting and preparing small animals to eat. Thinking they might be useful, I added them to the pack.

Picking up my mom's tin, I held it in my hands. I opened the lid and pulled out the picture of my mom and dad. Dav probably wouldn't think it was something I needed, but if I lost my dad, all I had left of him and my mom was in this little box. I couldn't leave it behind. Pushing it to the bottom of the pack, I tied it shut and headed outside.

***

"There she is," Master Orin said as I opened the door. He was getting ready to climb into his carriage to head to Yorkshire. Dav was standing next to him.

"Good morning, Master Orin." I pulled the new pack over one shoulder and walked over to join them.

"Good morning, my dear." The old man smiled, taking my hand and kissing me on either cheek. "I'd ask how you slept, but from what Dav has told me of what you went through the last few days, I'm sure it wasn't well."

"I got a little sleep," I said kindly, not wanting to offend his hospitality.

"Wonderful," he replied. "Please take some comfort that I will see to it that your father stays here. Lord Atwood is a loyal Warrior of Baleloch. He will make use of your father's skills and make sure he's protected." He kissed my cheek again and told me he wished we had more time to talk, then turned to Dav. "Protect her, my son. She is very important to all of us."

"You have my word," Dav responded and helped the old man into the carriage.

"And pay attention," the old man added, pointing to me. "I believe she has a lot she can teach you."

"Yes, sir." Dav bowed his head and secured the gate on the carriage. He glanced at me and back at the old man.

"Semmi," Master Orin said, holding his hand out the window to take mine. "Don't let his blank stare scare you." He motioned with his head toward Dav and grinned. "He's the best man I know. Trust him. Maybe you can help him learn to smile every now and then." He chuckled and waved goodbye as he headed down the road.

I heard Dav clear his throat to get my attention. "Are you ready?"

I nodded, and he walked over and grabbed another pack that was sitting near the front door of the house. Next to it was a small sword. When he returned to where I was standing he held it out to me.

"Do you know how to use one of these?"

"No"—I shook my head—"but I can use a sling." I hoped maybe I would impress him a little with the fact I knew how to use a weapon of sorts. Slings aren't easy to use, and it took me years before I could consistently hit a target.

"What's a sling?"

My heart sank a bit. Trying to convince him that I wasn't a useless girl would be a challenge. Setting my pack down, I took out a small bag that contained my sling and a dozen or so stones and showed it to him. "I used to use it to hunt small animals for eating," I explained. He looked at it and raised an eyebrow.

Seeing he didn't believe such a simple weapon could be effective, I took it out. Hooking the loop on one end of the sling around my finger and grasping the other end in my palm, I set a stone in the leather pouch in the middle. I looked around and saw a cup on a wooden barrel near the barn about thirty feet away. Taking a step away from Dav, I spun the sling a few times over my head then released the end of the sling, sending the stone flying. It hit the cup and knocked it off the barrel.

"Yes," I whispered, excited that I hit it on the first shot. It had been awhile since I'd used it and I was glad I didn't miss. When I turned around, Dav gave me a nod of approval but still handed me the sword.

"In case someone gets too close to use that."

When we reached the village, it was alive with people moving all about. Shops had their doors and windows open to show off their wares for sale. Toys, trinkets, and brightly colored fruits and veggies along with fresh-baked bread were available for purchase. Patrons and dealers bartered for what they felt was a fair price for their goods.

Two men walking down the street caught my attention. They wore red and brown matching uniforms each with a long sword hanging from their belts. The townspeople glared at them and hushed their conversations as they passed.

To my surprise, when one of the men grabbed a piece of fruit from a basket outside a shop without paying, no one tried to stop him. Even when he egged on the owner to come try to take it from him as he rested a hand on the hilt of his sword, no one did.

"Who are those men?" I asked quietly.

"The Calvar's minions." Dav's eyes narrowed as he watched the soldiers walk down the road. "They come here every week and force the shop owners to pay taxes, saying it's to help improve the town, but they pocket the money and do nothing to help the people."

"And the council approves of this?"

"Most of the council is made up of the Calvar elite members," he said, his voice tight. "Only a few aren't and they're frequently outvoted. Over the years, the council has taken more control over our people." He went on, detailing that the council was put in place not to dictate every facet of people's lives but to protect and preserve their freedom. The original goal was to make sure each person had control over their own lives and that their future was of their own choosing and not left up to those who knew nothing about them.

"I'm surprised Master Orin is still there. I'd be afraid for his safety." I assumed because of his high position among the Warriors of Baleloch that he was probably well guarded.

"They're not dumb enough to get rid of him," Dav replied. "His family has sat on the council for hundreds of years. The people trust him, but they know he's getting old and has no heir to take his place."

"He has you," I commented, since he told me how Master Orin had raised him as his son.

"I'm not blood, and they know that."

I continued to question Dav during our walk, trying to understand why the people wouldn't want to fight back if they hated the Calvar so much. He told me the Calvar used the new belief that declared them the only pure race to elevate themselves above the people. To defy them would condemn one's soul. Since most people here believed that there was another life after this one, they were afraid to fight back.

He further told me how the Calvar twisted their words to convince the people that giving them total control would be for the betterment of everyone. That their lives would be improved, but from what I could see of these people's lives, they didn't seem that well off. Most of the buildings were in dire need of repair. The people I saw wore old tattered clothes, and there seemed to be more beggars than shop owners. Those who did own shops looked like they could hardly feed themselves, let alone sell what little they had.

Dav shared a few sad stories about the ones begging for spare change and how they'd once been farmers or merchants, but the Calvar taxed them out of their homes and businesses. My heart felt for them. I was no stranger to being poor, but my dad always found a way to keep us fed and clothed. Work was easy to find in my world.

"That's why it is so important to prove the Order of Calvar wrong," he stressed. "With the Calvar's growing numbers, there're not enough Warriors of Baleloch to stop them. If we prove to the people they've been lied to, we hope they'll rise up and fight with us."

"Won't a lot of people die?"

"Maybe," he answered, "but that's nothing compared to how many will die if we do nothing. I think the Calvar will fall faster than Master

Orin believes. I've fought these men. They're not well trained and most of them are cowards."

After we turned a corner, he quickly changed the subject. Not far away, the Calvar soldiers were giving a store owner difficulty. We both kept our heads low and I followed him down another street until he finally approached one of the shops. The sign over the door was written in a language I didn't recognize. When Dav saw me stop and stare at it, he cocked his head to one side.

"Don't tell me you can't read the language you speak," he said jokingly.

"Your writing is different from mine," I replied, "but I think I can read it. It says *Fine Shoes,* right?"

"Yes," he answered slowly with a curious tone. "If this isn't the form of writing you use, then how do you know what it says?"

"Like I said, I can read over a dozen different languages." I straightened my shoulders and gave him a teasing smile hoping to get a reaction from him, but his expression didn't change.

He nodded with his usual lack of emotion and opened the door, allowing me to go in first. Somehow I had hoped for a different response. If Orin truly wanted me to teach him to smile, I suspected it might be more difficult a task than finding the proof of the Hvaldi. I took a defeated breath and walked past him into the shop.

A bell on the door rang and a man turned around, pushing his glasses up on his nose. He was an older gentleman with shaggy gray hair, wearing a long brown apron. In his hands were samples of leather in various colors. He was placing them on a rack, so customers could see the different options.

"Welcome," he said in a raspy voice. "How can I help you?"

"She needs shoes that won't hurt her feet," Dav told him, stepping past me.

"Lord Davik," the man said with a cheery smile. "It's good to see you."

"Sir Otto." Dav greeted the man with a handshake.

"Still as stoic as ever, I see." Otto chuckled at Dav's expressionless face. "I don't think I've ever heard you laugh. To what do I owe this pleasure?"

"Semmi, this is Sir Otto." He placed his hand on my back and guided me forward. "Sir Otto, Semmi. She's in need of some good shoes."

"Well, you've come to the right place. Come sit down, my dear, and let me see what we have." He took my hand and led me over to a long wooden bench in the center of the room.

I took a seat and Otto squatted down to look at my boots. I gripped the sides of the bench and winced in pain as he pulled one of my boots off, quicker than I expected. Seeing my reaction, he was more careful when removing the other. Even though it wasn't as bad as yesterday, it still hurt.

"I'm sorry, love," Otto said and examined my boots, then my feet. "No wonder your feet hurt. These were made all wrong for you."

He threw my boots to the side and began measuring my feet from heel to toe as he grumbled something about the poor quality of workmanship from other shoemakers. He promised me when he was finished, my new shoes would be the best I ever had.

"How long will this take?" Dav asked.

"Shouldn't take more than an hour," Otto answered without looking up.

"Very good." Dav instructed me to stay while he picked up a few more items. He left our bags by the front door and gave me a longer than normal look. "And Otto, be sure to make them tall to protect her legs. Where we're going, I want to make sure she doesn't get hurt."

"You got it, Lord Dav." Otto gave me a smile and a wink. "So, Lady Semmi, where are you from?" he asked after Dav closed the door.

"Um, Perth," I answered, reciting what Dav had told me before. "From the Great Valley...just outside of it I mean."

"Ah, I see. Never met anyone from there," he said. "You have a beautiful voice. Welcome to Sweetwater."

I asked him about the significance of the town's name, and he told me how it was named after the river to the south. Along the shore grew a special type of reed that gave the water a slightly sweet taste. He mentioned a few of his favorite fishing spots and best places to pick berries.

Otto continued jabbering on while he took the last few measurements he needed and walked over to a shelf filled with all different colors of leather. He looked at me then back at the shelf and pulled out a piece of black leather to match my pants.

He never stopped talking the entire time he cut, folded, and stitched my shoes. As he worked, he asked me a few questions, which I answered as best I could. I enjoyed his bubbly personality and smiling face. He told me that he had known Dav since he was a boy and offered to tell a few stories about him.

"What was Dav like when he was younger?" I asked, wondering if he was always so serious.

"Shorter." The shoemaker chuckled, bringing over my finished boots to try on. "He's a good man though. Never known a better one, and he seems to like you."

"I doubt that." I laughed, knowing he had to be joking with me. "I've seen how he looks at me."

"You simply don't know him well enough yet. I've known him since he was a child. He used to grow out of his shoes so fast." He helped me into the tall boots and secured the straps up the sides, so they stayed in place. "He saved my life once," he added.

I walked over to a mirror to see how my new shoes looked and was about to ask him how Dav saved him when the shop door opened. Dav had returned and was carrying an armful of supplies.

He looked me up and down as he set down the items and began organizing them in our packs. "Better?"

"Much better," I replied, thanking Dav and Otto. I took a few steps around the shop and looked at them again in the mirror. "These are incredibly comfortable. Thank you, Sir Otto."

"My pleasure, Lady Semmi." Otto winked and gave Dav a quick glance. "Just remember what I said," he whispered. "You'll always be in good hands with him."

He walked us outside and I heard Otto whisper something to Dav but couldn't make out the words. Dav thanked him and shook his hand, giving him a few coins before joining me.

"Where to?" I asked as I pulled the straps on my pack tight over my shoulders.

"North. Ready?"

"Lead the way, Lord Davik," I said jokingly.

He looked at me, raising an eyebrow before heading down the road. I tried to look closer at him for any subtle differences in his otherwise blank expression. Otto may have said he liked me, but I couldn't see it. If anything, I think he was probably only being polite. I smiled to myself. Otto was at least right about one thing: I did feel like I was in good hands with Dav near. Whether he thought so or not, I considered Dav my friend.

CHAPTER TEN

We headed out of town along an old road that looked rarely traveled. Only once were we passed by a horse and wagon carrying a man and young boy. They offered us a ride, but Dav declined and thanked the man. Little by little, we left the open farmlands behind and headed back into the trees and mountains. Even our fading road eventually disappeared.

Dav hardly spoke a word, only to check how I was doing or if I needed a rest until well after nightfall when he was finally satisfied with our progress and decided to make camp. He instructed me to collect wood for a fire and headed into the forest. When he returned, he was carrying a small animal in one hand. He seemed pleased to see I had already started the fire and offered to prepare the creature for cooking.

"So where exactly are we going?" I asked as I skinned the animal he called a Horned Taren. The creature looked like something you would get if you crossed a rabbit with a large rat and with the coloring of a skunk, except for its ears, which had long, bright yellow hair at the tips.

Dav took a map out of his pack then waited for me to get the Taren on a stick over the fire. I sat next to him and he laid out the map, so I could see. The edges of the map were worn from use and it appeared quite old. It showed all of the sacred lands, including the surrounding stone border as well as a few of the roads and villages along the outer perimeter. The area was massive and larger than several regions of Europe combined.

Each of the ancient cities was labeled with the writing form that Dav's people used as well as Hvaldi writing underneath. Dav explained that many of the cities were given names by his people. On this map, they included what was believed to be the names given by the Hvaldi. I saw Storm Wood and Thorn Valley as well as the abandoned road.

"We're here," he said, pointing to a location southwest of Thorn Valley. "We're almost to the border of the sacred lands and should cross it early tomorrow." He went on to explain the details of our journey over the next few days. "We'll keep to the forest and stop at these cities on our way to this one, which Orin requested I take you to."

I looked at the names written on the map by his people and then the Hvaldi name below it. "Hmm," I said, translating it in my mind. I chuckled at the similarities. Like the Hvaldi, Dav's people also seemed to name their towns and villages after the area they were located in.

"What is it?" Dav asked.

"The names," I answered.

"Are we that far off?"

"Actually no, if I'm reading your writing correctly." Being unfamiliar with his people's writing, I needed a little help with a few of the names. "They're very close. This city where you found me, a sign I saw called it Storm Wood and your people named it Thunder Forest. The same here." I pointed to the city Orin requested Dav take me to. "You have Towering Oaks, and this reads Valley of the Giants. I wonder why they named it that?"

"I'm not sure. I've never been that far north. Maybe once we get there, we'll find out why. It lies in the valley between the two tallest mountains. Said to be so tall the peaks stick out above the clouds." His knowledge of the various cities he'd been to in the sacred lands was impressive. Being a guard and a warrior, he didn't seem the type to spend much time examining the layout and inscriptions. To my surprise, he possessed an ability to remember everything he saw, a talent I wished I possessed.

He asked the names of a few more locations, explaining that the Hvaldi names on the map were decided by inscriptions found in the area, though he wasn't sure if they were even right since it was merely a guess.

"Orin said few know of this city's existence and even fewer have been there, but it's the largest and best preserved."

"How long will it take to get there?" I asked.

"After we stop at the other two cities, and if we don't run into any issues, it will take at least three weeks. Probably more."

To hear it would take so long to get to the Valley of the Giants, not including the time it might take me to find what I needed to free my dad, if it was even there, saddened me. For all I knew he was locked in a cage, hungry or even hurt. I only hoped Master Orin was able to do as he said, and my dad would survive until we returned.

The thought that we might fail entered my mind as I sat on the ground watching the fire slowly go out. A knot formed in my throat. Pulling my knees into my chest, I tried to push it from my mind and looked over at Dav. He was sitting with Jorunn's journal in his hands, slowly looking from page to page.

"D-do you want me to read more of that to you?" My voice cracked as I spoke.

"Orin said I should learn from you. Can you teach me to read this?" He held the journal out for me to help him.

I smiled at his request. This was exactly what I needed to keep my mind focused on our goal. "If I do, will you teach me how to use a sword?"

"I'd be honored to teach you." Something about the sound of his voice and the way he looked at me warmed my heart. My evening conversations with my dad were my favorite part of the day, and I missed that. By asking me to teach him, Dav, in his own way, had given that back to me and he didn't even know it.

I took the empty journal and my bag of pencils out of my pack. Sitting next to him, I opened the journal to a blank page and showed him the basics of the Hvaldi written language, starting with their letters. We spent about an hour before calling it a night.

Dav checked my feet before I lay down. There was no need to wrap them again. The pain was gone, and the skin was nearly healed. I was happy with the wonderful boots Otto made. They were definitely the best shoes I'd ever had.

***

Dav woke me early in the morning. The sun had yet to rise, but the light of the two bright moons made it easy to see. I gathered my things and got ready to leave when he stopped me. Keeping with his side of the deal, he handed me my sword.

"Are you ready for your first lesson?"

"Yes," I answered and followed him to an open area nearby where we could practice.

He instructed me how to correctly hold my sword and helped me get my body in the proper stance to begin. Walking around me, he explained the reason for this stance as I held the pose. Every time I wavered even a little, he corrected me.

I needed him to know that I could do this. In his world, I felt so foreign. The last thing I needed was for something to happen to him because I couldn't protect myself.

Once he was satisfied that I could hold the stance properly, he had me do a few simple steps and blocks with my sword, making sure to return to the same ready position after each movement. He assigned numbers to each movement and would call them out for me to perform.

"No, like this." Dav walked behind me, placing one hand around my waist and the other over my sword hand. Slowly, he moved my hand and body with his through all the movements in a fluid motion.

At first, I was nervous, having never been this close to a man before, but at the same time, I found his touch comforting. He quietly called out the movements in my ear as we went through each one. It was almost like a dance. After three passes, he stepped away and let me do them by myself.

We worked until the light of the sun peeked through the trees. He didn't say anything after we finished, and I wondered whether he was disappointed. My movements weren't smooth but very rigid and a little shaky. Everything takes time, I told myself. It took a lot of practice with my sling before I could even get close to hitting my target.

Each passing day went by like the first as we continued north. We walked from sunup to a little before sundown, only stopping for brief periods to get a drink of water or for a short rest.

I still couldn't get over the bright and vivid colors of all the plants, animals, and bugs around the forest. It was like something out of a fairy tale. Trees grew with yellow, pink, and even teal leaves. Some plants growing out from crevasses in the rocks or the spaces between branches had a rainbow of buds in every color imaginable.

I must have asked Dav a thousand questions about everything I saw. His answers were short and to the point, but he didn't seem bothered by them. And even though his expression never changed, his voice was kind and he took the time to point out unique things about some of the plants and animals. One flower in particular, which grew from the side of a tree, had long green leaves with a tall colorful flower that grew out of the center. When touched, it changed from red and orange to blue and purple.

"That's amazing," I whispered. I wished my dad could be here to see all this. I knew exactly the look he would have had on his face seeing the colors change.

Dav asked about the forests in Balfjord, which were difficult to describe. I did my best to tell him about the landscapes in the different places I had traveled. From deserts of sand, rocky mountains, and miles and miles of flat plains, to tall pines and rolling hills, I rambled on for what seemed like hours. Thinking he'd probably stopped listening a long time ago, I was surprised when he asked me more questions.

Each night after we reviewed the map, I sat with Dav and continued teaching him the Hvaldi language. I was impressed by how much he remembered from our previous lessons. Before beginning, he reviewed everything we had gone over and only made a few mistakes. The progress of my lessons, on the other hand, wasn't nearly as impressive as his. My movements were still a little rigid, and I stumbled more times than I could count.

One morning, Dav noticed my frustration and calmly reminded me to relax so I could maintain my focus. "Didn't you ever watch your father use a sword?"

"My dad never carried a sword," I huffed and slumped my shoulders, knowing I was disappointing him.

"How did he defend himself?" He cocked his head to one side. "Did he use a bow?"

"No, he had a gun for protection."

I could see he didn't recognize the weapon I spoke of and I did my best to describe it in a way that would make sense. It was hard to tell what Dav thought of such a weapon, but he nodded as I spoke.

"Can you shoot one of these guns?"

"No, he never taught me," I confessed, "and he didn't have a bow. When I was a kid, an old man at one of our dig sites taught me to use a sling. Although I think he did it so I would stop asking him questions all the time."

"Smart man," Dav commented with a straight face.

"Hey!" I gasped and swatted him on the arm. For the first time since we met, nearly a week ago now, I heard him laugh and saw a smile stretch across his face. "I'm not that bad, am I?"

"No." He chuckled, tapping my leg with his sword and raising his to continue our lesson. "Come on, the sun will be up soon."

"Okay." I positioned my feet and raised my sword to his. One side of his lips still curled up as he looked at me, and I knew what he was thinking. "You'd tell me if I was, right?" Dav only looked at me the way he always did. His brief smile disappeared and he remained expressionless.

We finished our lesson and headed out. I was looking forward to today. According to Dav, we would reach the first of the two cities we planned to explore before heading to the Valley of the Giants. He estimated that we would get there sometime in the early afternoon.

The name of the city was Moonstone. I imagined an entire city constructed of light gray and white stones as Dav had described to me the night before. He said at the northern end was a temple, and inside, there was a tablet twice the height of a man covered with line after line of text. All I could think about was what we might find. Would it be the story of their true beginnings, the history of the Hvaldi who once lived here, or maybe a prayer?

With all that was running through my mind, I didn't realize I hadn't said a word since we left. Dav looked back at me several times as if making sure I was still there, until he pointed out a tall stone in a clearing nearby. It was engraved with a few lines of writing similar to the marker stone my dad and I had found on the abandoned road.

"The top one is the name of the city we're headed to and the bottom one is to another city named Briarwood," I told him.

"Stones like these are found all over," he said. "There was probably a road that went through here at one time."

"My dad and I found one when we first got here."

"You've been quiet today," he commented, looking down at me.

"I thought your ears would appreciate the break," I replied, remembering our conversation from this morning.

"Your questions don't bother me. If I was in your realm, I'd have questions too."

"Thank you." I smiled. "Honestly, I've had a lot on my mind. I'm hoping we find something."

"Me too."

CHAPTER ELEVEN

The white stones of the city became visible through the trees but instead of being motivated to get there, Dav stopped and held his hand out for me to do the same. He glanced around the forest. Unfamiliar with this realm, I found everything a bit strange. The bugs and birds sounded different from what I was used to, but I didn't notice anything that seemed unnatural.

"Stay close," he whispered and slowly moved forward keeping near the trees.

"What is it?" I asked quietly.

"Someone's been here." I watched how intently he scanned the area. From his years of training, he could sense minute changes in his environment, which indicated when danger was near.

With one hand on the hilt of his sword, he reached back and took hold of my hand. As we proceeded forward, he pulled me close behind him. Nearing the city, I quickly realized what put Dav on alert. The magnificent ancient city he described to me the night before had been reduced to a pile of rubble. Barely a single wall remained standing.

"They destroyed it." There was sadness in his voice and anger in his eyes.

"The Calvar?" I asked already knowing who he was referring to.

He nodded and stared at the devastation shaking his head.

"When was the last time you were here?"

"A few months maybe," he answered. "This isn't my area to patrol, but I know the warrior who does. I was hoping he'd be here. I can't believe it's gone."

"It's not gone, Dav," I told him only to get a sharp comment on whether or not I was blind. I understood his frustration and hoped I could provide him some reassurance that it wasn't lost. "In my realm, nearly all ancient cities are in far worse condition than this," I said, "and we still managed to put them back together, so we could learn about the people who built them. All the pieces are still here."

"Do you know how long it would take to rebuild this?" he snapped.

"Yes, I do as a matter of fact." I echoed his sharpness to get his attention. "The point is, it can be done. Obviously not today but someday. It's all here. You said you wanted me to see the tablet in the temple. If you show me where it is, I may be able to at least reassemble it. Or would you rather give up?"

"Fine," he huffed and led me through the city.

His face may have not shown his dismay, but it was obvious in the tone of his voice. I crossed my fingers that the tablet would reveal something to encourage him that, while the city was now a pile rubble, it was still possible to repair someday.

I thought about the village in Europe where my dad and I first discovered the existence of the Hvaldi. When we first came upon the area, the average person would have never known it was once home to a few dozen people and probably thought the stones were a bunch of scattered rocks, but my dad saw it right away. It took several months to clear and reassemble what we could, but we did it.

Observing the damage as we walked by, I wasn't nearly as disappointed as Dav. Of course, if I had seen it before, I might have been, but it wasn't as bad as he believed. Most of the city looked like a battering ram of some sort was used to knock down the walls of the various structures.

Many of the stones weren't even broken and could easily be restacked. Sadly, all the statues had been broken apart with large hammers. Still, they were salvageable. In the past, I had reassembled artifacts that were broken down into pieces smaller than my fingers. However, we didn't have that kind of time. I prayed the tablet wasn't buried underneath the walls of the temple or it could take weeks to dig it out if we were strong enough.

Even through the rubble, I could make out the design of the city. It wasn't as big as the city in Idaho, but it was much larger than the small village in Europe. It would have been home to a few hundred residences or so, which was pretty large for ancient times. We walked past areas of housing along with small canals that could have been used to bring water into the city.

I was amazed that the vegetation that grew all around the city hadn't reclaimed it, as nature often does in Balfjord. More often than not in my realm, nature and time were the primary culprits to the devastation of ancient civilizations.

Looking this way and that at everything we passed, I didn't notice that Dav had stopped until I walked right into him. He turned to stop me, and I could hear him say not to look, but it was too late. Behind him lay the bloodied body of a man wearing the exact same uniform as him. I gasped and covered my mouth at the gruesome sight.

Dav pulled me to him, putting himself between me and the dead warrior. I could feel his arms around me. "It's okay," he said, holding my head to his chest. He quickly turned me away and took me behind the rubble of a collapsed wall where I could no longer see the dead man. "Look at me," he said as he sat me down.

I took a deep breath and opened my eyes. "I'm sorry." All I could see was red and I closed my eyes again. Banks was the first person I saw killed and the sight of him getting shot was horrible, but this was much worse. So much blood.

"There's no reason to apologize." I felt his hand cup my face and turn it up until I was looking at him. "Are you all right?" I nodded, and he instructed me to stay there while he tended to the man.

Before he could walk away, I grabbed his hand. "He's the warrior you told me about, isn't he?" My voice cracked as I spoke.

"Yes," Dav answered. He gave my fingers a squeeze and stepped around the wall.

It took a few minutes to collect my thoughts. *Pull it together, Semmi. You have to be stronger than this. Dad is counting on you and you don't need Dav thinking you're more useless than you already are in this place.* I took another deep breath and stood and joined Dav.

He had finished wrapping the man's body in his cloak. I could no longer see the injuries he had sustained, only the blood that stained the stones around him.

"Can I help you?" I asked. He looked at me for a moment then asked if I could assist him with carrying the warrior to a nearby clearing.

We took the man to the northeast edge of the city. Then Dav led me over to the location of the temple. Explaining the man we found appeared to have been killed not long ago, he instructed me to stay there while he patrolled the area,.

His voice was nearly a growl as he spoke, and his eyes didn't have the kind look I was used to. It was obvious he knew the man well. Being alone didn't make me feel all that comfortable, but it seemed Dav needed some time to himself. I promised to stay, and he assured me I would be safe.

After he left, I walked around the temple to assess the work ahead of me. Whoever was working to destroy the city must have ended up in a rush when they reached the northern part of town. Some walls were still fully intact or only toppled at the top, leaving the lower portions standing. This was true with the temple.

It wasn't a large building and was probably used for individual worship or small ceremonies. No more than a few dozen people could fit inside comfortably. The entrance to the temple received the most damage and was almost obliterated, but the side walls were only partially collapsed. It was sad to see the beautiful statues inside were now smashed to bits. The large tablet as well had been broken apart.

To my relief, the stones of the walls had fallen almost straight down, making it easy to separate them from the ones belonging to the tablet in the center of the room. Plus, the tablet was made of a different type of stone. It was almost completely white.

Picking up a few pieces, I could see it was much denser than the wall stones, and the face of the stone was smooth as glass. Unfortunately, because it was more dense and heavier than the surrounding stones, it shattered into hundreds of pieces when it hit the ground.

I stood at the broken base of the tablet sticking up out of the ground, looking at all the pieces. "Where do I start first?" I asked myself. "Dad, I wish you were here." He was the master at rebuilding crumbled cities. I remembered watching him in Idaho. He was able to look at the marks on a wall where it broke and tell which direction all the pieces would have gone. Ninety percent of the time he was right.

Luckily for me, all the pieces were here. No digging was needed to find them. It was a matter of putting them back together in the right spot. The tablet had been rammed near the base causing it to fall backward. Some pieces were rather large, but most were about the size of my hand or smaller. To save time, I decided reassembling it where it fell would be the best option.

First, I cleared away all the wall stones and moved the pieces of the tablet closer together. Once I was sure I had found all the pieces, I began putting it together like a gigantic jigsaw puzzle, starting at the bottom.

I had barely put together two feet when I realized it was getting dark. Several hours had passed and Dav hadn't returned. My stomach instantly turned as I walked to the temple entrance and looked around. The area was clear and silent. Although he'd told me to stay, after seeing the dead warrior earlier, I was worried about what was keeping him.

Quietly I walked through the city, looking and listening for any sign of Dav or if there was danger nearby, but all I heard were the bugs chirping that night was coming. The only place I could think to go was the clearing where we left the man's body, so I headed that way.

When I got to the perimeter wall, I stayed behind it and slowly peeked around the corner. I breathed a sigh of relief to see Dav. He was arranging a pile of wood into a rectangular platform, the type I had seen used to cremate people after they'd passed away.

The body of the man was no longer covered but laid out. His face and uniform were cleaned and straightened. With the blood gone, he looked almost as if he was lying on the ground asleep. Not wanting to disturb Dav, I ducked back behind the wall and walked back to the temple.

I felt horrible that Dav had lost one of his fellow warriors. Seeing him prepare the platform made me wish there was something I could do to help. As I looked around, it suddenly hit me: flowers. In my realm, it was customary to have flowers honoring lost loved ones and I remembered picking tons of them when my mother died. She would have loved it here. Flowers were not in short supply and they were more colorful than any I had ever seen before.

I hurried to gather an armful of blue, purple, and teal along with a few bright yellow ones and sat down to arrange them into a wreath. It had been a while since I had done this, but within about fifteen minutes I had a small but pretty wreath of flowers. The dark green leaves around the edge made the colors stand out even more.

Satisfied with my creation, I headed back to the clearing. Dav had laid the man on the platform and was securing his hands around the sword over his chest when I returned. I stood quietly waiting for him to finish when he noticed me holding the flowers.

I hoped I hadn't disturbed him. He walked up to me and looked down at the wreath in my hands. "Um, I made this for him," I said nervously and handed the wreath to Dav. "When, ah, when my mother died, my father was insistent that we not forget the flowers. He told me that she believed it was important to lay flowers over the person we had lost. That they symbolized the completion of the circle of life and a return of the body to the Earth after the spirit was released." As I explained the significance of the flowers, my eyes watered and my voice became shaky as I spoke.

When he took the wreath from my hands, his fingers brushed mine. With a slight nod, he took it and I stood with him as he laid it on the man's body. "Thank you, Semmi," he said quietly.

"He was your friend, wasn't he?"

"Yes," Dav answered. "His name was Tomar. We'd been friends since childhood. Trained together."

"I'm so sorry, Dav."

"He's not the first we've lost and I'm sure he won't be the last."

Hearing him say that broke my heart and filled me with guilt at the same time. Here his childhood friend was murdered, and I had been stressed about whether or not I would get to see my dad again. At least my dad was alive, I told myself. For the first time, I truly realized how important it was for his people that we succeed.

Dav said we would wait to light the fire to burn him until we were ready to leave. The smoke would be seen for miles and he wanted to make sure we were long gone before anyone noticed. We returned to the temple and I showed him the progress I had made. With his help, we could possibly finish putting it together tomorrow.

That night, we skipped studying. While Dav examined the map to find a different route for us to take, I used my sling to hunt something to eat. I was able to find another Horned Taren and when I returned, Dav had gathered some wild fruit to add to our meal.

As the Taren cooked, Dav explained he'd found evidence that the Calvar who killed his friend and probably destroyed the city had headed in the same direction he'd planned for us. By the number of tracks, he estimated there were over a dozen of them, and with only the two of us, he didn't want to chance running into them.

"What are you thinking?" I asked with regard to our new direction of travel.

He moved over next to me and laid the map over my legs. "I'm thinking we'll go in this direction." I followed his finger as he traced our new path to the northwest to an empty part of the map then east back to the Valley of the Giants.

"What's over there?" I asked, curious as to why that area was empty of any villages, roads, or trails.

"Don't know," he answered. "I don't know anyone who's ever been through this part of the forest."

I lifted the map toward the firelight to read the name. "I don't recognize this word," I said, pointing at it for him to read. His people's writing was so much different from mine that it took me time to decipher it, almost as if it was an entirely different language, but names were a struggle for me. He looked at the word then back at me but didn't respond. "Dav? What is it?"

"Baccoba," he replied. "It's the name of a giant hairy beast from an old scary story parents tell their children to keep them from getting out of bed at night. Your realm must have those stories that the Baccoba or some monster will get you if you get out of bed before the sun comes up."

"We have those stories." I laughed. "But the monsters were always said to hide under your bed or in the closet. Since I didn't have a bed or a closet, it didn't work very well on me."

Dav chuckled and further explained the significance of the child's tale and the name of the forest. He said that a long time ago, rumors spread that evil spirits lived in this part of the forest, causing the trees to grow bigger, blocking out the sun. Over time, it came to be known as the home of the Baccoba.

"Tomar said he stood at the border of the forest once," he continued. "He told me that a dense fog lingers below the canopy and when the wind blows, strange ghostly sounds echo off the trees."

When I laid down to sleep, Dav was still watching the fire. I silently made a promise to him that I would do everything I could to help his people, so he wouldn't have to see any more of his friends die. This was no longer about my dad and me but about the freedom of everyone in this realm.

CHAPTER TWELVE

The glow of the two moons was the only light in the sky when I woke. Dav lay asleep not far from me. Quietly, I grabbed my sword and tiptoed away from camp along the outer wall of the temple where there was an open space.

I set my feet and got into position. Slowly I practiced the moves Dav had taught me. I told myself I had to start making improvements, and if it took a little extra practice then that's what I would do. Too much was at stake and I didn't want us to fail because of me.

I closed my eyes and pictured Dav showing me how to strike and block and repeated the movements over and over until I saw a bit of light in the sky. Little by little, I crept back over to our camp. Dav still lay asleep. Thankful I hadn't woken him, I lay back down and pulled my cloak over me. He was doing so well with our short lessons; I didn't want him to know that I wasn't excelling quite as quickly.

I had barely drifted off to sleep when there was a thumping on my feet. Opening my eyes, I looked up to see Dav tapping my feet with his boot.

"Morning. Ready to practice?"

"Yep." I hopped to my feet and grabbed my sword.

I followed him to the place where I'd practiced earlier. Silently, I prayed that my little bit of extra practice would help show some improvement.

Without being asked, I got into position to begin. Dav nodded his head as he called out strikes and blocks. After he called out all the movements twice, he stepped in front of me and drew his own sword, then called out the movements again. This time he used his own sword to block or strike against me. It was the first time he presented himself as my opponent, so I could gain experience performing my moves on someone else.

We continued going through each movement over and over. I almost didn't notice that he had stopped calling out what to do and I was reading his movements to determine whether I needed to strike or block. My steps were still a little rigid, but I was more comfortable with the motions.

"Good," Dav commented as he stepped back and lowered his sword to signal we were finished. "You did well today."

Finally, I heard the words I'd prayed for: his recognition that I was at last making progress. I followed him back to camp, smiling to myself. The extra practice paid off, a ritual I would have to continue if I wanted to keep up.

Our camp was a few yards outside the temple and Dav said we could leave our bags there while we finished the tablet. He gave me instructions to get started while he checked the area again. With the Order of Calvar close by and if there were as many as Dav believed, it was imperative that we not cross paths. Even though I had made progress, I was nowhere near able to mount an effective defense. If Dav got hurt trying to protect me, I would never forgive myself.

"How much longer do you think it will take?" he asked before leaving. "It would be best if we didn't stay here much longer."

"With your help, probably by the end of the day. I hope you're good at puzzles."

"What's a puzzle?"

"This." I waved my arm at the scattered stones. His bland expression made it difficult to know whether he understood or not, but I didn't want to slow us down. "I'll explain when you get back."

I watched him leave then turned my attention to the pieces around me. Normally, reassembling something like this would take days, but we didn't have that kind of time. Working as fast as possible, I moved the pieces closer together, matching up the broken edges of the stones and engravings on the front. I made quick progress. The inscription was coming together, but I still had a long way to go.

When Dav returned, I had completed another two feet of the tablet. Four feet down, eight more to go, I thought to myself. I explained to Dav how I had all the pieces laid out and how to match them together. It took a few minutes for him to grasp the concept, but after he lined up a few pieces, he started moving much faster. I was a little embarrassed when I looked back and saw that he was moving quicker than I was.

"Is there anything you're not good at?" I asked.

Watching him work, I was caught somewhere between being impressed at his skills and disappointed in myself for lacking the speed at which he excelled in everything he did.

"I can't speak any other languages," he replied, glancing my way.

"At the rate you're going, you'll be able to read another language in no time."

"Only because I have a good teacher."

His comment made me smile. I had never taught anyone another language before and the only language I didn't learn on my own was Gaelic, which I learned from my mother as a child. It felt good to know my method of teaching was working well for him. I hoped he didn't think my poor progress was a result of his teaching. Because he already knew his own language, he already possessed the knowledge of how written language worked. I had never had to defend myself before. Teaching me to fight was like starting from scratch.

We barely spoke the rest of the day except for when Dav would let me know that he was going to do a perimeter check. Concerned for our safety, he would leave every couple of hours. During his last check before nightfall, I finished the last bit of the tablet and started translating it.

"Are you finished?" he asked quickly when he returned to the temple. He was breathing heavily and I could hear the concern in his voice. I squatted next to the tablet, writing the translation of the tablet in Master Orin's journal.

"Almost," I replied, not looking up.

"How soon until you're done?"

"Why?"

"We're going to have company in about ten minutes if we don't leave soon."

Dav instructed me to continue while he gathered our things. I was already working as fast as I could. Adding the threat of the Calvar approaching didn't help. To avoid mistranslating something, I opted to copy the inscription as it was written so I could finish translating it later. It took only a few minutes to copy what was left, and I ran out of the temple to where Dav was waiting with our bags.

"You got it all?" he asked, handing me my pack.

"Yes." I tucked the journal away and quickly slung the pack over my shoulders.

"Good, we have to go. Now."

We sprinted through the village. When we passed the platform with his friend's body, I slowed. "What about Tomar?" I asked, remembering Dav was going to light a fire, to burn him according to their traditions.

"There's no time," he replied, grabbing my hand and pulling me with him.

As I chased after him, the sound of people's voices echoed through the trees. It felt like Idaho all over again, but this time I couldn't scratch runes into the ground to escape to another realm. Jorunn had only given the runic code for this realm. If they found us, we would have to fight to save ourselves.

"Did they see us?"

"No, but they'll know we've been there soon enough."

We ducked around a large grove of bushes that looked like giant bright green ferns with long blue flowers. He pulled me down and motioned for me to stay quiet. He scanned the forest behind us and listened for signs that our trail had been discovered.

"Stay here," he whispered, setting down his pack.

"What?" I gasped, my mouth gaping open. Without thinking, I reached up and grabbed his hand as he stood up. "No," I pleaded. The last time I was told to stay out of sight, I lost my dad. If I lost Dav too, I didn't know what I would do. That thought scared me more than anything.

"You'll be okay," he replied. "I won't be gone long. Keep your head down."

"It's not me I'm worried about," I said, still holding onto his hand.

As if reading my mind, Dav knelt in front of me and cupped my face with his hand. "It's my job to protect you." He looked into my eyes. "I'll be back. I promise. Okay?"

I nodded and he squeezed my hand before letting go. Within seconds he was out of sight and I was alone. To try to stop my hands from shaking I clenched my fists and held them to my chest. My heart was beating out of control and I could hear it thumping in my chest. I closed my eyes for a few moments in an attempt to control my breathing and slow my pulse.

Through the pounding of my heart, I listened to the voices of the Calvar in the distance. They had reached the city. From this distance, I couldn't make out their words, but the change in the volume and pitch of their voices told me they had discovered our presence there. Someone began shouting. His voice was deep, and his orders to find who had been there carried through the trees.

"Hurry back, Dav," I whispered. I made sure the straps on my pack were tight and I grabbed Dav's bag, ready to run in an instant as soon as he returned, which I prayed was very soon.

Movement through the trees caught my attention and I ducked lower to stay hidden. A light-haired man moved through the trees toward my position, wearing the same Calvar uniform I had seen on the soldiers in

Sweetwater. He gave no indication that he could see me as he searched the area.

Where are you, Dav? I kept my eyes trained on the soldier.

I was so focused on him that I didn't notice another was approaching me from behind until it was too late. A large hand clamped over my mouth and around my waist, lifting me off the ground. I tried to scream but the sound of my voice couldn't be heard through the man's hand. I squirmed and kicked my feet trying to break his grip.

The man holding me shouted to the other for help as I kept kicking. I could feel the man's hand around my waist start to slip but when I thought I might be able to wiggle free, he threw me to the ground and slammed his boot into my stomach. Gasping for air, I felt his knee press into my back as he tied a rag around my mouth to keep me from yelling.

The man pulled my hands behind my back and started to tie them together when I sensed him being yanked away from me. He flew past me, hitting the light-haired man who was running toward me. Dav stepped over me, putting himself between them and me as he pulled a knife from his belt. Both men came at him with their swords drawn.

"Stay down," he said to me, stepping forward to engage them.

I jerked the rope off my wrist and quickly yanked the gag from my mouth. Taking out my sword, I looked up from the ground and saw Dav defending me against these two men with only a knife to their two swords. I had never seen anyone move the way he did. Dodging their swings, then delivering a powerful kick or slice with his knife, he fought them almost effortlessly.

Another dark-haired man with a beard emerged from the trees behind him carrying a bow. When he saw the fight going on, he reached over his shoulder for an arrow. The pouch with my sling hung from my belt and I quickly took it out along with one of the egg-shaped stones.

Before the man could pull the string to fire his arrow, I spun my sling and released the stone. Dav looked over at me as I sent the stone flying. Turning, he followed its path, watching as it struck the man in the head. The man's eyes rolled back, and his body slumped to the ground.

I had killed animals before but never a person. Not wanting to think about whether or not he was dead, I turned my attention back to Dav. The light-haired man was lying facedown, not showing any signs of life. A growing pool of blood oozed out from underneath him.

I looked over at the other man he was fighting. Dav had dodged a swing from his sword, then stepped forward taking a slice with his knife. Blood sprayed out from the man's neck and all over me. He fell to his knees before me, gripping his neck as I watched the life drain from his eyes.

"Semmi." I could hear Dav, but I was still focused on the dead man at my feet. Dav stepped in front of me and took my face with both hands to get my attention.

"Huh," I mumbled and looked up at him.

"Are you hurt?" I shook my head and told him no. "We need to move before they realize their men are missing."

***

We ran for what felt like hours. I kept my eyes on Dav's back as I chased him through the forest, listening intently for any sounds indicating that someone was behind us. My legs burned, and it seemed as though at any moment I was going to fall on my face from fatigue.

"Dav, please." I gasped for air. "Can we stop for a minute?"

"We'll stop up there, okay?" He pointed to an outcrop of rocks ahead of us.

"Okay," I replied in between breaths.

As soon as we stepped behind the rocks, I dropped to my hands and knees to catch my breath. Dav handed me a leather pouch filled with water and I immediately sucked down a big gulp before he snatched it away.

"Easy, Semmi," he snapped. "You'll make yourself sick if you drink that fast." He handed the pouch back to me but held onto my wrist until

I said I understood. "Are you sure you're okay?" he asked again. "You're not hurt?"

"I don't think so." I didn't realize the rag the man had tied over my face was still hanging around my neck and I quickly yanked it off. The wrist he managed to get a rope around was a little red and my ribs felt tight where he had kicked me, but there was no pain. With all the adrenaline running through me, I seemed fine but was sure I would feel the pain later.

"No, I'm not hurt," I told him. "Are you okay?" I peered at him curiously, worried one of the men he'd been fighting had landed a blow.

"Yeah, I'm fine."

I took another smaller sip and sat back, taking a few more deep breaths. "Are they following us?" I asked after a few minutes.

Dav sat by the edge of the rocks where he could watch behind us. "I can hear them out there," he answered, "but it doesn't seem like they know which way we went. We need to keep moving. If they know anything about tracking, it won't be long before they find our trail." He pulled the map out from inside his shirt and took a quick look.

Before he could put the map away, I was back on my feet. Even though my legs protested, I knew we were still in danger and they would have to wait. After Dav took a quick drink of water, we set out again heading north farther into the mountains. To my relief, we continued at a slower pace, giving my thighs a break.

Our journey was quiet. Dav only spoke to tell me which direction we were heading and that we wouldn't stop unless he felt it was safe. Every now and then, he would stop and listen.

At first, there were voices in the distance, but after a few more hours, all sounds of people were gone. I took it as a sign that they hadn't discovered our path and breathed a sigh of relief, although Dav was not as convinced.

The sun was long gone, and the moons were the only light we had to make our way north. The thick canopy of trees above made it much darker on the ground. I struggled to see and stumbled a few times but refused to stop until Dav finally insisted we take a break.

"No, I'm fine," I argued as I got up off the ground after tripping over a large tree root.

"Your legs are tired and so are mine," he said, "and I'm sure you're hungry. If we don't get some rest and food, we won't be strong enough to fight back if they do find us."

"I'll gather some wood for a fire."

Dav instructed me to keep it small and left to catch something to eat as he checked the area. When he returned, I had a little fire going, which I had stacked stones around to further hide the glow of the flames.

After he handed me two birds he'd managed to kill, I hurried to get them cooking. He sat and watched me work without saying a word. As I cleaned the birds and placed them on a stick to cook over the fire, I thought about the attack.

Although I found myself intently trying to wipe away the blood that had sprayed all over me, surprisingly, it wasn't seeing a man killed right in front of me that affected me the most. It was the way Dav fought that stuck in my mind. From his hands to his feet, he used his entire body as a weapon, and he was so fast, I found myself mesmerized by his skills as a warrior.

While our food cooked, I took out the journal and reread the inscription to see if it had information useful to our mission. Inscribed on the large tablet was a long quote, speaking about wisdom, respect, and prosperity. It was quite beautiful and full of wonderful information about life, but sadly it wasn't what we were looking for. I read it to Dav and he commented on what powerful words of wisdom the Hvaldi put forth to guide their lives.

We ate our meal in silence. Dav seemed disappointed in the translation. Had his people not been in this situation it would have been different. I crossed my fingers that we would have more success in the Valley of the Giants.

"Thank you," Dav said to break the silence, "for what you did for me today. You're very good with that sling of yours and it's more effective than I thought."

I shook my head, knowing who the real hero was. "You shouldn't be thanking me. I was so focused on the man in front of me that I didn't hear the one behind me. It's my fault. Had I been more observant—"

"I shouldn't have let them get that close to you," he cut in. His jaw clenched as he stared into the fire, his eyes narrow. He blamed himself, but he was wrong to.

I reached out and touched his knee, getting him to look at me. "You stopped them, and I'm okay."

He nodded and his face relaxed. I turned my attention back to tending our food, which was nearly ready to eat.

"Do you think I killed that man?" I asked after a few moments.

"If not, I'm sure he'll have one heck of a headache when he wakes up," Dav replied, the corner of his mouth curling up slightly. "Have you ever seen anyone die before?"

I nodded. "My mother. I was sitting next to her, holding her hand when she passed."

As we ate, Dav asked me how she died, and I told him about the illness that took her life and nearly mine. I could still clearly remember that night, sitting by her bedside as she took her last breath. "That's when my dad took a job as a master mason building a church in a small village. I begged for months to leave before he finally gave in."

"You didn't like living in the village?"

"I hated it," I replied, poking at the fire. "I was used to being on dig sites with my parents. In the village, I couldn't go with him and he made me attend school. I had such a hard time. The other children were still learning how to read and write their own language and here I was already able to speak three languages and read five. They teased me for being smart and made fun of my accent. No one wanted to be my friend."

"That was their loss." When I looked over at him, he was watching me. His eyes no longer showed his anger, and the look I had enjoyed had returned to his face. It made me smile. When we first met, it bothered me when he would watch me, not knowing what he was thinking. Now, I felt comfort in it. Safe. Although I still struggled with reading his lack of expression, I was getting better at noticing the subtle differences.

"Does that mean you consider me your friend?" I asked him.

The corner of his mouth curled up again and he gave me a wink. "Get some rest," he said. "We'll want to get moving again before the sun comes up." He threw some dirt on the fire to put it out and we both lay down.

I waited until I heard Dav breathing heavily before sitting up again to do my nightly ritual of practicing with my sword. I was careful not to go too far away in case anything happened. My body felt stiff as I tried to practice my moves and I was starting to feel where the man had kicked me in the ribs. Standing in the moonlight, I lifted my shirt and could see several bruises starting to form.

"That's going to hurt in the morning," I whispered.

Taking it slow, I kept practicing until something in the forest caught my eye. A light moving through the trees. From the color, it looked like a torch, but I didn't want to wait and find out. I hurried back to wake Dav.

"What is it?" he whispered and sat up after I shook him.

"I saw a light in the forest." He was on his feet in an instant and I led him over to where he could see it. The light was definitely a torch and it was getting closer. We both knew there was no more time to rest. We had to get moving.

Dav grabbed my arm before heading back to gather our things. "What were you doing wandering around?"

"I couldn't sleep," I lied, not wanting him to know the truth.

He only nodded and let go, but I could tell he was hesitant to believe me. In the week since I'd arrived in this realm, we had gotten to know each other, and I considered him my friend. After all we'd been through, I hated lying to him but still felt like I needed to prove that I could do this. Not only to him but to myself as well.

When I reached down to grab my pack, I gasped at a sudden, sharp pain in my ribs. My immediate reaction was to grab my side and clench my teeth. I took a few breaths and waited for the pain to subside before continuing. Unfortunately, my hopes that Dav hadn't noticed while he was getting his own things together didn't pan out.

"I thought you said you weren't hurt," he snapped. When I turned to face him, he was glaring at me.

"It didn't start hurting until I got up," I told him, which was the truth. "It's only a few bruises from where he kicked me. I'll be okay. I'm not as fragile as you think."

As I moved to walk past him, Dav stuck out his arm and held on to my waist. "And what makes you think that that's how I see you?" he asked quietly, his dark eyes burning into mine.

"Then how do you see me?" I asked without thinking and instantly regretted it, unsure if I wanted to know the answer.

I had a great deal of respect for Dav. For his willingness to do all he could to help his people and the training he'd endured to become a gifted warrior. He was a hero in my mind, and I appreciated him for everything he was doing. He was what pushed me to better myself.

"Not fragile," he replied and dropped his hand but kept looking at me. "You're stronger than you think, Semmi." Dav didn't wait for me to respond but grabbed his bag and moved out.

I didn't know what to make of his comment. Now, I was curious about what he thought of me. He was not at all what I expected from our first meeting. Though he rarely expressed how he felt, I had seen small changes in his behavior toward me. Although I didn't know what they meant, I liked the way they made me feel.

Even the way he touched my face or hand was never harsh but tender. After watching him make short work of the men who tried to capture me, it was difficult to imagine how a man so strong and fierce could also be gentle at the same time. You could say I admired and cared for him in a way I didn't yet understand.

When I fell into step behind him, we hurried to put some more distance between us and whoever was wandering through the forest before they located our camp. Dav had kicked out the fire but there was no way to hide that we had been there. He chose a rockier path that would make it more difficult to follow our trail.

"When do you think we'll reach the Baccoba Forest?" I asked.

"Before nightfall, if we hurry."

"Do you think they'll follow us in?"

"Maybe, if they don't believe all the scary stories about it."

"What, that there're ghosts there?" I teased.

Dav stopped and looked back at me. "Not exactly. But as far as anyone knows, no one who's gone in has ever come out."

"What?" I muttered, my eyes opening wider.

"What's wrong, Semmi? Scared?" There was smugness to his tone and I knew he had to be messing with me, but still, his comment was unsettling.

"No," I replied, trying to sound as convincing as possible. He turned away and kept walking, but I could hear him chuckle and had to admit that even I wasn't convinced. I hoped he was joking, but I guessed I would soon find out.

CHAPTER THIRTEEN

We reached the border of the Baccoba Forest as predicted. A narrow canyon with a river running far below divided the two forests. Tomar's description, while accurate, didn't do it justice.

The trees stretched hundreds of feet into the air making the trees in the forest where we were standing look like mere saplings. They towered so high above I had to lean my head back to see the tops. Not far overhead, wisps of fog hovered around the tree trunks. As the wind blew, I heard an awful sound, something between a howl and a moan and so eerie, it made the hair on my neck stand up.

"Are you sure we have to go through there?" I asked.

"It would take weeks to walk around it," Dav replied. "Not to mention we would probably run into the Calvar in the process. I think if we cut through here, we could get to the Valley of the Giants in less than a week."

"All right," I murmured, looking through the mammoth trees. Besides the spooky sounds and darkness, I couldn't see signs of life. The forest appeared empty, as though even the animals were scared to go in.

"Good. We'll follow the canyon that way," Dav said, pointing east past where I was standing. "Looks like there's a downed tree we can use to cross."

The day was nearly over. Only a few of the sun's rays still lit the sky and the moons were starting to rise. The colors created by the setting sun and the encroaching moonlight were so beautiful. No sunset on Balfjord could compare.

Where the yellow and orange rays met the approaching twilight made a ribbon of purple, blue, and green that rippled through the sky. I looked forward to a day when I could stop and enjoy being able to see the beauty of this realm without the fear of being hunted down.

Taking another look up, I turned and followed Dav's directions with him behind me. I had barely taken five steps when the snap of a twig caught my attention. I felt Dav's hand on my back before I had a chance to look for what had caused the sound.

"Run!" Dav snapped, pushing me forward.

I didn't hesitate and took off as fast as I could toward the downed tree, but it was still some distance away. From behind a tree a man wearing the Calvar uniform stepped out, his sword already swinging toward my head.

There was no time to think about form or stance. My immediate reaction was to drop to my knees and slide under his arm. I barely dodged the blade as it swooped over my head. I grabbed my sword and, in one motion, I pulled it from its sheath and swung it behind me cutting a deep gash into the man's leg.

For a moment, I watched him drop to one knee, grabbing at the wound and leaving his side unguarded. I stepped forward and plunged the end of my sword through his ribs as hard as I could, then ripped it back out. The man dropped his weapon to the ground and gasped once before falling over.

"Keep going," Dav yelled, jumping over the body of another man, blood dripping from the blade of his sword. He turned me around and guided me ahead of him.

We ran as fast as we could. Through the trees, I could see more men hurrying to cut us off, but they weren't quick enough. We made it to the tree first. The trunk was huge and Dav had to give me a lift, so I could reach the top and pull myself up.

Seeing the river so far below made me dizzy and I nearly lost my balance. Dav grabbed the back of my pack to steady me.

"Keep your eyes on the tree," he ordered. "And don't look down."

"Got it." I trained my eyes on the dark coarse bark of the tree in front of me. One step at a time, I walked as quickly as I could across the log and slid down the other side.

Dav jumped down right behind me, barely dodging an arrow fired by one of the men. "Into the forest," he yelled as another arrow flew by hitting the ground at my feet.

I didn't need him to tell me again. More arrows rained down on us, as we made our way past the tree line. One grazed my arm, but with no time to do anything about it, I gritted my teeth and kept going. They finally stopped firing arrows as we ran deeper into the forest. I slowed and looked back over my shoulder to see that the men hadn't followed us across and were now heading back the way they came.

"I guess they do believe the stories," I said between breaths. I reached up and rubbed my arm. My shirt was torn, and I could feel where the arrow had ripped through my skin. I touched the wound lightly, but that's all it took to feel the sting. Lightning bolts of pain shot down my arm and I quickly pulled my hand away, blood covering the tips of my fingers.

"Take off your jacket," Dav ordered, seeing the blood on my hand. He dropped his pack and helped me with mine.

I took off my cloak and unbuttoned my leather jacket. The burning of my arm made it difficult to slip it off. Dav grabbed the collar and gently helped me. Without my coat, I was a little self-conscious. The only thing I had on underneath was a thin, sleeveless leather top that barely covered my belly.

I wrapped one arm around my waist to hold the bottom of the shirt down when I noticed Dav staring at me. He quickly looked away and turned his attention to preparing medicine for my injury. I watched him mix blue, purple, and yellow powder from the medicine box he removed from his bag. Next, he sprinkled the mixture over my open wound, slowly adding more until the bleeding stopped. He wrapped it with a clean dressing before returning the box to his pack.

"Thank you."

"How are your bruises doing?" he asked as I picked up my jacket.

I dropped my arm from around my waist and he lifted my shirt a little and examined the large purple bruises that covered one side of my ribcage. I let him know that it didn't hurt to breathe, only when I pressed on the area or tried bending to that side. When he lightly ran his fingers over my ribs around the edge of one of the bruises, my heart quickened and goose bumps raised up on my skin.

"Did I hurt you?" he asked, pulling his hand away.

"No," I replied, quietly trying to hide a smile. "It…it tickled." He didn't say anything, but I could see him smile a little as he helped me with my jacket, picked up my pack, and offered to carry it.

Dav said he wanted to go a little farther before we stopped for the night. Even though I didn't believe in ghost stories, this dark forest with its patches of dense fog slowly blowing through the trees above made me extra jumpy. As I looked around, the forest lay still. No birds flew around or bugs chirped unlike the sacred lands.

A gust of wind blew by and the howl I heard from before called out over our heads. The gasp that escaped my lips was nearly a scream and I jumped, grabbing hold of Dav's arm. My heart leaped into my throat and every hair on my body felt as if it was standing straight up. I had turned my face into his shoulder when I heard him start to laugh.

"I thought you said you weren't scared," he teased.

"I ah…it startled me," I lied, a little embarrassed. My body still shook and I guess he must have felt it too. He took my hand in his and walked forward a few steps looking up at the canopy.

"There's your ghost, Semmi."

I followed his hand as he pointed up at one of the nearby trees. Tied to several of its branches was a collection of wooden wind chimes and what looked to be some kind of flute. When the wind blew through them, it created the howling sound I heard earlier. Several other trees in the area had the same items hanging from them. What an ingenious idea to scare people away.

The idea that such a simple thing had scared me made me even more embarrassed. I shook my head and looked down at the ground. I felt so silly.

"You know your cheeks are turning red," Dav whispered in my ear and squeezed my hand. "I promise I won't tell anyone."

"Thanks." I laughed.

We only walked for another hour before stopping. My eyes were heavy, and my body was drained from lack of sleep the night before. There was not much point in making a fire since we had yet to see any animals scurrying about that we could catch for a meal. Dav promised to find something in the morning and laid his stuff down in a flat area behind a downed log.

Knowing now what was making the howling sounds still didn't completely calm my nerves. When I set my things down, I tried not to make it too obvious that I had made my bed a little closer to his than usual.

I felt safer near him and it seemed the longer we spent time together, the more I wanted to be near him. I could see now what Otto meant when he said I simply didn't know Dav yet. At first glance, it might have seemed he showed little to no emotion, but now that I'd had the chance to be around him, I noticed when he smiled slightly and the way the look in his eyes changed depending on how he felt. The only thing I seemed to struggle with was what he thought when he looked at me.

"Are you all right?" Dav asked quietly.

"Yeah," I responded and checked the bandages on my arm.

"I wasn't referring to your arm," he clarified. "You killed a man today."

"I know," I muttered, sitting on my cloak and staring at the ground. "Is it bad that killing him isn't what's bothering me?"

"Then what is?"

"The moment I saw him swinging his sword at me, everything you taught me seemed to go right out of my mind and I reacted out of instinct, forgetting about proper form." I was so upset with myself. I felt like I'd failed Dav.

"That's what you're supposed to do." Dav's answer surprised me and I looked up at him for an explanation. "Fighting is about reaction and instinct. Training helps to improve those. You did well."

"I'm working on it. Your realm is so different from mine. I'm trying to learn as fast as I can." His comment made me feel better. I was worried I had disappointed him again with my lack of experience in fighting.

"You're doing fine."

"Yeah, if I have you there to protect me when a wind chime scares me," I replied, making fun of myself for letting an old monster story get the best of me. Dav chuckled and gave me a wink before lying down.

As I looked up at the canopy above, my thoughts drifted to those of my dad. I wondered how he was doing and if he had gotten a chance to talk to Master Orin. I hoped Orin told him I was okay and safe, but somehow, I didn't think my dad would consider what I was doing safe.

It didn't take long for sleep to find me. The silence of the forest and the sound of Dav's breathing, put my nerves at ease and I was able to relax.

***

The sound of a fire crackling and the smell of food cooking woke me up in the morning. When I lifted my head, Dav was sitting next to a fire and there were two small animals on a stick sizzling over the flames. The sun was up brightening the forest. The canopy still blocked most of the light, but a few rays snuck through, and in spots where the light touched the ground, patches of grass, flowers, or mushrooms grew in bright colors.

"Good morning," he said when he saw me sit up. "Hungry?"

123

"Yes." I heard my stomach grumble and scooted over next to him. "Good morning to you too," I added. "How long have I been asleep?"

"A while," he answered. "You looked like you needed a good night's rest."

"I did."

After we finished eating, I asked Dav what the plan was for today. He took out the map and showed me roughly where we were and our planned direction of travel. Because no one alive had ever been in the Baccoba Forest, all that was known was where the border was and what could be observed from the outside looking in. We had no idea what we might encounter on our way to the Valley of the Giants.

Based on distance alone, Dav expected us to be able to cross it in about four days if we didn't run into anything that would slow us down. Less than three hours into our trek, that's exactly what we found. In the middle of the forest, a nearly vertical cliff made of mammoth gray stones stretched more than a hundred feet overhead.

The cliff extended in either direction as far as we could see. It made me wonder what made everything in this particular part of the forest larger than anywhere else. The farther in we went, the bigger everything became. The trees were so huge you could live in them and I had yet to see a rock smaller than a wagon wheel.

"That might slow us down a little," I said sarcastically.

"Yeah," was Dav's only comment. He took out the map and walked along the cliff trying to determine which way we should go.

Examining the walls of the cliff, I looked for a possible way up. Close by was a crevice going all the way to the top. I stepped inside and found there were plenty of cracks, small ledges, and notches that could be used as footholds on all sides. After testing it out, I climbed up about twenty feet.

"Dav," I yelled to get his attention, pulling myself up higher. "We can go this way." I looked down and Dav was standing below looking up.

As he stepped into the crevice to start his ascent, I realized for the first time how much smaller I was than him. I knew he was a good head taller than me, but his broad shoulders nearly touched either side. Add his pack, bow, and other weapons, and it was a bit of a tight fit for him. I could hear him grunt as he pulled himself up a step at a time.

"You couldn't have found a spot that was a little roomier, could you?" he asked after he barely squeezed by a tight spot.

"Sorry," I replied, trying not to laugh as he struggled to pull himself through another narrow section. "I didn't realize it was that tight."

Poking my head over the top of the cliff, I came face-to-face with the strangest, and honestly, cutest creature I had ever seen. The animal was about the size of a small short-legged dog with dark brown fur and a thick shaggy mane around its neck. Its long tail wagged as it stared at me with its bright yellow eyes. It sniffed the air but seemed unafraid of me.

"Oh, hello," I slowly said to the creature. Waiting to see how the little beast would react to me, I didn't move.

"What is it?" Dav asked from right below me when he noticed I had stopped climbing.

"An animal," I replied quietly.

"Does it look dangerous?"

"Not exactly." I watched it step closer to me and sniff again. "He looks adorable actually, if it's a 'he.'" Out of nowhere, the little beast licked my face. "Ahh," I laughed and tried to turn my head away from the licking animal. "I'd have to say he's friendly."

I had never seen a small creature with such a long tongue. Since it obviously wasn't ferocious, I climbed the rest of the way over the side.

"Easy, little fella," I said to the beast that was now running around my feet and trying to jump up on me. I knelt and started petting him to keep him occupied while Dav finished his climb.

"Semmi, step away from the furball," Dav said slowly and placed his hand on my shoulder.

"But he doesn't seem dangerous." I looked up at him, but he wasn't looking at me or the creature. His eyes were locked on something else in front of us. My attention had been so focused on the friendly animal that I didn't realize we were being watched.

Not fifty feet away stood a being unlike any I had seen in Polarious. Standing not quite my height was a dark gray-skinned being wearing tan leather pants, coat, and cap. His eyes looked black in the poor light, but his bushy eyebrows and long mustache were as white as could be. He held a long stick that was sharpened at the end and pointed it at us. He growled and took a step forward.

Dav tried to pull me behind him as he drew his sword, but I pushed him back recognizing the being from a description in one of Jorunn's journal entries. "Dav, wait," I snapped and stepped around him. I held my hands up. "You're a Norranian, aren't you?" I asked. Everyone was quiet except the furry creature that was still jumping around my feet and barking.

The being lowered his stick a bit and cocked his head to one side. "And 'ow do you know what I am?" he growled.

"From writings left by the Hvaldi," I answered, still holding my hands up. "Lower your sword," I whispered to Dav. He was hesitant to drop his guard but did as I asked.

"Don't know no Hvaldi," the gray-skinned man said. His accent was thick and gruff. With Dav lowering his weapon, he lowered his spear as well.

"But you are from Norranheim, yes?" He nodded in approval but seemed confused by my question. "How did you get here?" I asked, hoping he might know about traveling between realms that could help us.

"Chasin' dat vermin," the Norranian replied, pointing the end of his spear at the furry creature sitting at my feet. The little beast was smiling up at me with its tongue hanging out. "And 'e don't listen. Chased 'im into a tunnel when 'e took off afta a critter and didn't come back. When we came out, we was 'ere." The furry little beast looked back at his master and snorted at him as if knowing he was being talked about. "Yeah, it's you I'm talkin' about," the Norranian snapped. "Where is 'ere anyways? Been 'ere for years now and every time I try to talk to one of you, dey call me Baccoba and run away screamin'."

"This is Polarious," Dav answered.

"Pole-ar-ee-us," he repeated slowly. "Like dah realm, Polarious."

"You know about the realms?" I asked.

"Everybody knows about dah realms," he spouted. "Never wanted to go to none. Can't figure out 'ow I ended up 'ere."

"I don't understand." I looked up at Dav. "I had to carve the runes to open the door to get here. How did he get here by accident?"

"You'd know better than I would," he replied, still watching the Norranian.

"Carve runes? You not from 'ere?" the Norranian asked me, hearing our conversation.

"She's from Balfjord."

"Great!" he boasted. "You know den. Send me back."

"I can't," I replied sadly. "I only know the runes that got me here."

"So, you stuck 'ere too, eh? Figures." He turned to walk away, calling for the creature to come with him.

"Wait!" I waved and walked toward him. "Maybe we can help each other."

"Semmi, what are you doing?" Dav hissed. It was obvious he was leery of the Norranian, but from what I had read about them, they were supposed to be friendly beings.

"If he's been here for years, he may know the fastest way to the Valley of the Giants," I said. Whether Dav liked the idea or not, we needed the help, and it was clear he understood. We were already well into our second week out here and hadn't found anything that would help prove where his people came from. "Wait. Sir," I yelled after the Norranian. "Please, I don't know what to call you."

"Fye'Gor," he growled.

"What?"

"Fye'Gor," he slowly repeated and turned around. "Me name is Fye'Gor. Fye'Gor Tremble'oof."

"I'm Semmi Bastian and this is Dav," I said.

"Dav what?" Fye'Gor asked, looking him up and down.

"Just Dav," he replied.

"Mm," Fye'Gor grunted. "And 'ow can you 'elp me, and what do you think I can do fur you?" He had a sour look on his face.

"You know this forest," I told him. "We don't. We're trying to get to an ancient city in a place called the Valley of the Giants. Can you help us find the quickest way there?"

"And 'ow does dat 'elp me?"

"At that city, I may be able to find out how to send you home." That caught his attention and he looked at us with excitement in his eyes.

"Why didn't you say so in dah first place?" he snapped. "Which way is dah city?"

CHAPTER FOURTEEN

Fye'Gor agreed to help us but insisted that we stay the night at his hut, saying we both looked like we needed a bath and a good meal, which I couldn't deny. Although a bucket of water and a rag wasn't quite what I would call a bath, it was still greatly appreciated. With it, I was able to wipe away all the dirt that had collected on my body over the last several weeks and even wash my hair. I had almost forgotten how good it felt to be clean.

The Norranian's small, domed mud hut consisted of three rooms: the main living area, a sleeping room, and a small storage room, where Fye'Gor allowed me to clean up. There were a dozen pots from small to large filled with different plants and roots he had gathered to eat. From the roof, a few bundles of herbs hung to dry. He was nice enough to hang a large animal pelt up over the door, so I could have some privacy.

After getting dressed, I came out and found Fye'Gor and Dav hunched over a table near the door discussing the map. Fye'Gor was helping Dav draw in features from this previously unknown forest. In the center of the room, a stone kettle hung over a crackling fire filling the room with a delicious smell. Wisps of smoke floated up through a cone-shaped hole in the roof.

"Did you guys get our route figured out?" I asked, walking over and sitting next to Dav to view the map.

"Yes," Dav replied. He showed me all the land formations Fye'Gor had told him about. Several rivers, lakes, valleys, and mountains were now drawn in. Dav outlined our new path of travel. "It will take a little longer than expected, but had we kept going the way I initially planned, we would've had to backtrack at least three times. It may have taken us over two weeks. Thank you, Fye'Gor."

"Ah," he grunted and waved a hand like it was no big deal. He walked over to the kettle and stirred the soup. "I 'ope you're 'ungry."

"It smells delicious," I commented.

Fye'Gor grabbed some bowls to fill and set them on the stone hearth. The whole time, his little furry friend was darting around the room and between his feet. He growled at the creature as it darted off and jumped onto my lap. I tried to lean my head away from the impending lick, but I wasn't quick enough and he caught me right across the check. Even Dav had to admit he was cute.

"Fye'Gor, what's his name?" I asked as I gave the fuzzball a scratch behind the ears.

"Dung 'eap," he replied, causing me to stop what I was doing.

"Does *dung* mean the same here as I think?" I whispered to Dav.

"Uh-huh," he replied and let out a laugh.

"W-why did you name him after, um"—I cleared my throat—"a pile of poo?"

"Wait and you'll find out," he grumbled. "As usual, 'e won't listen, barks all dah time, always gettin' me into trouble wit 'is dang curiosity. You'll see."

After we ate, Dav went to clean up while Fye'Gor busied himself with gathering his things and preparing some provisions for our journey. He made several loaves of bread and half a dozen pouches of dried veggies; we could easily add water to them to make a soup. I kept Dung Heap entertained with a stick. Like a dog, he enjoyed playing tug-of-war and barked when I managed to get the stick away from him.

When Dav came out of the storeroom from washing, he had his cloak in his hand and his jacket hung open revealing his bare chest underneath. His dark wet hair glistened in the firelight and I found myself staring at him. I didn't notice that Dung Heap had taken the stick from me and run off.

"Did I miss a spot?" Dav asked, noticing I was staring at him.

"Huh? No," I replied a bit surprised and looked away as a warmth spread through my body. When I glanced back, he was still looking at me as if he was waiting for me to say something. To my relief, Fye'Gor came out of his bedroom with a couple of blankets that he laid out on the floor for us.

"I don't get company much 'round 'ere." He laughed and clarified that he had actually never had guests and that we were the first people who hadn't run away screaming when we saw him. "I 'ope dis'll work fur ya."

"It's fine," Dav told him, offering him his hand in thanks for his help and hospitality.

Fye'Gor bid us good evening and retired to his bedroom, calling for Dung Heap to come with him. It got quiet fast. I was still embarrassed that Dav saw me staring at him longer than I should have. I don't know what came over me, I thought to myself. That was a lie. I knew exactly what it was. Dav was an attractive man and the longer I was with him, the more I liked him.

"Are you going to sit over there staring at the floor, or do you want to lie down?" he asked, sitting down on the blankets.

I looked up and noticed there wasn't much floor space, which meant I would be sleeping right next to him. "Ah yeah, I mean no. I mean…Argh," I grumbled, so embarrassed I couldn't even talk. I was sure my cheeks were bright red which only made it worse. "Yes, I'm coming."

Dav didn't say anything, but he had a slight smile and I could see he enjoyed watching me repeatedly embarrass myself. He gazed at me as I walked over and sat down next to him on the floor.

"So," I said to break the awkward silence, "did you learn anything else about this forest?"

"Well, there's no Baccoba," he said, almost sounding disappointed.

"No?"

Dav shook his head. "Fye'Gor said he hasn't seen any animal that resembles the monster. He told me most of the animals here are small except for a giant owl that lives in the trees and a few packs of wolves to the west." He looked back at the fire then back at me before talking again. "I'm glad you asked him to come with us."

"I thought it couldn't hurt to ask. He knows this place and we could use the help," I replied. "I know how important it is that we succeed."

"I only hope that when we do, your father will forgive me for my mistake." He looked down as he finished what he was saying. Clearly, he was trying to remain positive.

"I know he will," I said. "Because I have."

"You have?" His brows crinkled. "But your father's still a prisoner because of me. I haven't earned your forgiveness yet."

"Yes, you have," I told him, taking his hand. "You've saved my life more than once, patched me up, taught me to defend myself even if I'm not that good yet, and protected me from ghosts." I added the last one in hopes of making him laugh and to my delight it worked. "And like it or not, you're my friend. That means a lot to me."

"Thank you." He squeezed my hand and continued to look at me as I pushed a lock of hair out of my face. I had almost forgotten about the injury to my shoulder until then. I cringed as I felt a sting run down my arm. "Speaking of patching you up, let's change your bandages."

My arm was healing well. The colorful powders he used were better than any medicine I had ever seen. My feet had healed quickly and now my arm was doing so as well. The pain had dulled and Dav told me it would be nothing but a scar in another couple of days, adding that I could leave the bandage off after tomorrow.

We talked a little longer about what we would do when we got to the city. I tried not to sound too depressing when I let him know that I was unsure of how long it would take to find the information we needed, but I promised I would work as fast as possible. He asked if we could read a little more of Jorunn's journal to keep up on his lessons, so when we reached the city he would be able to help in some capacity.

It was late, so we kept the lesson short before lying down. I entertained the idea of sneaking out to get a little extra practice with my sword but felt I wouldn't be able to slip out without waking Dav. I reminded myself that after tonight, I needed to keep up my own lessons. Considering how hard he'd worked for me, I had to do all I could for him too

***

Caught somewhere between asleep and awake, I lay still on the floor waiting for Dav's customary tap on the feet to get me up, but it was a slobbery lick to the face that yanked me into consciousness.

"Ahh," I yelled, throwing my hands up to block Dung Heap's tongue from catching me again. I tried to scoot him away and rolled halfway on top of Dav, who was still asleep next to me. My sudden movement must have woken him, and he wrapped one arm around my waist as he helped me fend off the licking fuzzball with the other. I couldn't help but laugh hysterically.

"Dung 'eap!" Fye'Gor snapped, walking into the room. "Leave 'em alone." I was still laughing too hard to respond but managed to roll off of Dav and sit up. His hand still rested on my back.

"Is the sun up yet?" Dav asked.

"You think dat mangy mutt would allow anyone to sleep in dat late?" Fye'Gor huffed. "Probably 'bout another hour."

Now that we were awake, Fye'Gor hurried about grabbing the last few things he thought he would need. This could be the last time he'd see this place. Some of the items he packed last night were now sitting out as if he couldn't decide if he needed them or not.

"Would you like to get in a short lesson?" Dav asked, getting to his feet and grabbing our swords.

"Absolutely." He offered me his hand to lift me off the floor and gave me my sword. I almost didn't notice that Jorunn's necklace had fallen off until Dav called for me to stop. In my haste to fend off Dung Heap's licking attack, I must have somehow knocked it loose. He brought it over and carefully clipped it back on letting his finger graze across my neck, sending a tingle through my body. "Thank you," I told him, looking down at the pendant. "I never would've known it was a key if you hadn't shown me. I keep wondering what it was meant to open."

"Maybe we'll find out when we reach the city." I could feel his eyes still on me as I tucked the necklace inside my shirt. "As much as you've told me about the Hvaldi, I don't think they would have bothered making something so intricate if it wasn't for something important."

We went outside and began my lesson. I was becoming more comfortable swinging the sword and my steps were more graceful instead of choppy and rigid. Since I was showing improvement, Dav said it was time to start adding some new moves.

These were focused on using more of my body to fight, such as using my free hand or a foot to deliver a blow to my opponent while blocking with my sword. He explained that not relying solely on my weapon to fight would make it more difficult for an assailant to defend against me.

At first I protested. I wasn't nearly strong enough to hurt anyone with my fist, but Dav pointed out a well-placed punch could be more effective than I thought. He pointed out several places on the body where you didn't have to hit very hard to inflict pain. Also, he said that I shouldn't make my target what I was trying to hit but to aim right behind it. Doing this would increase the force of my swing.

I noticed Fye'Gor had started listening in on Dav's lesson and added a few pointers of his own. It was hard not to chuckle when he talked. With his rough, gravelly voice, combined with the sour look he constantly had on his face, he reminded me of a grumpy old man. Even the way he walked with his short legs was like someone who had been riding a horse for too long. But he seemed like a good man and I knew his help would improve our chances of success.

Our lesson lasted a little longer than expected, but it was probably the most productive. Because Fye'Gor was small like me, he had his own tricks for using his size to his advantage, which he was happy to share. I enjoyed listening to Dav and Fye'Gor discuss tactics with each other. It was as much a learning experience for them as it was for me. Fye'Gor told us that at one time, he too was known as a top warrior among his own people.

***

The sun was already shining through the canopy when we got underway. The new plan for our journey had us heading north for the next few days, avoiding a rather tall and treacherous mountain—a place Fye'Gor said was home to creatures that we would be wise to stay away from.

Once we were within sight of a river he named the Serpent's Trough from the creatures that lived in it, we would follow it to a lake where we could cross. Fye'Gor mentioned he had a boat there he'd used on previous trips. From there it would only take a day to reach the edge of the Baccoba Forest and another half day to the Valley of the Giants.

Apparently, this dark and gloomy forest did have its share of monsters, but for the most part, they were territorial and seldom ventured out, as our new guide explained. The large wolves stayed to the west, the giant owls above, and woolly spiders inhabited the mountain we were traveling around. Fye'Gor said the spiders weren't much bigger than your hand, but he had seen them take down a stray horse in seconds.

He said we would come across the serpents but advised us to keep our distance, describing them as a large four-legged reptile with teeth like daggers and a long, armored tail. My first thought was it sounded like an alligator, which I had never seen but always wanted to, mostly because it's said they've existed far longer than people.

Fye'Gor was much more talkative than I had expected. As he led us through the forest, he told us about his time here and the things he had encountered. To Dav's surprise, he mentioned coming across several abandoned villages in the forest. As far as Dav knew, no one had ever gone into the forest and lived to tell about it. To discover some of his people lived here at one point was astonishing.

From above, another wind chime howled in the breeze and sent a shiver up my spine. Without turning my head, I knew Dav had seen me flinch and I could hear him chuckling behind me.

"Not a word," I whispered, pointing at him. "You promised."

"Your secret is safe with me, my lady," he whispered back, still chuckling.

The chimes, which resembled a flute and were responsible for the howling sound, didn't always have quite the same tone. Some were a little higher and some lower. When only one or two sounded, it was rather spooky, but with a strong enough breeze, dozens would sound in harmony all at once and it was beautiful to hear.

Fye'Gor said they had been here since before he arrived and didn't understand why people would place them in the trees until Dav told him about the Order of Calvar. Then, he said it made sense, explaining people might have moved here to escape the Calvar. The chimes and flutes were used as a safety tactic, preying upon people's superstitions to scare them away.

Even Dav had to agree it was a pretty smart idea but wondered why the villages were now abandoned. Fye'Gor had no answer for him, only that they appeared to have been abandoned a long time ago.

***

All the talking back and forth made the next few days go by quickly. Before I knew it, we were standing on a ridge overlooking the river Fye'Gor had described. It meandered through the distant mountains from the north to the southeast toward the lake. From here, I could see an abundance of animals lying on the banks of the river. Fye'Gor said they were the serpents he told us about.

By sundown, we made it down into the river valley and kept our distance from the creatures. Fye'Gor said the beasts never crawled farther from the water than a few yards up the bank. As I gathered some wood for a fire, I was able to get a better look. These gigantic reptiles looked like a cross between an alligator and an iguana. Their teeth were as Fye'Gor described but their claws were even longer making it easy for them to shred their prey to bits.

There were dozens of them everywhere. I could see why Fye'Gor recommended we cross at the lake instead of the river. It would be nearly impossible to make it without becoming a meal for one of these huge monsters.

"What do you think?" Dav asked, walking up next to me.

"I think every day I see something here that amazes me. I hope someday I'll get the chance to show all this to my dad."

"You will," he assured me. "There're creatures out here even I've never seen."

"Does that mean you'd like to come with us?" I asked, hoping he'd say yes. I had grown so accustomed to having him near, it was difficult to imagine being without him.

"If you'd like me to." His voice caught a little as he responded and I smiled, nodding my approval.

He helped me gather a few more pieces of wood then headed back to camp. Fye'Gor had taken over cooking each night, and for not being from Polarious, he knew all the best plants to use for spicing up a meal.

As he cooked, I gave Dav his evening lesson. It would still take some time before he would be able to translate the way I did, but he was making great progress. While our spoken language was the same, our written language was very different, which caused a brief setback.

Even though I could roughly read his language, translating between it and Hvaldi proved challenging. Dav gave me a few lessons on his people's writing structure and we were back on track. He was now to a point where I could write a Hvaldi sentence and he could rewrite it in his own language with only a few mistakes.

"So how much longer will it take to reach the lake?" I asked Fye'Gor while Dav sat on a nearby log translating a few words I had written.

"Day and a 'alf," he replied, checking the meat that was cooking and sprinkling them with a few bits of a flower he'd crunched up. "But we'll 'ave to wait 'til afta nightfall before crossin'."

"And why is that?" Dav asked, looking up from his work. Fye'Gor hadn't mentioned this before.

"Didn't I tell ya why dah serpents stay away from dah lake?" We both shook our heads. "Mm, it seems me mind's not what it used to be," he said, still attending to the food.

"Please say it's because the food is more plentiful in the river," I muttered under my breath, but somehow, I suspected I was wrong and didn't know if I wanted to hear the truth.

"Or there's something bigger than them in the lake," Dav added, having heard my comment. Which is exactly what I didn't want to know.

"It's not bigga," Fye'Gor corrected him and I started to breathe a sigh of relief until I heard the rest of it. "But it does 'ave a fierce appetite and one sharp set of teef. The lake is filled with these meat-eatin' fish. They're so 'ungry dey'll devour anyting dat touches dah wada."

"Wonderful." Rolling my eyes, I took a nervous breath. "Does that include the boat?"

"Mm-hmm," Fye'Gor grunted in response to my question. "Dat's why we cross at night and quietly while dey're sleepin'."

"How long will it take to cross?" Dav asked. I could hear the concern in his voice, but at this point, we had no choice. This was the fastest route to the city, and we had already been traveling for nearly a month.

Time seemed to keep adding up. We hadn't even made it to the city and I knew it could easily take another month to find the information we needed. Then, of course, there was the trip back and the Calvar would still be after us. And how long would it take to distribute the information to the people? Would it start a war? Would they even believe it? All these questions made me wonder if I would ever see my dad again.

Without knowing what Master Orin was able to do for him, I couldn't shake the thought that he was spending his nights in a cold cell and his days being worked to the bone. I took some comfort that I had at least told him I loved him before they took him.

"Semmi?" Dav said, placing a hand on my shoulder. I had been sitting on the ground next to him in silence for quite some time. "What's wrong?"

"I was thinking about my dad," I replied and wiped a tear from the corner of my eye. "I hope he's okay."

"I'm sure Master Orin was able to keep him here." He squeezed my shoulder and I placed my hand on top of his. "And if he was able to tell Lord Atwood anything about what we were up to and your father's expertise, I'm sure he's being treated better than most."

Keeping my hand on his knee, I leaned my head against his leg. "Thank you, Dav," I whispered.

Dung Heap came and lay down in my lap as if he knew I was sad. For as ornery as Fye'Gor made him out to be, he had proven to be a good traveling companion. He was perfect at growling to notify us when something was near, and his goofy nature was always good for a laugh.

He was a creature from Norranheim, called a Prickly Bullbash, who Fye'Gor had gotten as a boy. I wasn't sure why he was referred to as prickly since his fur was as soft as a rabbit's. His purring was soothing and soon I fell asleep with my head still against Dav.

CHAPTER FIFTEEN

We reached the lake a little earlier than expected, giving us nearly an entire day to relax before our nighttime voyage across it. I knew Dav didn't want to waste any time, but it was nice to rest in a place where we knew the Calvar weren't trying to hunt us down. I think he knew it too.

Dav took the opportunity to get in some of his own training. Fye'Gor offered to spar with him to give himself a little practice as well before we were out of the Baccoba Forest and the odds of having to defend ourselves from the Calvar increased. Dav agreed and they both shed their jackets.

It was the first time I'd seen Dav without a shirt and I had to remind myself repeatedly not to stare. His muscles were well defined from his years of training. If I got caught admiring him, at least I had an excuse: I was watching them fight. Although, I did find the sparring match educational.

Their fighting styles were so different from each other's. Fye'Gor's long stick was his weapon of choice, while Dav favored his sword. They both used their entire bodies, yet Fye'Gor was shorter and aimed his shots low, focusing his punches or kicks at joints or what he called *sensitive* locations.

After watching for nearly an hour, I decided to take a walk around and look at the lake with Dung Heap by my side. He chased a few birds and small rodents scurrying around but seemed to know to stay away from the water.

It was such a lovely lake that I found it hard to believe it to be so deadly. Surrounded by a rocky shoreline and the usual mammoth trees, it was like something out of a book. The water was crystal clear and as I looked over the edge of the rocky bank, I could see a school of the ravenous fish. They ranged in size from two to three feet with long, slender, striped bodies.

Dav soon joined me on the rocks, still not wearing his jacket. There were a few scars across his stomach and back, which I hadn't noticed when he was practicing. He'd carried over a large tree branch he had picked up on the way. I didn't need to ask to know what he planned to do with it.

"Come here, Dungy," I called to Dung Heap and picked him up as Dav flung the branch out into the water.

The fish near the rock darted toward the splash. The water all around the branch bubbled and turned violently, almost like it was boiling. In less than a minute the branch was gone, and the water calmed.

"I guess they will eat anything," Dav said. "That explains why it's so clear."

"Lovely," I replied. I almost thought it would have been less dangerous to take our chances with the Calvar. "Are we sure there's no other way?"

Dav shook his head, "Fye'Gor said there's a river on the southern side like the one we've been walking along. It's either the serpents or the fish unless we want to add another two weeks to our journey."

"Fish it is," I said reluctantly without any enthusiasm. "He didn't happen to say how long the trip across would take. Three, four hours maybe?"

"Two days."

"What?"

Dav explained that while the fish were dormant at night, loud splashing could easily wake them and trigger an attack. We had to row

141

carefully. He did mention that Fye'Gor thought we could make the full distance in one night with Dav's help, but it would be close and Dav didn't want to take the chance. It was decided we would row out to an island halfway across tonight, then complete the remainder tomorrow night.

"Out of curiosity," I said, thinking of another question that had been running through my mind as I picked up a flat stone off the ground, "why does Fye'Gor come out here? We're awfully far from his hut."

"I wondered that myself. It appears there's an oversized rodent on the other side that's good eating."

"Well, he does like to cook." I chuckled and looked over at Dav, then flung the stone out to the lake, watching it skip three times before a fish jumped out of the water at it.

The hours couldn't go by fast enough as we waited for the sun to set and the moons to rise. Dav and I both got in a translating and fighting lesson, which I appreciated since I knew I wasn't going to be able to sneak in my nightly training.

Fye'Gor busied himself with cooking a small meal. I thought for sure he would have made fish considering the way he boasted about how fun they were to catch, but after he showed us why, it all made sense.

As we waited for our food to finish cooking, Fye'Gor grabbed a long chain with a hook on the end from the boat he had pulled near shore for our voyage. He cast it out into the water and as soon as it touched the surface, a fish hit. Fye'Gor held onto the chain for dear life as it fought him. The other fish in the area must have sensed it was in distress and raced toward it. The surface of the water came alive as it had with the stick. By the time he pulled the hook back in, all that was left of the fish was the jaw.

"Oh my," I said, looking at the remains he held up.

Fye'Gor laughed, commenting on what a rush it was to fight a fish that strong. Dav decided to give it a shot. His feet slid on the gravel beach as he pulled the chain back. Fye'Gor hooted, saying he must have hooked a big one. They both hooked a few more before our Norranian friend said we needed to let them settle down so they would slumber for the night.

Finally, it was time. With no sign of the setting sun and the moons high above, we gently eased the boat into the water and climbed inside. Fye'Gor was at the bow, Dav at the stern, and I was in the middle with Dung Heap on my lap.

"One peep out of you and you're bait," Fye'Gor whispered to Dungy to keep him quiet, even though I knew he'd never do it. He'd had him nearly all his life and it was obvious they were best friends.

The small rowboat was barely large enough to fit all of us and our gear. I'm sure Fye'Gor never intended to have more than Dungy and him in it, but he assured us it was strong enough to carry us all. He and Dav each had an oar and he showed Dav how to carefully lower it and slowly take a stroke without disturbing the water too much, to avoid making a splash.

Tonight was the longest leg of our two-night voyage. The paddling was a slow and methodical process, but little by little, we got closer to the island where we would stop. Part of me wished we could talk to make the time go by faster. It would have helped to calm my uneasiness of being in a lake full of ravenous fish, but for our safety, we all remained silent.

Under different circumstances, being out in a rowboat, under the moonlight, in the most beautiful crystal clear lake would be kind of romantic. Every now and then Dav would look up from his rowing to check on me. Unable to speak, I would nod and smile to let him know I was okay.

***

The first half of the trip went off without a hitch. We reached the island with plenty of night left. Fye'Gor tried to talk Dav into completing the second half, but Dav wouldn't budge on his decision, making it clear he was not willing to take the chance when the result was death if they failed.

I knew it wasn't an easy choice. Both of us had started getting increasingly anxious the closer we got to our destination and little delays were becoming progressively more irritating. At least for me.

For Dav, it was difficult to tell, but sometimes I'd see him sitting alone, which I took as his way of clearing his mind. I too would take short walks to calm myself. Mostly I feared the thought of failing at our mission, and I'm sure the lack of sleep from my nightly training wasn't helping.

After we dragged the boat on shore, I walked around the little island. There were some giant trees clustered in the center with berry-producing ferns at their base. I could tell we were approaching the border of the forest because the trees were getting a little smaller. Not that they still weren't bigger than the trees in the sacred lands, but those on the interior were considerably taller.

When I returned, Dav was arranging our bags up by one of the trees where we would have shade to rest once the sun came up. For now, the moons were still shining down on the lake and I took the opportunity to stand out on the shore. The clear water and nearly white sandy bottom made it almost glow in the moonlight.

Looking across the surface, out of the corner of my eye, movement under the water caught my attention. When I turned to see what it was, it was gone. I waited and was about to leave, excusing it for something reflecting off the surface, when I saw it again. A shadow darted around under the water, but it was too far away to see what it was.

I walked around the edge of the little bay where we came ashore to get a clearer view. Again, the dark shadow moved through the water staying deep enough so as not to cause a wave or ripple. I couldn't make out what the creature looked like—only that it was fast and much larger than the fish I had seen earlier. It was easily twice the length of our little boat.

"Hey," Dav said from behind.

I had been so focused on the water I didn't hear him walk up. The sudden break in the silence made me jump.

My heart raced and I covered my chest with my hand. "You startled me."

"Are you okay?"

"I thought I saw something in the water," I replied and turned back toward the lake.

"Maybe something disturbed the fish," he suggested. "That's why I didn't want to take any chances."

"What I saw was much bigger than the fish." I scanned the water, but the shadow didn't return. "I swear I saw a large shadow under the water." Frustrated, it figured now that Dav was here, it was gone.

"Maybe you're just tired." I was exhausted, but I also knew what I saw, and I shot him a glare for not believing me. "Or maybe there's another creature that comes out at night," he added, trying to recover from his earlier comment. "We can ask Fye'Gor."

We walked back to the interior of the island where Fye'Gor was waiting for us. He had gathered a bowl full of deep red berries that looked almost like cherries but smaller. He said they would help us relax so we could get some rest while we waited for the day to pass.

"Fye'Gor, have you ever seen any other creatures in the lake?" Dav asked.

"Not dat lived long," he joked. "Why you think dah serpents won't even come down 'ere?"

Dav looked over at me and I could tell he believed Fye'Gor over me. "I know what I saw," I snapped then left to go lie down by our bags. It bothered me that after all we had gone through, he would take someone else's word over mine. I was tired, but I wasn't delusional.

When the sun started to come up, I heard Dav walk over to where I was lying and sit down next to me. He brushed a few locks of hair out of my face and draped his cloak over top of me.

He whispered my name, but I pretended to be asleep. I didn't want to talk to him right now, fearing I would say something I would regret because I was tired and irritable. So many things weighed on me and I needed his support. Maybe a little sleep would help alleviate some of my stress.

***

Dav and Fye'Gor were still asleep when I woke. The sun had already passed its highest point and was starting its descent, but it would be several more hours before we could get on our way. I looked over at Dav. It was so hard to stay upset with him and I felt bad for how I behaved. I knew it wasn't his intention, but I had an unsettling feeling about the shadow I saw. The way it darted around was like it knew we were here.

Quietly, I slipped away and returned to the beach for some time alone. Although there was no sneaking away around Dungy, at least he knew what it meant to keep quiet. I had become accustomed to his company during my nightly training and he was good and never made a peep. We played fetch for a while, until I saw Dav coming over to join me.

"Hi," he said softly, handing me a pouch of water and some dried meat.

"Hi." I didn't know quite what to say, but I smiled lightly and thanked him for the food.

"I didn't mean to upset you," he said. I nodded, but inside I was still concerned. "Are you sure you saw what you did?"

"Had I only seen it once, I would have thought it was my eyes playing tricks or that I was tired," I admitted, "but I saw it more than once, Dav. Something else is in there. It swam around right where we came in like it was looking for us."

"Well, it didn't bother us last night. Hopefully it will leave us alone."

"I hope you're right"—I looked back at the water—"because it was much bigger than our boat." I wasn't sure if he believed me or not, but it didn't matter. We were on an island in the middle of a lake. Unless we wanted to spend the rest of our lives here, we had to move forward.

146

We walked back to the shade of the trees and I sat down on the ground while Dav and Fye'Gor chatted about our path of travel once we reached the other side, and of course, Fye'Gor's favorite topic, what was good to eat.

He was always talking about food and how he would travel a hundred miles to pick berries or hunt down a specific animal if it was good. I had never seen anyone with such a fascination with cooking. I had to admit though, I'd never eaten such tasty food. Watching him talk about food was as entertaining as watching him cook. He was so passionate and animated. He would even talk quietly to himself as he added a dash of this or a pinch of that when he thought we weren't listening.

***

With the sun gone, it was time to shove off again. We took our respective places and rowed toward our destination. Dav must have seen my nervousness and reached out and put his hand on my knee. Unable to speak, I smiled and placed my hand on his in appreciation. I wrapped my other arm around Dungy and pet his soft fur to pass the time.

The night started out the same as the last and the gentle rocking of the boat made my eyes heavy. Suddenly a shadow off the stern behind Dav darted past. My eyes widened, and I sat straight up in my seat looking past him. When I looked at Dav his eyes were on me and he cocked his head to one side, as his way of silently asking what I saw. I motioned with my head behind him and mimicked the movement of a fish with my hand.

He nodded for me to continue watching the water behind him as his eyes scanned the water ahead. Dungy let out a little growl, but I quickly shushed him and continued petting him. Dav kept looking my way and I could tell he was starting to feel a little on edge. He waved to Fye'Gor to watch the water, but Fye'Gor shook his head, indicating he hadn't seen anything.

The shore was nearing. In five minutes, we would be close enough to safely jump out if need be. Seconds felt like minutes as the dark shadow swam past us again not ten feet away. How I wished we could row faster, but then we would take the chance of waking the sleeping fish and I had already seen what they could do. So far, this one hadn't done anything besides swim by.

Without any warning, something thumped the bottom of the boat. I almost screamed and lifted my feet off the bottom.

"Fye'Gor," Dav whispered through clenched teeth. "You said there was nothing else in here."

"I've nevah seen anything else in 'ere," he whispered back. They both began to row a little faster, but they were limited in how fast they could go without creating any noise.

Three minutes from the shore and there was another thump on the bottom of the boat, this one harder than the last. "It feels like it's trying to determine if we're predator or prey," I whispered to Dav. I barely got the words out of my mouth when the dark shadow below revealed itself.

Its head came out of the water at me, mouth opened, and teeth bared. With the head of an alligator and body of a walrus, this beast lurched at me. A growl emanated from deep in its throat that sounded like a bear. I pulled Dungy to my chest and leaned back nearly falling over the other side. Dav jumped up, grabbing me with one hand and slicing through the neck of the creature with his knife.

The animal fell back into the water turning it a bright red. "Are you okay?" Dav asked, pulling me to him. There was a fear in his eyes I'd never seen before, and his hands were nearly shaking. All I could do was nod.

"Row!" Fye'Gor shouted. "Row! Row!"

The blood and noise had woken the real danger in these waters and they were headed toward us. The water around the large beast came alive as they worked to devour it.

There was no use keeping quiet anymore. We needed to get to shore and fast before we were their next meal. I strapped my pack on and grabbed the other two, so I would be ready to leap out.

"Go! Go! Go!" Dav yelled when we were within jumping distance. I could hear the fish hitting the bottom of the boat as they started feeding on it. The sound was like a million people beating on a wall at the same time.

Fye'Gor tossed Dungy to shore and jumped. I was right behind him tossing the packs out first. I felt Dav grab my waist, pulling me with him. We tumbled over the ground, and as we hit the loose gravel on the beach, Dav turned to take the brunt of the fall with me landing on top of him.

"Are you okay?" I asked, hearing a grunt as we hit the ground. My heart was still racing, and my body shook like crazy.

"Well, we won't be goin' back dat way," I heard Fye'Gor say almost laughing. Dav and I looked back in time to see the last of the boat disappear below the bubbling water. "I've paddled across dis lake over a dozen times and nevah seen a creature like dat," he said apologetically.

"It's not your fault," I told to him. "You didn't know."

"But you did," Dav said to me. "I'm sorry I didn't believe you."

"I was hoping you were right. Thank you for saving me. Again."

***

Now that we were on the other side of the lake, it was a straight shot to the city in the Valley of the Giants. We would hike between the two tallest mountains to reach the valley. Rather than rest, we set out immediately and by morning, we had reached the edge of the Baccoba Forest.

Until now, I hadn't realized how much more colorful the sacred lands were. The trees, flowers, and animals were all so bright. I looked back at the giant trees behind me. Most everything there was a shade of brown, deep green, or gray.

Part of me didn't want to leave. The age-old ghost stories had made it a safe place to hide. We were able to travel without the fear of the Calvar attacking at any given moment. Besides the boat ride, it was the first time Fye'Gor stayed quiet. He kept Dungy at his side with a snap of his fingers so as not to draw any unwanted attention.

Dav took the lead and picked up the pace trying to make up for lost time. Fye'Gor grumbled when I pushed for Dav to keep going through the day. I reminded him he would have plenty of time to rest when we reached the city as it could take me a while to find what we were looking for.

"And what exactly are we lookin' for?" Fye'Gor asked.

To fulfill our promise to him, I explained we needed to locate a tablet containing a long string of runic symbols, which the Hvaldi used to open the doors between realms. During one of our rests, I showed him the symbols in Jorunn's journal to better explain how they were used.

For us though, we needed to find something explaining how Dav's people came to be in this realm. It needed to be solid proof, a journal or detailed inscription of some sort. I prayed it wouldn't take me long. I so wanted to see my dad and tell him all about what we'd seen.

We stopped at midday to rest and make sure we were still on the right track. Fye'Gor took the opportunity to take a quick nap and rest his short legs. I sat beside Dav and looked at the map with him. We had made good time and, it appeared, we should reach the city by nightfall.

"When this is all over, what do you want to do?" I asked him. I only knew him as a warrior and most of our other conversations were either about our mission or our past. I was curious about what he liked to do when he wasn't being a hero.

"I hadn't thought much about it," he replied. "You said you'd like to bring your father out here. I could arrange for that."

"I'd like that." I imagined the look on my dad's face when he saw all these cities. He'd probably think he'd died and gone to heaven.

"How about you?" he asked.

"Besides coming out here with you and my dad?" I asked jokingly. I looked at the dirt on Dav's hands and noticed mine were every bit as filthy. "I think a bath would be nice too." I tried to wipe some of the dirt off on my pants.

He chuckled and agreed it would be nice to clean up a bit then suggested we get moving. Fye'Gor wasn't as easy to coax back on his feet but didn't put up too much of an argument. Of course, Dungy was full of energy.

We were tired, but as soon as we got our first glimpse of the Valley of the Giants, it made it all worth it. The white of the stone walls and buildings stuck out from the green, gold, and red of the trees. We were still some distance away, but everything appeared to be pristine, with no crumbling walls or toppled monuments. Even a few of the roof's wooden beams were still in place.

There was no question of where the city's name came from. A grove of mammoth trees grew around the city. They were every bit as tall as those in the Baccoba Forest, but instead of resembling pines, they looked like the ancient oaks I had seen in northern Europe, with their huge branches twisting out over the city.

Thus far, we hadn't come across any sign that the Calvar had been in the area and I hoped it stayed that way. Judging from the size of this city, it would likely take me awhile to find what we needed, and the closer we got, the bigger it looked.

We walked through the main entrance before nightfall, a little ahead of when we expected to arrive. As excited as we were to get here, we nearly ran the last bit of the trek. However, once we were inside, Dav slowed down and began moving through the city carefully, his head swiveling from side to side. He and Fye'Gor kept me between them for protection, both with their weapons ready to strike if needed.

We passed by a few structures that were used as shops and houses until Dav found one he felt would be good for making camp until morning. He instructed me to stay with Dungy while he and Fye'Gor surveyed the immediate vicinity to make sure it was safe.

They were only gone a few minutes, but it was long enough for me to walk through the structure. It was once someone's home. Inscribed on the wall in the main living area, I saw one of the many blessings I had seen before. There was a hearth on one side that still looked usable. Fye'Gor would enjoy finally having a better working area to prepare meals. There was even a stone kettle on the ledge nearby.

I didn't find any artifacts, but that was typical of other cities I had investigated. Most of the information we found came from temples, libraries, and other public buildings.

"Semmi?" Dav called. I had walked back into one of the sleeping areas leaving Dungy in the main room.

"I'm here," I answered and walked back. "I was looking around."

Fye'Gor brought back some wood, but we didn't make a fire. He lay down and was asleep in less than a minute with Dungy cuddled up next to him. Dav helped me lay out our things and we talked about tomorrow.

"We're going to have to do a full sweep of the city once it's light," he explained. "Is there anywhere you would prefer to get started so you're not waiting on us?"

"You didn't happen to see a temple or large building while you were out, did you? That would be the best."

I explained from past experience there was little to be found in the residential areas, so there was no point in going through them until we exhausted all other locations. He said he hadn't wandered that far but promised to look for one first thing in the morning.

"Will you do one other thing for me?" he asked.

"Sure," I replied, curious as to what he would want from me.

"Will you keep Dungy with you at all times?" I was confused by the request and he better explained that Fye'Gor told him that Dungy might be small, but he was very protective. "I'm confident in your ability to defend yourself, but he's already shown he can sense danger earlier than we can. I only want you to be safe."

"Okay," I agreed.

CHAPTER SIXTEEN

The giant creature from the lake leaped toward me, its jaws open with its razor-sharp teeth about to chomp down when I awoke and sat straight up, gasping for air. Thankfully, my nightmare woke only me and everyone else seemed undisturbed. Fye'Gor still lay snoring by the hearth and Dav was next to me. I pulled my knees to my chest and rested my forehead on them.

I had only taken a few breaths when I felt a hand on my back. Dav lifted his head and looked at me. "I'm okay," I whispered, knowing what he was thinking. "Just a bad dream."

"You seem to have a lot of them lately," he commented. "You're restless and talk." I hadn't realized I wasn't sleeping as well as I thought. "I'm sorry you had to be brought in the middle of all this. I'm sure this isn't what you thought would happen coming here."

"It's not your fault."

"Actually, it is," he replied.

"Don't start that," I jumped in. "I already told you I forgive you. You have to know that by now." He acknowledged that he did. "Besides, my mother always said everything happens for a reason."

"I guess that's one way to look at life." He sat up, letting his hand slide down my back until his arm was around my waist.

"When I think about it, I wouldn't be here if it wasn't for her," I told him. Dav looked confused at my comment. I hadn't told him much about her besides how she died.

Opening my pack, I took out my mother's tin and showed him the items inside, explaining them the way my dad did when he gave it to me for my birthday. It wasn't even a year ago, yet it felt like a lifetime. Upon seeing everything, Dav was as astonished as I was. He looked at the picture of my mom and dad as well as the one my dad and I had taken in Idaho.

"You look a lot like your mother."

"That's what my dad says," I replied. "He says I'm as stubborn as her too."

Dav raised his eyebrows and I swatted him before he could comment back, making him smile. I considered what Master Orin had asked of me: to teach Dav to smile. It wasn't a big smile, but I loved it. When I reached the bottom of the tin, I took out the broken tablet.

"My mom found this on one of her first digs before she met my dad," I said. "She thought it was from a culture we called the Vikings. Her passion became my dad's and mine. It wasn't until my dad gave me this that I learned she had found the Hvaldi long before we did. She didn't know and died before I realized it."

Dav took the tablet and examined the runes on it. I explained the difference between these ceremonial runes and the writing I had been teaching him. "These here are the same as the last few runes written in the back of Jorunn's journal," he pointed out.

"What?" I asked, not noticing it before. He took the journal out of my pack and flipped to the back page where the runic code was written. He was right. The third line down on the tablet contained the last four runes in the list from the journal. "Then these other lines must be the last few runes needed to get to the other realms. If we had the other piece of this, we could send Fye'Gor home."

"And you."

"Why would I want to leave?" I asked. "Everything that I care about is here." Part of me wanted to say that that included him, but I was afraid. Someday I would tell him, I promised myself, hoping he might feel the same.

With all that we'd been through, it was hard not to care about him. I had learned so much from him, and his passion to save my dad and his people had become my driving force to work as hard as I could to do the same. For him.

We both lay back down to get a little more sleep. I scooted over enough to rest my head against his arm. Tomorrow was a big day—the first of who knows how many to find the answers we needed. I rubbed my fingers over the runes on Jorunn's necklace, which hung around my neck, and prayed for our success.

***

At first light, we ventured out and I got to see the entire city. It was bigger than any I had been in before. Thousands of people could have lived there with plenty of room to spare.

Rather than having only one city center with a temple and a couple of public buildings like libraries or meeting centers, this city had been laid out in sections and each residential area had a city center. By my count, there appeared to be six sections, arranged in a semicircle. At the center was a large statue with a road leading up the mountainside.

Not all sections had the same public buildings in them. I assumed some of them could be educational buildings or council chambers.

When Dav asked where I wanted to start, I hardly knew the answer. There was not enough time to map out the city, and we needed to move through it quickly. I suggested we tackle it in sections and exclude all houses and small shops for now as we had discussed the night before.

After Dav and Fye'Gor completed a quick sweep of the city, I showed them where I wanted to get started in a large temple at the far end of the city. I gave instructions for them to look through the other buildings for books, scrolls, or tablets with long inscriptions.

And so, the hunt began. From sunup to sundown, I translated. My nightly training, when the others were asleep, was swapped out for more time spent translating. The days blurred from one to another. After a while, I stopped translating and started skimming through inscriptions, looking for anything mentioning the race of man in this realm.

Dav promised to help once he and Fye'Gor completed a thorough search of the city so they could better guide me through it. The only time he would pull me away was if he thought he might have found something important, but so far, I had found nothing about his people.

From section to section I worked my way through, carrying my bag so I would have my brushes, pencils, and anything else necessary within reach. What I needed was my dad. We were a team when it came to digging into the past. Without him, I felt like all the responsibility rested on my shoulders alone, and the stress was weighing on me. About the only time I saw anyone was when they brought me food or water or came to tell me it was getting late. My only company was Dungy who stayed at my side.

My eyes heavy with exhaustion, I kept dozing off from lack of sleep and had to go back repeatedly to reread what I had already gone through. I heard Dav call my name as I struggled through a rather lengthy inscription about the Hvaldi's creation story. I was hoping somewhere they would mention a race other than themselves living here, but so far, nothing. It was taking me forever.

"Semmi!" Dav called again, walking into the temple. By the way he was breathing, he must have run over here. "I think we found something. You have to come see."

I grabbed my bag as he helped me to my feet. I knew better than to get excited too early. We had already had several disappointments. The library was empty as well as what I believed to be an educational center. Like all the other cities, it appeared that the Hvaldi had gathered their things and moved on, leaving next to nothing behind.

He led me up the road to the mountainside where a mural had been carved right into the rocky face. Fye'Gor stood nearby and looked as excited as Dav at the find. I recognized the scene that was depicted in the carving immediately—the discovery of the four realms. Every corner had a scene from each realm: Lothenbrow and Norranheim in the top corners, and Balfjord and Polarious at the bottom.

I explained the significance of each section to them both but didn't understand why he thought the carving was so important. We needed solid proof about his people and I didn't think a carving about the four realms was quite the evidence Master Orin wanted.

"Not the carving," Dav clarified and walked me closer to it and pointed to the center where the four realms came together. "There."

In the very center of the mural was a round white stone different from the others. It was the same smooth dense stone used for their tablets. Five evenly spaced notches were carved around the edge with an impression of the key I wore around my neck in the middle. I slipped off Jorunn's necklace and twisted it the way Dav had shown me and placed it in the impression. It fit perfectly.

When I pushed on the key, the white stone could be pressed in, but nothing happened. I tried to use the notches around the edge to turn the stone, but my hands weren't big enough to press and turn the stone at the same time.

"Can you help me?" I asked Dav. He stepped up behind me and I placed his hand over the key. I instructed him to push in and turn, using the notches.

He did so and with a little effort, the stone moved a quarter turn. A loud clunk echoed behind the mural followed by a release of air and dust from around the edges of the carving.

"What 'appened?" Fye'Gor asked. "Is der something be'ind dat?"

"It seems like it," Dav replied and pushed on the mural in different places. "It feels like it should move." Toward the edge, it finally budged. "It's a door." He gasped and gave it another hard shove. There must have been something running through the center that allowed it to spin on its axis.

The open mural revealed a tunnel leading into the mountain. Inside, the walls had been polished to a glass-like finish. As far as I could see, there were dozens of sections containing line after line of inscribed text.

It was an incredible find, but I also knew it would take weeks or more to read everything.

My head dropped, and tears streamed down my face. "Semmi, what's wrong?" Dav asked. "I thought you'd be happy."

"I am. It's…" I tried to think of the right words to say, but my mind was on overload, so I blurted out the first thing that popped into my head. "I'm so tired." I cried unable to stop the tears. "It would take an entire team of translators weeks to go through all this. I haven't slept since we got here, and I've read so much my brain hurts. And yet I've found nothing about your people or a way to send Fye'Gor home. I've failed all of you."

"Semmi." Dav stepped toward me.

"No," I snapped and tried to move away from him, but in my exhausted state, I stumbled, sending the contents of my pack scattering across the ground. "I just need a minute." I dropped my pack on the ground and walked away.

I found the first side street and followed it to the edge of town where I could sit and cry alone. It didn't take long for my little companion to find me. Dungy pushed his way under my arm. I hugged him to my chest, running my fingers through his soft fur and humming a song my mom used to sing when I was a child.

After a few minutes, the tears stopped. Dung Heap's soft purring was soothing and I dried my cheeks. "Why is everything going wrong, Dungy?" I whispered. My furry friend snapped his head up and quietly growled the way he did when danger was near. I looked around but saw nothing and decided I should head back.

From around the corner, a tall man jumped out in front of me wearing the uniform of the Order of Calvar. Sidestepping a swing from his sword, I landed a hard punch to his lower back. The man howled in pain. I didn't think I had hit him that hard but when I looked down for Dungy, I saw my furry friend had bitten the soldier and his leg was covered in white quills. When I glanced at Dungy, bony spikes were

159

sticking out of his fur. Now I knew why he was called a Prickly Bullbash.

The man tried to take another swing at me only to get another bite to the leg. I pulled my own sword and delivered a solid strike across the man's abdomen, dropping him to the ground.

"Come on, Dungy," I yelled and ran back toward the mural. Out of the corner of my eye, I saw more movement in the city. "Dav!" I screamed when I reached the main road. I saw him already running in my direction. "They're here," I yelled to him.

He pulled his knife from his belt and flung it past me. When I turned, I saw it stick in the throat of a Calvar who was behind me. Dav retrieved his knife from the dead man's body.

"Head to the tunnel," he ordered and fell in step behind me.

Two soldiers moved in ahead to intercept us. The thought that I should've slept last night instead of staying up working briefly crossed my mind. My limbs felt heavy as they fought to cooperate.

"Take the one on the right," I heard Dav yell.

Still running forward, I moved to take on my opponent with Dungy a few steps ahead. The soldier tried to take a swing at Dung Heap, but he was too fast. The furry beast darted through the man's legs, fanning out his quills. The minor distraction allowed me to take a swing catching the man across the face. The other Calvar was no match for Dav and the battle was over in seconds. Dav barely broke step as we kept running.

When a soldier holding a bow stepped out from behind a nearby statue, I tried to skid to a stop. He had the arrow drawn and before I could react he let go. Dav reached around my waist and stepped in front of me. There was nothing I could do as the arrow struck him in the side.

"No!" I screamed, holding on to him as he dropped to his knees. "Dav! No!"

The man was about to fire another arrow when I saw the tip of a wooden spear plunge through his chest. When the man fell to the ground, Fye'Gor was standing behind him.

"We have to keep moving," Dav moaned and I helped him back to his feet. Fye'Gor picked up Dav's sword and we moved as fast as we could into the tunnel.

Fye'Gor pushed the mural closed then turned another white stone on the wall. A loud clunk sealed the door shut, leaving us in the dark.

"Gimme a moment," Fye'Gor said. I could hear him rummaging around in a bag before I heard a clack and light filled the tunnel.

In Fye'Gor's hand were two stones emanating a white light. Each had a leather strap hooked to one end. He hung one stone around his neck and the other around mine. Up ahead, our bags sat near the tunnel entrance where muffled shouts of the Calvar soldiers indicated they were trying to open the mural door.

Dav pulled Jorunn's necklace from his pocket and gave it back to me. "They'll have to break it down to get in," he said, his voice straining through the pain. "Show her what we found," he told Fye'Gor who nodded and gathered our bags. I followed him, helping Dav as he headed down the tunnel.

When we reached the end, there was a waterfall pouring out of the stone wall and into a pool, but I couldn't tell where the water was coming from or going to. There was no stream leading to the pool, yet it wasn't overflowing.

"It's a doorway to another realm," I said.

"Look at the pedestal," Dav instructed me. Fye'Gor took Dav's arm so I could investigate.

Near the pool was a pedestal and set on top were two flat stones. I instantly recognized one of them as the missing piece to my mother's tablet. The other stone had been carved to replace hers. The completed tablet contained four lines of runes each eighteen characters long. The third line contained the runes from Jorunn's journal.

I picked up the pieces and looked back at Dav. He was holding out his knife to me. "Carve the runes."

"Which one do I choose?" I asked. A loud boom echoed through the tunnel. The Calvar were trying to break down the door. Dirt and rock fell from the ceiling above us.

"Not Lothenbrow," Fye'Gor blurted. "We'll freeze before we can get back."

"It doesn't say which is which," I told them, looking at the four lines.

"Do the meanings of the runes give any hint?" Dav replied, gritting his teeth together and struggling to stay on his feet.

I knew the third line was for here. The next line up had several runes that symbolized winter, snow, and ice. I hoped that meant it was Lothenbrow. Kneeling next to the water, I carved the top line into the dirt and stepped back.

A vibration rippled through the water and the ground around us. I watched as a stone lifted out of the water and the falls parted, revealing a dark tunnel. Another boom echoed down the tunnel. There was no time. I grabbed Dav's arm and Fye'Gor yelled for Dung Heap as we ran over the stone and into the tunnel.

CHAPTER SEVENTEEN

We tumbled out the other side and the tunnel closed behind us. The stone around my neck was going dim and Fye'Gor asked for it, so he could refresh the light of the stones. I could feel Dav on the ground next to me, but he hadn't moved.

"Dav," I said to him, but he didn't respond. I called his name again and lightly shook his body as Fye'Gor held the rejuvenated stones over him. His eyes were closed, and he appeared to be dead. "No, no, no, no. Dav!" I yelled, shaking him harder. "Please, no." My worst fear flashed through my mind and it terrified me.

"Semmi," Fye'Gor said, taking my hand. "Calm down, 'e's not dead. Look 'e's breathin'."

Dav's chest rose and fell, and I closed my eyes in relief as a few tears trickled down my face. My hands shook as I rested them on his chest. Fye'Gor told me to pull the arrow out and patch him up while he had a look around. He called for Dungy to go with him while I cared for Dav. With the dim light, it was hard to tell where we were. It was a cavern of some sort, but the walls looked veiny like the inside of a tree.

Dav's pack wasn't far away. I took out the medicine box and removed the powders he had used on my arm along with the stone saucer and clean bandages. The end of the arrow must have snapped off when we fell, leaving only a few inches of the shaft sticking out. Carefully, I unbuttoned and opened his jacket, gently pulling the arrow through so I could see his injury better.

With shaking hands, I grasped the end of the arrow. I had never done this before and was afraid I might hurt him even more. Taking a deep breath, I gave it a hard yank, pulling it free. Dav sat straight up and yelled out in pain.

"Dav," I said and tried to coax him back down. "Please, you have to lie down."

"Semmi," he gasped and grabbed my arm.

"I'm here." I turned his face toward me and forced a smile. He let out a long breath and leaned his head against mine for a few moments. I asked him again to lie down, so I could attend to his wound. He finally complied and guided me through how to patch him up.

First, he had me mix the blue, purple, and yellow powders and sprinkle a little of the mixture inside the wound. Then I stitched it closed and sprinkled more powder on top. Within a few minutes, the bleeding had stopped, and I was able to wrap the wound before putting everything away.

He watched me, making it hard for me to focus as I fought back the tears. I couldn't erase the thought that I'd almost lost him, and it only made my hands shake more.

"Why do you try so hard?" he asked as he watched me.

"What? I-I don't understand."

"You don't think I know that you get up every night when you think we're sleeping?" he said. "First it was to practice your training. Once we got here, it was to work extra time on the translations. Why?"

I looked down, placing my hands in my lap, unsure how to respond. I had no idea he knew what I had been doing. "Be-because I'm not like you," I confessed. "I'm not that strong and I wasn't taught how to fight. You were doing so much better than I with your lessons and I didn't want to let you down." Tears trickled down my cheeks and I stuttered over my words. "I know it's your job to protect me, but the last thing I wanted was for you to get hurt trying to defend me because you thought I was too weak to defend myself. But it happened anyways, and I thought I lost you."

"Semmi." Dav pushed himself up and lifted my face to look into my eyes. "I have never thought of you as weak." He continued holding my face. "You are the strongest woman I have ever met. The smartest too. I didn't step in front of the arrow because it's my job or because I thought you couldn't defend yourself. I did it because I care about you. A lot."

Hearing his words made my heart jump and I smiled. "I care about you a lot too," I squeaked out. Dav smiled the biggest smile I had seen from him. He leaned closer and lightly kissed my lips. "Please don't ever scare me like that again," I whispered when our lips parted.

"I promise," he whispered back, then kissed me again, pulling me against him. For my first kiss, it was the most amazing kiss ever. His lips were warm and soft against mine and a rush of heat spread through my body. Gently, I ran my finger up his neck and through his hair, which had gotten a bit shaggy over the weeks, and held on to this moment as long as possible.

"Well, it's about time," I heard Fye'Gor blurt out when he walked in on us.

"How did you know?" Dav asked him.

"Why is it dat when two people love each other, dah last ones to know are dah two people in love?" he asked, laughing at us. "Glad to see you're doin' bettah, me boy."

"Thank you," Dav replied and took my hand in his, giving me a wink. "Where are we?"

"Well, your lady picked dah right one. We're in me realm," he answered proudly and bowed his head to us. "Welcome to Norran'eim."

"Are you sure?" Dav asked.

"Wit outta doubt," Fye'Gor replied. "'Dis place you're in, is a tree. I don't know about dah trees in your realm, Semmi, but I never saw 'em like dis in yours." He pointed to Dav with his spear. "Everything's big in Norran'eim." He laughed, producing a berry nearly the size of a watermelon. "Except us Norranians, of course."

"I'm so glad we were able to get you home," I said, trying my best to be happy, but inside my emotions were a mess. I was relieved that Dav was alive, happy beyond belief that he liked me and even kissed me but crushed that we failed at our mission to save his people and my dad.

"Yes, but now you're not," Fye'Gor replied.

"We have the tablet with the runic codes," Dav told him. "We can get back."

"But dat wasn't our deal," Fye'Gor said. "I was to lead you to a city where you could find what you needed to free your people and den you would send me 'ome. I 'aven't fulfilled my side. Which gives me an idea." He held up a finger.

Fye'Gor sat down next to us with Dungy by his side and told us about an ancient tale among his people. "No one knows when it started but it 'as been told in me family for over a 'undred generations," he began. "A very long time ago, some visitors came to our realm we called dah White Ones because of deir white 'air and clothin'. It's even said dat deir skin looked as though it 'ad nevah seen dah sun. Deir eyes were a crystal blue like dah sky in Polarious in the early afternoon." He paused for a moment then continued. "Dey told our people dey were looking for a place of peace and asked if dey could stay a while. Our people agreed, and dey built a city of stone far to dah west beyond our borders and were nevah 'eard from again."

"Is the story true?" I asked. The thought that the Hvaldi came here renewed my hope that maybe we could still find something.

"I don't know 'ow true it is," Fye'Gor confessed, "but I know dah stone city is dere. I saw it once from a distance. From what I saw of dah statues and dah carvin's in Polarious, I think dah Hvaldi and dah White Ones are dah same."

"So, no one's ever gone to see if anyone's still out there?" Dav asked him.

"Well, you see," Fye'Gor said slowly like he was trying to come up with the right words, "me people, um, we're not very *sociable* creatures. We're kind of quiet and keep to ourselves."

The blank look on Dav's face, with his mouth hanging open, was indescribable and I struggled not to laugh. From the moment we met Fye'Gor, he rarely stopped talking. With the exception of the boat ride, the only other time was when he was sleeping, and even that wasn't a given. More often than not when I returned from my nightly getaways, he was mumbling something.

Dav winked at me then inquired as to how far away this city was. Fye'Gor told him that he recognized our location, and it would only be about a day and a half's walk. He also offered to take us there as soon as Dav was ready to travel. Dav suggested we wait until morning and insisted we could all use some much-needed rest, commenting about the dark circles that had been forming under my eyes over the past few days.

There was no argument on my part.

***

That night was the most restful night's sleep I had ever had. Curled up next to Dav with my head on his chest and his arms wrapped around me, not a single scary thought entered my mind. All I could see was his face. The way he smiled at me before we lay down and the warmth of his lips against mine as he kissed me good night were all I could think about until my eyes opened in the morning.

Dav was sitting up next to me. He still had one hand on my back while he was looking through some of the notes I had written down from the Valley of the Giants.

"How long have you been up?" I asked, sitting up next to him.

"A while." He gingerly leaned over and kissed my cheek and I could tell by his clenched jaw that he was still feeling the pain of his wound.

"Why didn't you wake me?"

"Because you needed the rest." He let me know that Fye'Gor was out tracking down something to eat, saying how excited the old man was to show us his realm. "He's been humming a tune all morning," Dav said. "I thought he was going to wake you up."

For the first time in what felt like weeks, we got to have a conversation about what we had learned from the city rather than what we hadn't. The Hvaldi were an amazing and intelligent race. I hoped that even if we didn't find exactly what Master Orin requested of us, we could at least prove the existence of the Hvaldi and take back the teachings they left inscribed all over the city.

While we were waiting for Fye'Gor to return, I readied our packs and changed the bandages on Dav's wound. I was amazed at how much it had healed in such a short time. It was no longer a gaping hole in his side, the way it had been the day before. There was no sign of infection and he said the pain wasn't bad if he didn't move around too much. By tomorrow, the stitches could be removed and the bandage would probably no longer be necessary.

"I've never seen anything that can heal the way your powders do," I said in amazement as I lightly ran my fingers along the scab that was forming over his injury.

"Don't you have medicine in Balfjord?" he asked as if surprised by my comment.

"Yes, but not like these."

He told me what the different-colored powders did and that they were made from various flowers, mushrooms, and fruit seeds found in the forests. He couldn't remember how his people discovered them, only that they had been used for hundreds of years.

As we talked, I heard the sound of whistling coming from outside and a couple of minutes later, Dungy raced in, followed by Fye'Gor carrying a piece of bark filled with nuts and berry bits. He had a pep in his step and a smile on his face, which I hadn't seen. It was obvious he was happy to be home.

"Good, you're awake," he grumbled, setting the food down for us to eat. "For a while dere I thought you may not get up until tomorrow. And I see you 'ave everything ready to go. Good."

"Good morning to you too," I said sarcastically.

"Mm," he grunted and raised one of his bushy eyebrows. "I found us a ride. We may be able to reach dah city by nightfall, so eat up and let's get a move on." He grabbed his pack and headed back outside with Dung Heap on his heels.

"Are you going to be okay to travel today?" I asked Dav, concerned he could reinjure himself if he tried to move too much.

"Yeah." He groaned and climbed to his feet, taking a look from me. "I'll let you know if I need to stop," he assured me, but I knew he only said that to make me feel better.

I grabbed our bags and helped Dav outside where Fye'Gor was waiting with our ride. "Is that..." I stared at the huge creature, my mouth gaping open. "Is that an ant?" I finally asked.

The ginormous bug looked like your average worker ant only it was large enough to carry at least a half a dozen people. It had been equipped with some kind of halter on its head, and strapped to its torso was a leather blanket with metal loops along the side for the rider's feet.

"Do you 'ave dese in your realm?" Fye'Gor asked, surprised. "I looked all over Polarious and couldn't find one."

"Oh, we have them," I replied, hesitant to approach the animal. "Except they're about this big." I held my fingers apart to show the average size of a little ant from Balfjord.

"Mm," Fye'Gor grunted. "And 'ow are you supposed to ride 'em if dey're dat small?"

"We don't," I answered. "They're actually more of a nuisance than anything."

Fye'Gor crinkled his nose and eyebrows. "You must ride those furry mongrels his people do," he grumbled and waved a hand toward Dav. "Dese are much bettah. Docile, easy to train, and extremely loyal." He patted the beast on the head. "Well, load up. Time's a wastin'."

"I don't like bugs," I whispered to Dav.

He only laughed and urged me forward. Fye'Gor sat in front with Dungy in his lap, while Dav and I sat behind him. Our bags had been tied to the sides of the creature's saddle. It was nice to not have to carry them for once. In comparison to a horse, the giant ant was surprisingly a very smooth ride.

Being able to see Norranheim for the first time was unbelievable. I never felt so small. If I didn't know better, I would swear I had been shrunk. Everything was big. I saw flowers the size of my head, bugs and animals large enough to ride, and as for the trees, a simple description could not do them justice. While most weren't as tall as those in the Baccoba Forest, the trunks were twice as wide, resembling more of the ancient oaks we found in the Valley of the Giants.

There were mushrooms so big you could use them as an umbrella. Ferns and vines were everywhere covered in berries the size of grapefruits and cantaloupes, in every color imaginable. Fye'Gor pointed out which ones were sweet or tart but warned us to be careful eating them after they got too ripe as they tended to ferment. His comment was followed by a wink and a laugh.

CHAPTER EIGHTEEN

I was so focused on the forest around me, I didn't realize the city of the White Ones was in sight until Dav squeezed my waist and pointed ahead. The centuries of rain and constant fog had covered the buildings and walls in a layer of moss and algae, making it nearly invisible among the surrounding trees and plants.

As we got closer, the structures became more visible. The buildings were definitely Hvaldi in design, but the layout seemed different from all the others. There was no exterior wall and no main entrance or road into the city, which was a major focal point of the cities I had seen before.

We stopped outside and Fye'Gor secured our ride, so we could continue in on foot to investigate. "Do you think it's Hvaldi?" he asked.

Dav and I both replied *yes* at the same time, making me laugh. As much time as he spent guarding the sacred lands in his realm, I'm sure he knew their structures well. He also pointed out the differences in the design that I hadn't noticed on our approach. Despite the dozen-plus temples, libraries, and other public buildings at the city's center, there was a surprisingly limited number of houses and shops.

Barely a dozen or so were scattered around the perimeter of the town. Stone stairs led up to another level of the city. This level contained the public buildings arranged in a rectangle around the city center. To my surprise, the damp environment had done little to decay portions of the city not made of stone. The roof of nearly every building was still

171

intact. We climbed the stairs and walked between two of the buildings looking for an entrance, but it was what we saw in the middle of town that stopped us in our tracks: a graveyard.

Thousands of headstones were laid out in rows. Dav followed me as I descended the steps and looked at the first few stones. Each contained a family name inscribed at the top with the names of each individual underneath. In the very middle of the graveyard was a stone altar with the bones of a single person lying on top.

The remains were of a man dressed in a magnificently forged suit of armor with a long sword in his hands. Embedded in the center of the chest guard was what appeared to be another key resembling the one around my neck, only it bore different runes from Jorunn's.

"What do they mean?" Dav asked, pointing to the runes on the key. I told him they meant gift, knowledge, and new beginnings.

I reached up and ran my fingers over the piece. It looked like something we could pry away. Clipping the tips of my fingers underneath its edge, I tried to pull it free, but it seemed stuck. The chest guard didn't appear to have anything on it that would release the key from its slot. Thinking that time has a way of building up, preventing things from working the way they used to, I gave it a good hard tug. It popped loose and went flying across the grass with Dung Heap chasing after it.

"No," I yelled at him, but it was too late. Fye'Gor's furry pet took off with it in his mouth.

"I'll get it from 'im," Fye'Gor grumbled. "Now you know why 'e got 'is name." As he left, he grumbled a few more words that I couldn't make out, but it was safe to say he was a bit frustrated with the creature.

Turning my attention back to the Hvaldi lying on the altar, I thought about all the times I was baffled that not a single set of remains had been discovered at any site. It was part of what drove me to keep looking for them. Now, a part of me felt like my journey was over and I was saddened by what I saw.

"I don't understand," I said quietly. "Why bury all but one? Why was he not buried like the others, so he could rest with his family?"

"Maybe there was no one left," Dav suggested. He wrapped his arms around me and kissed the top of my head. "Did you expect to find them alive?"

"Not exactly," I replied. I told him how many great societies of man had existed in Balfjord, and while their cities were now abandoned and the way they lived had changed, the descendants of those people still lived on.

Dav looked up at the darkening sky and suggested we find a good place to make camp. We could do a more thorough search in the morning. To my surprise, Fye'Gor came running down the steps into the graveyard toward us waving his hands frantically.

"You 'ave to 'urry," he blurted between breaths. "It's incredible. Please, 'urry, 'urry." He waved for us to follow him. "I said 'urry!"

Not wanting to irritate him further, we ran behind him up the steps and over to one of the public buildings. "Dat thing Dungy took was a key like yours." He pointed to Jorunn's necklace. "Semmi, you won't believe what it opened."

Fye'Gor led us past several buildings with sealed stone doors until we came to one where the doors had been pushed open and I saw the key dangling out of a slot near the edge. Above the door were two lines of script. *Hall of Records* with *Polarious* written below. He stepped aside and let me enter.

I gasped and covered my mouth, unable to speak. For the first time, I entered a Hvaldi structure that wasn't empty. Stone shelves lined every wall and were filled from floor to ceiling with books, journals, and scrolls. Even the stone tables that filled the center of the room were covered in documents. I couldn't believe they had survived this long.

"Dav," I squeaked, giving his arm a squeeze before walking farther in to look around. "This is amazing."

"This could take a lifetime to go through," Dav said, looking at the shelves full of information. From the tone of his voice, he sounded disappointed and I didn't think he realized how amazing a find this was. Of all the buildings Fye'Gor could have opened here, this was the most important one.

"It may not take as long as you think," I replied. "According to the front door, this building contains records for Polarious, and it looks like everything on the shelves is organized by date." I peered at the books on a shelf near the door.

I looked at a few of the books on the tables and each one had the date it was written and the name of the person who wrote it. "I think if I start at the latest date and work my way back, I can find what we need." I walked around trying to locate the most recent documents.

"I'll let you get started," Dav told me. "Fye'Gor and I will find a place to sleep tonight."

"Okay," I mumbled, focused on reading the dates on the shelves.

"Semmi," Dav said to get my attention. I turned to look, and he smiled at me. "I'll come back and get you."

"All right." I watched Fye'Gor and him leave, thinking how much Dav had changed since we first met. Maybe it was because I knew him better or because I had grown to care about him deeply, but the emotionless expressions had softened, replaced by more frequent smiles. How strange that I had never given much thought to having someone like him in my life, and now I couldn't imagine a single day without him.

***

The light was fading fast and the constant foggy cloud cover meant that moonlight was probably seldom seen on the ground. Dav returned after about an hour to take me to our camp. I was excited to tell him I had located the section of records containing the most recent documents and planned to start going through them first thing in the morning.

Dav looked down at me and made me promise I would wait until morning and not try to slip out in the middle of the night.

174

"I promise." He lifted my chin and looked me in the eyes. "I swear, I won't leave," I added to reassure him.

"Good," he said, "then I have a surprise for you."

He took me by the hand and led me away from the public buildings and down into the small cluster of housing. We passed the structure where he and Fye'Gor had set up camp. Fye'Gor was inside making dinner. He waved to me and we turned into the structure directly across from it.

Inside was a long narrow room with a stone bench running down the center. On either side were three doors. Dav's cloak hung over the first door on the right and he motioned for me to go in. What I saw nearly brought tears to my eyes.

"A bath." It was one of the things I had said I wanted to do when all of this was over. "You remembered." In the center of the room was a bathtub made of solid stone with steps along one side to climb in.

Dav clacked together the two stones from Fye'Gor to produce light for me to see while I was there. On the side of the tub were two thick leaves that had been cut in half and he explained how to squeeze out the gel from inside to clean myself. He apologized that the water wasn't hot but before he could finish, I stopped him with a kiss.

"It's perfect," I whispered. "Thank you so much for everything."

"You're welcome," he replied and thanked me for forgiving him. I gave him a hug and he left so I could clean up.

The water turned from crystal clear to a dingy gray as I washed the weeks of dirt off my body. It was hard to imagine how much time had gone by. I didn't even know how long it had been. The time at the Valley of the Giants was a blur, and I hadn't yet recovered from the lack of sleep. All I knew for sure was that it had been well over a month since we started this journey.

For the first time, though, I felt we were close. There was something here; I knew it and could feel it. "Don't worry, Dad," I whispered. "We're gonna find it."

Sleep came quickly. When I came out of the bedroom, Dav was sitting next to the hearth on the far side of the main room eating a piece of a berry. I was still amazed at everything the small house contained. Most of the wooden furniture was no longer in usable condition and would fall to pieces as soon as we touched it, but the stone and metal items were perfect. We even found some hard clay cookware and plates that were in good shape.

There was a small fire burning and a slight chill in the air from the early morning fog. Dav bid me good morning and I sat down to join him for breakfast. The smell of sweet spices drifted up from a pot hanging over the fire. Dav said it was filled with a hot drink Fye'Gor had made. He explained that Fye'Gor had gone to gather some supplies and should return tomorrow. Now that we had escaped from Polarious, we were no longer in danger of attack by the Calvar and Fye'Gor had said the Norranian clans in this region were peaceful.

"Did you sleep well?" he asked. "You didn't seem to have any bad dreams the last two nights."

"I haven't." *Thanks to you.*

We had come so far together. From strangers to friends, and now, he was one of the most important people in my life. Over the last month, I had also grown as a person, more than I had in years. I had Dav to thank for that.

We talked about the plan for the day. Dav suggested that while I continued where I was yesterday, he would open the other buildings and report back later to help me with the translations.

"I know I'm not as fast as you, but I think I could help."

"That's perfect," I said. "It'll give me time to clear one of the tables, so we'll have a place to work."

It only took about an hour for Dav to unlock all the buildings and take a quick look around. While he was gone, I returned to the Hall of Records for Polarious and found the section with the most recent records that I'd discovered the day before. Nearby was a long stone table with benches. I carefully moved the scrolls and books stacked on top to another table.

One of the books caught my attention. It had Jorunn's name on the cover and the dates were from after she returned from my realm. I only read a few entries and set it aside for later. She was a big part of how I got here, and I looked forward to when I could again resume reading about her life. For now, it would have to wait until we had completed our mission.

When Dav returned, he was carrying a half dozen books in his arms. He explained they were empty and he thought we might be able to use them to translate what we found.

"Excellent," I said since the only journal we brought was filled from my lessons with Dav. I took a couple of the books and carried them over to the table I had prepared.

He told me there were five other buildings like this one with *Hall of Records* inscribed over the door. Three of them had the names of the other realms underneath and two had Polarious. This made sense since Polarious was the Hvaldi's home. He said four other buildings were also filled with books, but he wasn't able to translate the names on the buildings. Three contained an abundance of statues, jewelry, artwork, and trinkets. The remaining two were empty, but he mentioned one had a large statue inside.

Because he didn't recognize the names over some of the doors, he copied them down for me. The four that contained books were titled with the Hvaldi word for Library and listed a subject underneath: Health, Farming, Architecture, and Society. The ones with trinkets were museums. There were no inscriptions over the doors of the two empty buildings.

It was all so fascinating, but like the book with Jorunn's name on it, they too would have to wait until we finished what we'd set out to do. Showing him the section where I was working, I opened one of the empty books and wrote a list of key words for him to search for. I hoped anything containing these words would indicate a time when his people and the Hvaldi lived together. If we tried to read through everything, it would take months. Instead, we wanted to scan them for these words and, if found, translate the document.

With a bit of luck, this would make our search go faster. Dav grabbed a stack of books and a few scrolls and got to work. Anything he found containing the words from my list he passed to me. If not, he returned them to the shelf.

This turned out to work better than I thought. Within a couple of hours, Dav had me buried in books. When he ran out of space on the table, he began marking the books I needed to read later and placed them back on the shelf. By midafternoon, he was no longer finding those key words.

I looked at the dates on the shelves where Dav had marked the books. "Less than two hundred years," I said out loud. "I thought it would be longer." He seemed confused by my comment and I explained that this section of time should contain all the information about his people in Polarious while the Hvaldi were still there. And hopefully they would have the answers we were seeking.

"I'm sure as you start doing a more thorough search, we'll get a better understanding," he replied. I think he was hoping to raise my spirits, but I still thought that the time frame was awfully short.

Even more questions built in my mind beyond the ones I already had. The fact that his people were here at all baffled me. Balfjord was the realm of man. Why then, did they come here and how did they figure out how to get here? Or, were they brought here as Dav believed? And of course, if they were brought here by the Hvaldi, why then did the Hvaldi leave soon after?

Dav left me to get started on the in-depth reading while he got to work preparing an evening meal. Now that we had identified the section of books to go through, there was no need to work backward, so I decided to start with the oldest of the books and go forward. There were over three hundred books and scrolls in this section alone. If this was everything, I would definitely have to summarize it in my notes to take back with us.

The books and scrolls read a lot like some of my journal entries, documenting thoughts, educational sessions, or incidents the author had with Dav's people. Each entry was dated and titled. From the few I was able to go through, it appeared the Hvaldi were teaching them how to develop a prosperous society based on the way they governed their own people.

"Why were you teaching them to be like you?" I asked, thinking out loud. From what I knew of the Hvaldi, they traveled to the other realms to learn, not to teach. This didn't make any sense.

Taking a break from reading, I examined the dates on the journals and scrolls, and it appeared there were chunks of time where there were no writings. "I must be missing some," I whispered and started looking around on the tables.

A barking sound caught my attention and I looked up to see Dungy running over to me, his tail wagging. "Well, hello there, buddy." Leaning over, I scratched behind his ears.

Not far behind, Dav entered with Fye'Gor and a couple of other Norranians. "Look who's back," Dav announced.

"I thought you weren't going to return until tomorrow," I said to Fye'Gor with a smile. He introduced his friends as Halvor and Eamon.

Both Halvor and Eamon were about the same height as Fye'Gor, but instead of gray skin, theirs was brown. Halvor's was a bit darker, and they both had wispy gray and white hair. They wore clothes similar to Fye'Gor's in various colors of brown and green.

"I ran into me ole friends on me way," Fye'Gor replied. "I told 'em your situation and dey offered to 'elp. We may not be able to read dis but when you two return 'ome, you will still 'ave to deal with dose Calvar people. You'll need 'elp."

"We can't ask you to do that," Dav responded.

"You don't 'ave to," Eamon said in a raspy voice, then stepped past him to look at the place.

"I don't understand." I looked at them and at Fye'Gor. "You're home. Why would you go back with us into a potentially dangerous situation?"

"Because Fye'Gor is your friend, which makes you our friend," Halvor answered. His accent was much thicker than Fye'Gor and Eamon's. "It's dah way of our people. Plus, dis place has been a mystery to us for 'undreds of years. It'd be nice to finally 'ave some answers."

"I think we all have many unanswered questions," I said. "I'll do my best to find the answers for you."

"Wonderful," Fye'Gor replied. "But let's find yours first. Ours can wait."

"No," Eamon said. "First we eat. Wera is making us all a fine meal."

"Who's Wera?" I asked.

"Me wife," Eamon answered proudly.

***

That night was the most fun I'd had in a long time. Halvor and Eamon took turns telling funny stories and singing songs while Wera fed us an amazing meal of meat and vegetables with fruit for dessert. Fye'Gor tried to teach me how to dance, which I wasn't very good at, but at least it gave everyone a good laugh and made me quite embarrassed.

"I don't think I've evah seen someone's face get that red before." Eamon laughed.

I helped Wera clean up after eating. She was such a bubbly woman, singing a little song as she worked. Her skin was a very light gray and she had bright blue eyes and pure white hair styled in a braid. Her clothing was a simple light blue dress with a white apron.

She had also brought a change of clothes for Dav and me so we could have a chance to wash the ones we were wearing. Apparently, Fye'Gor had mentioned to her that we had been traveling for a while, which I took to mean that we stank. I hadn't noticed but wouldn't be a bit surprised.

After we both got a chance to bathe, we tried on our temporary clothes. My skirt was a little short, but the top fit. Dav's clothes were way too small. The pants barely covered his knees and he gave up trying to get the vest on. Thank goodness they were only temporary, and our normal clothes would be dry by morning. We both looked a little silly in the new clothes.

Toward the end of the evening, the men began passing around a gourd filled with the juice of some fermented berries. I had heard about alcohol but never tried any. After seeing Dav nearly choke on it, I was hesitant to taste it and once I did, I wished I hadn't. Everyone laughed at the two of us.

"It's an acquired taste," Eamon said, still chuckling at us and taking the gourd back.

When I finally lay down to sleep, my cheeks were sore from smiling so much. The night was chilly, and Dav wrapped his arms around me and pulled me close.

"I didn't get a chance to ask you tonight if you found anything."

"I only read through a half dozen documents," I replied. "I did find proof that your people and the Hvaldi lived together. The Hvaldi were teaching your ancestors skills to better their lives, but I don't know why or if they were responsible for your people coming here."

"You'll figure it out," he said. "I believe in you." His words warmed my heart. He had more faith in me than I had in myself, and that's why I worked so hard. I didn't want to let him down. "Finding out that we lived with the Hvaldi for a time is amazing."

"Why do you have so much confidence in me?" I asked, looking up into his eyes.

"Because you're smarter than you think you are," he answered. "And, because I love you."

My heart nearly stopped, and it was difficult to breathe. While he held me close, I lifted my head so that we were looking at each other face-to-face. As if reading my mind, he leaned over and kissed me, running his hands over my back and squeezing me against him.

"I love you too," I whispered.

CHAPTER NINETEEN

"So, where do you want me to start?" Wera asked as I led her into the Hall of Records. Her accent wasn't nearly as thick as everyone else's and her voice had a much softer tone.

Dav was already sitting at the table in the corner with a stack of scrolls and one of the empty journals. He smiled when he saw us walk in and went back to his work.

"I'm going to have you look at the books and scrolls on the tables to find ones that fall within the dates Dav's people were in Polarious," I said.

To help out, since she didn't know the Hvaldi language, I wrote down the number symbols she would be looking for on a scrap of paper. She took it and got busy, starting at the front of the building. Wera reminded me a lot of Tessa, so friendly and always running around with a smile on her face.

Remembering Tessa brought back the memories from Idaho. Everything had happened so quickly I never knew for sure what happened to her. I prayed with all my heart that she was okay and had made it out, but somehow, deep down, I felt she most likely met with the same fate as Banks.

"Dav, do you mind if I take a walk around?" I asked, my voice cracking as a rush of emotion came over me. Of course, I knew he didn't mind. He asked if I was okay. "Yes, I'm fine," I told him. "She reminds me of someone I once knew."

I picked up one of the journals to take with me and walked around the front of the buildings, glancing through their open doors. Once I made it down to the cemetery, I wandered through the gravestones until I was standing near the center altar.

"What happened to all of you?" I whispered to the bones of the Hvaldi man resting on top. The name Torger was engraved on either side of the altar along with the date of his birth, but the date of his death had only a year and was poorly carved. I assumed he must have been weak and near death when he scratched it into the stone.

Returning to the upper level, I was about to head back to help Dav with the reading when a glimmer inside the smallest of the buildings caught my attention. Dav hadn't figured out what this building was used for and told me it was empty except for a large statue. Sticking my head through the door, I quickly saw what had caught my eye. Water from a fountain in the center of the room reflected a small bit of sunlight peeking through a hole in the ceiling. This must have been the statue Dav mentioned.

I found no inscriptions on the walls, and the room had no tables or benches on which to sit, only the fountain in the center of the room. It was well over twice my height and contained a carved representation of a being from each realm. In a small bowl between each statue were a set of the glow stones Fye'Gor used for light. I clacked two of them together and they lit up, allowing me to get a better look.

Each statue faced the center with their hands extended as if holding an offering. Water filled their cupped hands and poured over the tips of their fingers creating a single stream of falling water. My eyes followed the stream as it dropped into the top of a globe in the center at their feet.

Around the edge of the globe was a shiny silver ring with the names of the realms engraved into it. It was breathtaking. I gazed at it for a few minutes and decided it was time to go, but before I stepped away, I noticed the names of the realms on the ring didn't match up with the beings that stood in front of them. Reaching out, I grabbed the edge and sensed that I could move it. I turned it until the names of the realms lined up with the correct beings.

As soon as I had the ring aligned, there was a vibration in the floor and I jumped back. The stones around the fountain began to descend into the floor creating a staircase that spiraled down into the ground. It was so dark I couldn't see beyond the fourth step.

Grabbing two of the glowing stones from the fountain, I carefully walked down the stairs. Before I reached the bottom, I completed two loops and followed a tunnel a short distance to a small room with a low ceiling not much taller than Dav. The room looked to have been carved into a single massive stone.

Shelves were chiseled into every wall from floor to ceiling and filled with neatly organized books. I examined a few of the titles printed along their spines. Instead of only dates, the titles also included the names of events that had occurred during the Hvaldi's history: the discovery of the realms, their various visits, and experiences with the beings they met.

As the stones dimmed, I clacked them together again to brighten the room. On the far side was another statue of a Hvaldi woman kneeling in a pool of water fed by a stream coming out of the wall. Her hands were holding a book up as if offering it as a gift. The title read *Our Final Chapter*. Barely able to breathe, I gently lifted the book out of the statue's hands and carried it over to the table in the center of the room. Taking a deep breath, I closed my eyes and prayed that this was what we had been searching for as I opened it to the first page and began to read.

***

"Semmi." Dav's voice echoed down the tunnel. I was so immersed in what I was reading that I didn't realize how much time had gone by. Jumping up, I hurried down the tunnel and shouted up the stairs to him.

A couple of minutes later, he found his way down and I led him to the small room. He told me when I didn't return, he had gone looking for me. "I'm glad you're o…k…" His voice trailed off when he stepped inside. "What is this place?"

"All these books contain the history of the Hvaldi," I answered and walked over to the table. "And this one"—I lifted the book for him to see—"tells about your people." I further explained, from what I'd read, his people were brought to Polarious by the Hvaldi.

"Why?" he asked.

"Because the Hvaldi race was dying and they didn't want everything they had learned to become lost. Passing their knowledge to your people was their answer, so they could live on through you."

"Then what happened? Why did they leave?"

"I don't know yet. I haven't gotten that far."

He suggested that we read it together, which I thought was a great idea. I grabbed the book and we headed back up to the surface.

We returned to the Hall of Records and sat down at our table in the corner. Dav pulled out one of the empty journals to copy down the information in his writing and take it back with us, and I started again from the beginning. Even Wera and the others sat down to listen as I read aloud from *Our Final Chapter*.

It took nearly a week to read and transcribe the words from this great race. I found myself having to stop several times to dry my eyes knowing every word was written in an attempt to not let the memory and knowledge of their existence disappear with them.

When the Hvaldi realized their race was dying and more and more women were unable to have children, they knew they needed to do something or everything they had learned and experienced would die with them. It was decided that they would pass their world and knowledge to the race of man.

The Hvaldi hand-selected thousands of people and their families to come to Polarious where they would pass on to them all they knew, a process that would take many generations to complete. They thought they would have plenty of time before the last of their kind was gone, but unfortunately, their population declined faster than expected.

They had barely scratched the surface of passing down their knowledge when they realized they were running out of time and a new plan was needed. The city in Norranheim was built not only to be their final resting place but to house all their knowledge and the knowledge they gathered about the other realms.

A small council of man was formed and taught how to maintain the society they were brought into. Materials were provided for them to learn the Hvaldi language along with the keys.

The Hvaldi felt that if those who were given the knowledge did as instructed, they'd figure out what to do with the keys and would be led here. They believed that if the race of man found this city, it meant they were ready for what was left for them.

The process took nearly a generation to complete. Two-thirds of the Hvaldi population was now gone. The remaining were moved to this city, to live out their final days. From the date on Torger's altar, the last of them died less than ten years after they left Polarious.

"There was never any pure or superior family," Dav commented as I finished reading. "We were all important and the Calvar tried to destroy it." I could hear the anger in his voice. Never had I seen him this upset. He stormed out of the building.

I tried to go after him, but Eamon stopped me and said to give him some time alone. Being in a relationship was new for me, and I wasn't sure how to help him with the pain and betrayal he was feeling now that he knew the truth. He had been raised with the stories that his people were brought to Polarious. However, I'm sure somewhere in the back of his mind he wondered whether or not the Calvar were right, even if he disagreed with the way they used his people to gain power.

"I'm sorry, Eamon. I can't wait any longer," I told the Norranian after Dav hadn't returned after ten minutes. "I love him, and I want him to know I'm here for him." He nodded, and I headed toward the far edge of the city in the direction I saw Dav go.

I found him sitting on a rock with his head down. His sword was stuck in the side of a tree where he had hit it, and from the looks of the tree, he'd hit it more than once. Not saying a word, I slowly walked up and stood in front of him. I lightly ran my fingers through his hair and felt his arms reach around my waist, pulling me to him. He rested his head against my chest.

After a couple of minutes, he let go and I sat next to him.

"I can't stop thinking about everyone who died at the hands of the Calvar when it was clear the belief they were pushing was false," he said quietly. "I don't understand why some people find pleasure in making others suffer to gain power and control."

"I wish I had the answer." Coming from Balfjord, I had studied many societies of man that all fought the same battles over and over against those who sought to oppress their people. "My dad told me once that power corrupts, and absolute power corrupts absolutely." It had been a repetitive behavior throughout our people's history, I explained.

"How do you stop it?"

"I don't think I'm the right person to answer that question," I confessed and looked down at the ground.

Who was I to tell him what to do? In my realm, as those in power continued to pass laws that only benefited them and not the people they governed, we didn't fight back. Though we knew it was wrong and we argued about it, we still obeyed. Even when our profession was made illegal, we didn't put our foot down and say no. Instead we hid.

How many generations of the Warriors of Baleloch had fought against the Order of Calvar to protect the people even when their people didn't believe in them? They didn't hide. They fought. They had honor and pride and cared more about the freedom of their people than their own lives. No, I had no right to offer advice and I was ashamed at not having the courage to stand up for what I believed in when my dad and I were running for our lives.

"Semmi, what's wrong?" he asked.

"I feel like such a coward," I answered. "Your people fight back in little ways every day against the Calvar. We didn't. We ran and hid. That's what we were doing when we came here. We were running for our lives while they slaughtered everyone in camp. We didn't fight. Maybe if we did, Banks and Tessa would still be alive." My lips quivered as the memory of Banks getting shot played in my mind.

"It was you and your father," Dav stated. "I'm sure saving your life was all he was concerned about." He lifted my chin and our eyes met. "Do you think my people have ever not run when we were outnumbered? There're more ways to fight back than with weapons. Master Orin taught me that. What we're doing here is finding the truth. If Master Orin is right, when we share this with our people, it will strike a blow stronger than any sword. And it's because of you. None of this would be possible without you."

"You've always had more faith in me than I have in myself." I smiled.

"It's because I've seen how amazing you are," he replied, kissing me and standing to retrieve his sword from the tree so we could head back to the others.

"I hope Master Orin is right."

"He has to be," Dav answered. "Or all of this is for nothing. I have faith in our people. They'll open their eyes when the truth is in their hands and they can see it for themselves."

CHAPTER TWENTY

Now that we had the translation complete, we needed to make plans to return to Polarious and get the book to Master Orin. We had the tablet with the runic codes and knew which one to use to get back. Being new to traveling the realms, we weren't sure where we would come out if we used the same door. We weren't even sure if the waterfall or tunnel were still there or if the Calvar had demolished it.

Fye'Gor explained to the others how to identify a location where a doorway could be concealed and Wera immediately clapped her hands together saying she knew exactly where one was: a place not far from their home. Eamon nodded in agreement, describing a small pond with a tree growing in the middle of it. He further explained that there was no stream entering or leaving the pond and that the tree was of a species no one had seen anywhere else in their realm.

As if reading my mind, Dav glanced at me then looked back at Eamon and asked how long it would take to get there. We were told it was less than a day's ride by ant. If we left in the morning, we could be back in Polarious by the end of the day.

The thought excited and frightened me at the same time. I wanted so badly to see my dad and to share everything I'd seen with him. I prayed this book would be enough to convince Dav's people. Lying awake, I thought about all we'd gone through to get here, but it was only half the battle. There was still a long way to go and a lot of uncertainties.

"Are you still awake?" Dav yawned, rolling onto his side and pulling me to him. Whenever he held me against his warm body, the rest of the world slipped away.

"Sorry," I apologized, sinking into him. "I can't stop thinking about everything. Will you tell me a story about when you were little?" I knew it probably sounded like a silly request and I asked that it not to have anything to do with war or people getting hurt.

I loved the sound of his voice. He had barely started talking and I was out. The next thing I knew, I was opening my eyes to Dav kneeling over me, tickling my nose. I giggled and swatted at his hand.

"Are the others awake?" My voice was still groggy from sleeping.

"Yep," he replied. "They've been awake for a few minutes."

Before leaving, we decided it would be best to leave the original copy of the book here where it would be safe. I returned it to the hands of the statue in the hidden room and looked around at the other books. Someday I hoped to come back to read them all. I also returned the other key to Torger's altar, placing it back in his armor. The Hvaldi was an incredibly intelligent race that had a lot to teach us. I hoped we were ready.

Climbing aboard another monster ant, I watched the city slowly fade into the forest as we left. It wasn't the biggest city the Hvaldi had ever built and with the giant plants and animals that lived here, it looked even smaller. But it was never designed to be lived in. It was to be their final resting place. The public buildings they built to house everything about them were magnificent: a last testament of a dying race.

***

We rode through the morning hours, only stopping to wait for the usual afternoon showers to pass. The smell of the damp forest was relaxing. The aroma of the flowers, moss, and soil created a unique and clean scent.

Dav and I shared an apple-sized berry off a bush we were standing under. It had bright green and yellow leaves and the berries hung in

191

bunches like grapes on a vine. The tart juice was like nothing I'd ever had before. I picked a few more to take with us and tucked them inside my cloak for later.

Another late-afternoon storm slowed our progress and it was well after dark when we finally arrived at the pond. I should have remembered Fye'Gor's comment about everything here being big, so when they told me it was a small pond I wouldn't have pictured a little body of water. Instead this pond was huge. Calling it a lake would have been a better description.

Wera explained that the tree was at the very center and pointed in the direction it was located, but it was too far away to see. We would have to take a boat to reach it. Visions of our last boat ride flashed through my mind, making me a little nervous.

The pond was beautiful. Large ferns and trees grew all around it. All of the sand and stones along the bottom were gray or white—an amazing sight and much different from the brown dirt and dark rocks found in the rest of the forest. The fish swimming about were a menagerie of pretty colors and didn't seem overly large or aggressive.

Due to the late hour, Eamon suggested we wait until morning, offering for all of us to stay at his and Wera's home, located not far from the water's edge. It was built in a similar fashion to the hut Fye'Gor had in Polarious, with the obvious added touches of a woman. Curtains, flowers, and intricate tablecloths decorated the inside, giving it a warm, welcoming feeling.

Tonight was our last night to stay in a place where our lives weren't in any danger. Tomorrow, as soon as we returned to Polarious, we would have to constantly keep a sharp eye out for anyone who might want to harm us. The Calvar were always looming somewhere ready to eliminate anyone who opposed them and their way of thinking.

We tried to make the most of the time we had here. I helped Wera prepare a nice meal and we each got the opportunity to take a bath. Dav and Fye'Gor did their best to prepare everyone for what to expect when we returned. He thanked all of them for their willingness to come with us given the danger involved.

"As we've said before, any friend of Fye'Gor's is a friend of ours," Halvor said. "Plus, the way I look at it, if dah book doesn't convince dem, a bunch of Norranians should."

"It would certainly help prove our point," Dav agreed, shaking Halvor's hand.

I had hoped the night would last longer, but morning came earlier than either of us wanted. In the little room where we slept, I lay quietly with my head on Dav's chest until I felt his hand rub my back.

"I thought you were still sleeping."

"No," he replied quietly and kissed the top of my head. "Just enjoying this."

From outside, I heard some movement. Someone was up. I let out a huff as I knew that meant it was time to get moving. We both got up and gathered our things, but before opening the door, Dav pulled me close and gave me a long kiss.

I wished this moment would last forever. We had been gone for over two months, although it felt longer, and we were about to head back into the lion's den.

"Are you ready for this?" he asked.

"As long as I have you."

He reached inside his coat and pulled out a simple silver bracelet. "When Master Orin found me as a baby, this was tucked inside the blanket I was wrapped in." He slipped it around my wrist. "It's the only thing I have from whoever my parents were."

He spun the bracelet until I could see the engraving on the top. It was a Hvaldi rune shaped like an X with a notch on either side and a dot at the bottom. The symbol had several meanings including gift, relationship, and love.

"You are everything to me," he said.

"As you are to me."

He kissed me once more and I followed him out.

Wera was busy packing provisions for our journey. She let us know that Eamon and Halvor were out getting the boat ready and that Fye'Gor wasn't yet up. She wasn't wearing her usual dress but had exchanged it for a pair of wide-legged blue pants and a matching blouse. Around her waist was a belt carrying half a dozen small knives.

"Can I help with anything?" I asked after Dungy jumped all over me. She smiled and started giving me a list of things I could do to help her finish.

Dav left us to our work. He took our bags along with two others Wera had sitting by the door and headed out to give Eamon a hand. Wera chuckled as I watched Dav leave.

"What?" I asked, not sure what she thought was so funny.

"I remember when Eamon and I were like that," she said with a giggle.

"Were?" I chuckled at her comment. I had watched the two of them together. They were always sneaking a look at each other when they thought the other wasn't looking, and Eamon never missed an opportunity to touch her when she was within reach. Whether it was a kiss, a pat on the fanny, or a rub of her cheek, their actions showed it was easy to see they loved each other very much. "From what I've seen you still are."

"Oh, well." She laughed, and her cheeks turned slightly rosy. "Some say love isn't easy, that you have to work at it for it to be successful. Loving him is the easiest thing I've ever done," she said. "I think love is what you make it."

As we worked, Wera told me about how she and Eamon met and gave me some pointers on what she felt made their relationship last. They had been married for over ten years and she told me that she loved him more every day. I had never been in love before, but I prayed we would be like them in ten years.

"What are you two gagglin' about in 'ere?" Fye'Gor yawned as he walked into the room and sat down at the hearth.

"Love," Wera told him and we both smiled.

"Oh dear," he replied, making a funny face. Standing, he headed for the door.

"Don't grumble at me, old man," Wera said with a glint in her eye. "I remember someone else who was as silly in love."

"Augh," Fye'Gor groaned and waved a hand at her. "I don't know what you're talking about." His tone made it obvious he was lying. Before he stepped out the door, he looked back at her and shook his head. "Come on, fuzzball!" he shouted to Dungy as he shut the door. I could hear him chuckling outside.

"Don't let his rough exterior fool you, my dear," she said. "When his wife Thaydra was alive, oh my. I never saw two who loved each other so much." She shared a few stories before Halvor came in to let us know it was time.

I grabbed the last two packs Wera and I had filled with supplies and we left to meet up with the others. Eamon and Fye'Gor were untying the ropes for the wooden boat, which looked like the barges used to carry wagons and horses across rivers in Balfjord. Several long wood poles were tied to the railing, which I assumed were to be used to move the boat through the water by pushing off the bottom.

Dav was holding the reins of a much smaller ant. This one was about the size of a large horse or pony, not like the bigger ones we rode before. He took the last two bags I was carrying and tied them with the others on the ant's back then led the creature onto the boat and secured him.

"I hope you didn't forget anything!" Eamon grumbled loudly at his wife, seeing all the bags that were tied to the poor creature.

"You'll thank me later," she snapped back at him and went on with getting herself settled on the boat.

Looking around at the others, I could see that they took Dav's words about the dangers of the Calvar to heart. Fye'Gor had a new long spear, Eamon carried two shorter spears on his back with long metal points, and Halvor had a small ax and long knife hanging from his belt.

Dung Heap, I think, was having the most fun, splashing about in the water. Fye'Gor threw a rock into the water for him and he swam out and

195

dove to get it. He laughed at his silly pet and yelled at him to get in the boat. The soaking wet critter hopped in and ran between Dav and Eamon before shaking the water off. Eamon cursed the little beast, swinging his hand and foot in the air to shoo him away.

When everyone was aboard, Halvor and Fye'Gor shoved off from the back. Dav and Eamon stood up front with their own poles. For as large as the pond was, it wasn't very deep. Less than ten feet in most places making it easy to see the ground below the surface.

"I thought the fish would be bigger," I commented, looking over the side. Of all the fish I saw darting around, most were about a foot or two long, with the longest no bigger than three.

"In every other lake dey are," Eamon clarified. "Dis is dah only one I've seen dat was shallow and 'ad fish smaller dan dis boat and one tiny tree at its middle. But she loved it, so I made 'er a 'ome 'ere." He winked at Wera making her blush.

"And 'ow 'bout you, Semmi?" Eamon asked. "What does your dream 'ome look like?"

"Um," I said, trying to think of my dream home. "I've never thought much about it. I don't remember ever living in a home."

"Never lived in a 'ome?" Fye'Gor gasped. "Where did you live?"

"In tents mostly," I answered, a little self-conscious. "We traveled a lot. Oh! I lived in a cabin once, for a little while. It was nice and had a loft. That's the closest I've ever come to having my own room."

"Well, maybe dis strong lad will build you both a nice 'ome someday," Eamon spouted and gave Dav a pat on the back. "What you think, me boy?" he asked, shaking Dav's shoulder as he chuckled loudly.

"Absolutely," Dav answered and looked at me.

"I'd like that." The thought of having a home, a real home, seemed hard to picture. I tried to think of all the homes I had been in to picture what I would like my dream home to look like. Nothing big that's for sure. Everything I owned fit in my backpack. I couldn't imagine trying to fill an entire house.

"Does dat boy ever smile?" Eamon asked loudly after seeing Dav's ever-so-popular straight face.

"Yes." I laughed. Dav only raised an eyebrow.

"You should've seen 'im before 'e kissed 'er," Fye'Gor yelled from the back of the boat. "Yep, 'e's a real ball of joy now."

They all took turns teasing Dav. Even Halvor got in a couple of comments until they finally got him to laugh. The men all cheered in good fun and Eamon handed Dav a small leather flask from his coat pocket. Dav cringed after taking a sip of it, making Eamon laugh even harder.

"Bet you 'aven't tasted anything like dat before," Eamon said as Dav handed it back, and he took a swig for himself. "Better dan dat weak stuff I gave you before. It's me own recipe. You won't find none finer."

"I'll take your word for it," Dav said between coughs. Eamon offered him another drink, but Dav declined and asked me for some water instead.

They continued pushing the boat along until the tree they spoke of came into sight. The voyage took a little more than an hour. The little tree grew out of the rocks of a tiny island that was no more than a few feet above the water. The trunk of the tree grew in a twisted shape. Its bark was thin and flaky showing the ivory color of the wood below, and the limbs all grew up to the same height creating a flat top.

"What do you think, Semmi?" Dav asked.

"It's definitely unlike anything else we've seen in this realm," I replied, staring at it. While all other plants, trees, and animals we'd encountered were so big, here, everything was infinitely smaller in comparison. The tiny island and tree combined stood not more than twelve feet out of the water. I tried to imagine how a door large enough for all of us could possibly open from this little place. "Let me see if I can open a door before we unload. I'm not sure there's enough room for all of us otherwise," I suggested, getting a nod in agreement.

Opening my bag, I took a quick look at the runes on the stone tablet that I needed to scratch into the ground then tucked it away and jumped out of the boat. The water was shallow, and I could feel the coolness through my boots. Dav handed me his knife and I walked up to the island.

The small tree was an amazing sight. It grew out of a pile of stones with its roots twisted through the rocks and down into the water. When I looked closer, what I thought were leaves were actually clusters of tiny pine needles growing together. Bunches of ivory pine cones grew in clusters like ornaments.

Realizing I was procrastinating, I knelt by the water's edge and moved a few stones, trying to find some dirt to scratch the runes into, but there was none. The whole island was a mound of stones and boulders, so I looked for a rock large enough to scrape the symbols on.

"Over there," I heard Dav say and turned to see him pointing at a long rock nearby. It was like he knew what I was thinking.

"You read my mind," I said and walked over to the rock. Using the knife, I scratched the runes on the stone, pausing for a moment before carving the last one.

Each door had been different, and I didn't know what to expect from this one—roots opening, trees untwisting, and waterfalls with opening stones I didn't even know were there. As I stepped back to the side of the boat, the thought of whirlpools and rapids popped into my mind. My thoughts were cut short when the ground beneath me fell away. I dropped into the water and my world went dark.

CHAPTER TWENTY-ONE

"Semmi!" Dav yelled my name over and over, but he seemed so far away and all I could see was darkness. Something was pressing against my chest. Slowly a blurry shape, which kneeled over me, came into focus. It was Dav pushing down on me with his hands. I heard him yell my name again, clearly this time, and felt a burning in my chest.

Coughing and gasping for air, I lifted my head. He helped me sit up so I could cough out the rest of the water in my lungs. I held onto his arm and leaned against him as I tried to suck in some desperately needed air.

"Wha…what…happened?" I asked between breaths.

"The bottom of dah lake dropped out," Fye'Gor said with excitement. "It was quite a rush." His comment received a swat from Wera. "Ah, I mean, of course, with dah exception of almost losin' ya."

"Who would've thought pushin' on someone's chest could get 'em to spit up dah water dey sucked in," Halvor said and patted Dav on the shoulder.

Wera explained how after I had dropped into the water, a tunnel opened below the island pulling the water and boat into it. As soon as we emerged on the other side, Dav jumped over the side looking for me.

"He saved your life," she said, taking my hand in one of hers and giving Dav's arm a squeeze with the other.

The boat drifted out of a tunnel in a giant rock face and into a big lake. The water was a deep dark blue surrounded by a variety of pines and oaks. They weren't as colorful as those I had seen in the sacred grounds, but I recognized them as those I had seen in the valley.

"Do you know where we are?" I asked Dav.

"Yeah," he replied, helping me to my feet. "And we need to get off of the water fast."

He quickly explained it was a large lake south of the farmlands widely used for fishing and that the people in this area tended to be supporters of the Calvar. No further explanation was needed to tell us it was unadvisable to be spotted.

The poles were too short to reach the bottom of the lake and we weren't drifting toward shore. Dav and the men jumped out and pulled the boat with them as they swam to the north shore. The angle of the sun told me it was still early in the morning, but already there were a few boats on the water. I hoped those aboard were far enough away to assume we were simply another fishing boat.

When we reached shore, everyone quickly jumped out and headed into the forest. Wera and I were left with Dungy and the ant while they looked for a shielded place where we could hide until sundown when it would be safer to travel.

I helped Wera secure the ant to a tree then kept an eye out for the men's return. Dungy stayed at my feet, but his nose was working overtime. The ant, on the other hand, was a curious creature. It made little clicking noises as its way of talking and it liked to be pet. He nudged Wera and turned the top of its head toward her so she could give him a rub.

Dungy let out a growl to notify me that someone who shouldn't be was close. I shushed him and looked through the trees for movement. Not far off, a couple of Calvar soldiers were walking through the woods, but they didn't appear to have noticed us. I pulled Dungy back with me and told Wera to duck down. She did as I asked and even got the ant she called Diddles, to lie down on the ground.

The soldiers got close enough for us to hear their voices as they walked past our location without even a glance in our direction. We stayed down until Dav and the Norranians returned. I started to tell them about the soldiers we saw on patrol, but when I noticed the blood on Dav's sword and Eamon's spears, I realized they were already aware.

"Let's move," Dav said and led us away from the lake to a cave not far away.

There we waited until the moons rose into the sky before setting out. At this time of night, the Calvar would still be out, but most other people would be in their homes or asleep, meaning fewer prying eyes. If it was only Dav and me, we could slip through unnoticed, but with the Norranians, a mangy furball, and giant bug, we would stick out a bit.

Fortunately, the lake was much closer to Master Orin's home than the Valley of the Giants. But, that also meant we would have to travel around several heavily populated areas, including the capital city of Yorkshire where my dad was being held.

Keeping to the forest around the lake and the Sweetwater River, we walked west, staying far outside any of the cities. It was near morning when we passed Yorkshire. I stopped and stared at the city in the distance, wondering where he was.

"I miss you, Dad," I whispered.

"I'm sure he's okay," Dav said as he walked up next to me and put his arm around my waist. I leaned into him and kept watching the city.

"How do you always know what I'm thinking?" I asked. He looked at me with his ever-so-slight smile and kissed my forehead. To make me feel better he told me we would know for sure how my dad was doing once we reached Master Orin's the day after tomorrow.

It still wasn't completely light and Dav was eager to put a little more distance between us and Yorkshire. It was the largest city, filled with thousands of people coming and going. The farther from it we could get, the safer we would be.

Wera reminded me of myself when I first arrived here. She was fascinated by all the plants, animals, and bugs. I showed her what an ant looked like here and she was shocked at how tiny they were. She held one in her hand, letting it crawl over her fingers before setting it back down.

I shared fun facts about the forest with her which I had learned from Dav when we first set out on this journey. "I can't get over how small everything is," she said, picking a little flower and holding it to her nose to breathe in its scent.

Ahead I saw Eamon waving for us to get down. Grabbing Wera by the arm, I pulled her behind a bush. She tugged on Diddles' reins and I called for Dungy who was already growling to signal danger. I waved to Fye'Gor who was walking behind us to let him know.

"What's goin' on?" Fye'Gor asked quietly when he reached us.

"I don't know." I looked straight ahead, waiting.

Eamon pointed at me and waved for me to join them. Staying low, I made my way up to him. He took my hand and motioned for me to move up to where Dav and Halvor were lying behind a mound of dirt.

Before I reached them, voices on the road caught my attention. I dropped down to my knees and crawled the rest of the way until I was next to Dav. He whispered to me that there were four Calvar soldiers on the road and they needed a diversion. Halvor further explained, that if we could draw them off the road and into the forest, they could take the soldiers down quickly and silently so as not to draw any unwanted attention.

"What do you want me to do?" I asked, unsure of how I could accomplish this.

"I need you to act like a scared girl," Dav explained, trying not to laugh.

"Seriously?"

"I know you can do this," he said. "Do whatever's necessary to get them over here."

"Okay," I replied. I buttoned up my cloak and messed my hair up a bit to make it look like I had been running through the forest. Dav took a little dirt and rubbed it on my face and cheeks. *Okay, I can do this.* I prepared to run out.

"Semmi?" Dav whispered, "Sword." He pointed at my waist. Quickly I unbuckled my belt and handed it to him then ran out onto the road.

"Help!" I yelled, waving my hands at the soldier. "Please, help me." I ran toward them. "Oh, thank goodness."

"What is it, my lady?" one of the soldiers asked.

"In the forest." I pointed to where Dav wanted me to send them. "A creature was chasing me. It was hideous. I've never seen anything like it before. It was growling and snarling with long claws and fangs," I babbled on the way I had seen feeble women do in Balfjord.

"It's all right, miss," the soldier said, taking my hand and ordering the other three to go check it out while he stayed with me. Knowing what I did about the Calvar made me want to pull my hand away, but I played my part and continued to behave like I was terrified of what I claimed to have seen. The soldier tried to console me as I looked back.

The fact that they all didn't go made me nervous about how to get away from him if I needed to. The three soldiers ran off the road and through the woods. Minutes passed, and they didn't return. I needed to do something else, I thought to myself.

"It was right behind me, I swear," I told the man, taking hold of his arm and acting panicked.

"Relax, miss," he said, turning his back to the woods.

I heard a whistle and saw Dav step out onto the road. The soldier turned and saw Dav coming toward him. He yanked me in front of him and tried to pull his sword, but it was too late. Dav flung his knife at him. It flew over my shoulder and sank into the man's neck. A gurgle came from the man's mouth as he tried to gasp for air.

Dav caught him before he hit the ground and dragged him off the road. Quickly, I kicked dirt over the blood that had sprayed out and rubbed out the drag marks.

As I was finishing up, Wera ran across the road with Diddles and Dungy. The others followed a few seconds after with Dav coming out last. There was no more walking until we reached a thick cluster of trees and ferns, where we would be well hidden for the rest of the day.

"You did great," Dav said once we were settled.

"Thank you. I was worried when they all didn't go."

"I figured one would stay."

"Really?" *How could he possibly know these things?*

"Mm-hmm," he answered. "Beautiful, scared woman in distress."

I didn't say anything, only stared at him for a moment with a teasing glare. "You think I'm beautiful?"

"You know I do," he answered.

CHAPTER TWENTY-TWO

Until the sun dropped below the horizon, we took turns standing watch in pairs throughout the day, so everyone had a chance to get some rest. We were all thankful Wera packed extra food for the trip. With having to travel so close to towns, it was impossible to hunt for anything or have a fire for cooking without being spotted.

Wera gave her husband an I-told-you-so look and he had to do a little groveling for picking on her before for over-packing. We all had a good laugh and the guys teased him about it.

Dav took out a map to show everyone where we were while we waited a bit longer for the last of the sun's rays to disappear. I recognized the location. We were east of where Dav and I had come out of the sacred lands when we first met.

Our goal for tonight was to continue west until we reached a small town Dav called Grassy Meadows. There we would cross the valley to the forest on the north side. Few people lived there making it easier for us to travel the remaining distance to Master Orin's.

He explained that after Grassy Meadows, most of the forest to the south had been cut down for farmland, leaving nowhere for us to hide or travel safely. It was also the narrowest part of the valley, making it the best place to cross.

"We should be able to reach Master Orin's by morning," Dav told everyone.

The excitement bubbled up inside me. We were in the home stretch. Once we reached Orin's, we would be safe and able to work on the next plan of action to complete the mission of delivering the truth to his people.

Dav thanked them all again for their help. They sloughed it off like it was no big deal. Eamon commented on how he was looking for a nice place to take his wife on vacation and Halvor said he was always up for an adventure. They were an amazing people. I hoped after this was over, the friendship we had built with them would continue.

It was clear Dav and Eamon were quickly becoming good friends. Of the three, Eamon was the youngest. He often referred to Fye'Gor and Halvor as the *old guys* which usually was followed by a wait-until-you're-our-age kind of comment. With Dav now the youngest of the bunch, he definitely got his share of the heckling. And I think he enjoyed it.

Looking up at the moonlit sky, I knew it was time to get moving. Grassy Meadows was only a few hours' walk. Dav and Eamon took the lead with Fye'Gor and Halvor in the rear, keeping Wera and me in the middle.

We made good time and reached the outskirts of the city after everyone had turned in for the night. The town was dark with only a few lights to be seen, but something had Dav on edge.

"What is it?" Eamon asked.

"I have a bad feeling for some reason," Dav answered. "Something doesn't seem right."

"Does dah place look different?" Fye'Gor asked.

"I haven't been here in months, but nothing is jumping out at me," he replied.

"Probably yer nerves," Halvor suggested. "You said we're gettin' close."

"Maybe," Dav said, "but in case, let's all be on our toes. We'll be vulnerable out in the open." Everyone agreed and Dav explained we would be crossing west of town where there was an old abandoned barn in the middle of a field. He suggested we could use it for cover if needed.

The rundown barn wasn't far away, but it was a good enough distance from the town that anyone up and about wouldn't think much of seeing movement in the field. Dav instructed us to stay behind the tree line while he and Eamon went out first to check the area and make sure the barn was clear.

I watched them slowly walk out into the field, keeping their heads down. Eamon was barely visible over the tall grass. They slowed their approach as they neared the barn and they spread farther apart. Without warning, a soldier wearing the Order of Calvar uniform walked around the corner of the building.

Dav tried to duck out of sight but as tall as he was, he couldn't get his head below the grass in time. The soldier saw him and shouted for backup. My heart jumped, and I tried to get to my feet, but a hand clamped over my mouth and held me from moving.

"Shh," I heard Fye'Gor say in my ear. "Stay quiet." He then let me go and I watched.

Dav didn't move for a moment then took off running toward town. I counted eight soldiers emerge from the old barn and take off after him.

"Where's Eamon?" Wera whispered.

"Dere," Halvor answered and pointed at a spot in the field. "Dey didn't see 'im."

We waited for Eamon to work his way back to us. When he was safely behind the trees, he let us know that Dav was leading them away and would double back.

"Dav said for us to keep goin' west until we reached Sweetwa'er and that you'd know where it was," Eamon said, looking at me. "And 'e'll meet us dere and den we'll cross."

"We better hurry," I said. "Sweetwater is still a good distance from here."

The farm fields made travel difficult. The only trees to conceal our position were along the edges of the fields. We had to zigzag back and forth, slowing our progress dramatically. I constantly looked back to see if Dav was coming, but after two hours, there was no sign of him.

Another hour passed, and Sweetwater lay in the distance. Dav still hadn't returned and I was beginning to worry he had been captured or worse, but we had other issues. Morning would be coming soon and there was nowhere to hide in the fields. We needed to cross and soon.

"If we follow dis line of trees, we can stay somewhat 'idden for most of dah way," Halvor suggested.

"Yeah, but it'll get us awfully close to dat farm." Fye'Gor pointed to a large barn with a small house nearby.

"It's still late," I said, "and it looks like the people are asleep. We're running out of time."

With no other options, we made our way north. Part of me felt the trees did little to shield us, but it was better than nothing. There wasn't much we could do to hide an eight-foot-long ant.

Eamon stopped ahead of us and began looking around frantically. "We need to 'ide now!" he quietly yelled and pointed to the east. A group of soldiers were riding on the dirt road, heading toward Sweetwater.

"And where do you suggest we 'ide?" Halvor snapped.

"The barn. Hurry," I ordered.

We weren't more than twenty yards away and we only needed to stay for a few minutes while the soldiers passed. I heard Fye'Gor grumble, but he knew as well as I did we had no choice. If we didn't get out of sight, we would be captured for sure.

I hoped the soldiers were still far enough away that they didn't notice us as we moved in behind the barn. Eamon crept around the corner and opened the doors, so we could all run in before the soldiers saw us.

As Eamon pulled the doors shut, I heard a sound that made my heart drop. Dung Heap started barking like crazy at an animal that was in one of the pens inside.

"No!" I gasped and tried to grab him, but he darted away from me and continued barking. "Fye'Gor!"

"Shut it!" he yelled and grabbed Dungy, but the beast wouldn't stop. Halvor grabbed a blanket off a nearby gate and threw it over the furball, finally getting him to quiet down.

Wera tied Diddles to a post and Eamon watched out the window to see if the noise had alerted anyone to our presence. The barn was filled with a large collection of farming tools hung on the walls. Three pens along one side contained a few animals that looked like goats with overly long ears and tusks, and an overhead loft was piled high with hay.

"We got company," Eamon said, backing away from the window and pulling out his spears. "Someone's coming out of dah 'ouse. An old man. Must 'ave 'eard us."

"I'm sure dey 'eard us all dah way in Norran'eim," Fye'Gor growled and glared at Dungy who was still being held under the blanket.

I looked around the barn. There was no place to hide, but some of the tools that were scattered across the workbench struck a memory. I had seen them before somewhere. On the edge of the table sat a shoe and I remembered.

"Shoes." My voice was a whisper. "Eamon wait!" I snapped as the barn door opened and Sir Otto stepped inside holding a lantern in his hand.

Eamon stood still holding his spear in the air, ready to defend us. Halvor too, had his weapons ready but didn't move, waiting for my instructions.

Otto jumped seeing the two Norranians with weapons raised. "Wait, wait," I said again and stepped in front of them. "Sir Otto."

"Lady Semmi, is that you?" he asked, squinting at me and patting at the pocket on his coat. "I don't have my glasses on."

"Yes sir, it's me," I answered and waved for them to lower their weapons.

"Is Lord Davik with you?" he asked, finally putting his glasses on and looking around the room at everyone. Strangely, he didn't seem scared or startled at the sight of the Norranians and the giant ant. "Are these friends of yours?"

"Yes," I answered slowly. "These are Norranians."

"From Norranheim!" he blurted in amazement, his mouth hanging open in shock.

"You know of Norranheim?" I asked, surprised.

"I was raised with the old beliefs, Lady Semmi," he answered, smiling and holding the lantern up so he could see them all. "Amazing. You are all welcome here."

Eamon resumed his post at the window as I introduced everyone to Otto and explained that we were trying to get to Master Orin's, stressing the importance that we get there as soon as possible. I told him about what happened in Grassy Meadows and that Dav was supposed to catch up, but we hadn't seen him.

Otto said we could stay until Dav returned. He would hang a light outside so Dav would know, explaining it was a signal for the Warriors of Baleloch that help was needed.

"Too late for that," Eamon interrupted. "We got company again, and it's not Dav."

I followed Otto to the window. The soldiers we had seen on the road to Sweetwater were now heading straight toward Otto's farm.

"Stay here," Otto ordered. "I'll get rid of 'em."

He grabbed the lantern he had set down on the workbench and went outside, closing the door behind him. I stood with Eamon watching from the window.

"Out for a stroll, old man?" one of the soldiers asked Otto, his voice carrying a harsh tone that sounded somewhat familiar, but I couldn't picture where I had heard it before. He rested a hand on the hilt of his sword. Like the other nine soldiers in his group, he wore the Calvar uniform, but his was more decorative. I figured that meant he was their leader.

"Checking on my pygmies," Otto answered. "Little devils are escape artists."

"Perhaps we can help," the soldier said and waved for a couple of his comrades to check out the barn.

"Yes, Lord Varick," they said in unison.

"No, no," Otto snapped. "I finally got them settled down. There's no need."

The men stopped and looked at their leader. The man chuckled, stepping closer to Otto, then backhanded him in the face. Otto fell to the ground holding his cheek.

"Dere's too many of dem," Eamon stated, eyes wide with panic. He glanced over at Wera. Clearly, he feared for her safety as well as ours.

"I have an idea," I said.

Moving quickly, I grabbed a dirty old brown cloak hanging next to the door and a rag off the workbench. I tied the rag over my hair and traded my cloak for the old one. "Wera, take this in case anything happens," I told her, handing her my sword and belt.

"What are you doin'?" Fye'Gor spat.

"She's buyin' us some time," Eamon answered, nodding my way to indicate that he knew what I was about to do. "She's dah only one dat can."

"I don't like it," Fye'Gor said, shaking his head.

"Like it or not, if dose soldiers come in 'ere, we're all dead," Halvor said, stating the obvious. We had little choice. We had to do something.

"If anything happens, make sure that book gets to Master Orin," I ordered. Pulling the hood over my head, I stepped out the door.

CHAPTER TWENTY-THREE

"I got 'em, Uncle Otto," I said loudly as I shut the door to the barn. All the soldiers stopped and looked at me as I turned around and tried to act startled. "Oh, hello," I said nervously, then turned my attention to Otto who was still on the ground. "Uncle Otto, did you fall down?"

I hurried over to him, but Lord Varick stepped in front of me before I could get to him. "Who are you?"

"This is my niece, Nel," Otto answered before I could. "She's here visiting."

"Is she? Where are you from, *Nel*?" he hissed, looking me up and down.

"Outside Perth," I answered. "My family has a farm in the Great Valley."

Varick slowly walked around me, not saying a word and keeping his eyes fixed on me. I held my head low but kept looking from Otto to Varick. *Act like a scared little girl,* I told myself. As Lord Varick walked behind me he pulled my hood down, taking the rag with it and yanked off the cloak.

"You know, I've been to Perth," he said, walking back in front of me. "Not too many of them have dark hair like yours." Varick reached up and ran his hand over my braid. "But you know what none of them have?" Leaning down, he looked me in the eyes.

"No," I whispered, realizing coming out may have been a big mistake.

He leaned closer, so his mouth was right next to my ear and whispered, "An accent like yours." As soon as Varick finished his sentence he grabbed my braid and pulled me with him toward the house. "Hold him!" he shouted to the other soldiers and they grabbed Otto, pinning him to the ground.

I screamed and grabbed Varick's hand as he yanked harder, nearly pulling me off my feet.

"Do you know who has an accent like yours?" he asked sarcastically, pulling me close so my face was right in front of his. "An old man I found in the sacred lands a while back, and I bet you know him. But, unlike him, old man Orin won't be here to stop me from interrogating you." He flung open the door and shoved me inside. I hit the corner of the dining room table and fell to the floor.

Varick shut the door behind him and walked around the room. It was a small house. A fireplace with a rocking chair was at the center of the room. On the far side was a bed covered in leathers and the dining room table I hit was by the door next to the hearth. Varick picked up a thick strap of leather hanging on the rocking chair and walked back over to me, twisting one end around his hand.

"So, this is how it works." His mouth turned up in an evil grin. "It's very simple. You see, I ask you a question, and you answer. If I think you're lying, I'm going to hurt you," he said. "Now, what's your name?"

"Nel."

"Lie!" Varick shouted. He raised his hand over his head and swung the strap at me. I turned away and it struck across my back. It felt like a thousand bees stinging me all at once and I winced in pain.

"Where are you from?" Came his next question.

"P-Perth," I answered, my voice shaking.

"Lie!" This time he struck me twice with the strap. "Are you seeing a pattern, *Nel?*" Varick reached down and grabbed me by the neck, lifting me to my feet. "Who are you?" he yelled in my face.

"Nel," I said as I struggled to breathe.

"Lie!" He threw me across the room, breaking the rocking chair with my body before I smashed into the bed.

A sharp pain spread through my ribs and I gasped for air. Tears filled my eyes as Varick walked toward me, flinging the broken chair out of his way. I crawled up on my hands and knees, holding my side with one hand. My brain told me to find a weapon to defend myself but there was nothing within reach.

"Why are you here?" Not even waiting for my answer, he backhanded me against the bed. "Answer me!" Varick yelled, whipping me over and over.

I tried to yell, but it hurt to breathe, and I tasted blood in my mouth. All I could do was cover my head and take the hits. He placed his hand on my shoulder and flipped me over onto my back. Grabbing the front of my jacket, he lifted me off my feet. I kicked my legs and tried to scratch at him, but it didn't faze him, and he only laughed.

"Who are you?" he screamed in my face, then flung me through the air.

The table smashed and collapsed on top of me. I hurt everywhere and wasn't sure how much more I could take. As I pushed myself up off the floor, I saw a knife that must have fallen off the table when I hit it. Looking back, Varick was already stomping toward me.

Shouting from outside stalled him for a moment and he took his eyes off me to look out the window. I knew this was the only chance I had. I snatched the knife and swung it at his leg, sticking it deep into his thigh.

Varick yelped in pain, grabbing his leg. "You bitch!" He took a swing at me. I turned my head and tried to get out of the way, but he still managed to catch me across the cheek.

I didn't deliver a lethal blow with the knife, but it was enough to slow him down a little. I crawled away and was waiting for the next hit when the door burst open. Varick turned, only to meet a fist flying at him. Blood sprayed from his mouth and he dropped to one knee still holding his injured leg.

Behind him, my savior came into view. Dav. He glanced at me and his eyes sparked with fury. Pulling Varick back to his feet, Dav proceeded to throw him across the room. Varick tried to fight back, but Dav blocked or dodged his every swing, landing one of his own each time.

Soon, Varick's face was a bloody mess. Finally, Dav landed a kick to his chest. He hit the wall and before he could fall to the ground, Dav pulled the knife from Varick's leg and slammed it through his throat and into the wall, leaving him hanging.

"Semmi." He hurried over to me. His hands shook as he reached out and gently cradled me in his arms. "I'm sorry," he whispered.

"I'm okay."

"No, you're not," he said. "I need to get you cleaned up."

"No. There's no time," I told him. "The sun's going to come up any minute. We have to go now." He knew I was right. If we stalled any longer, we wouldn't make it across the valley before morning, and we couldn't stay here. I hadn't been outside but was sure that Dav's presence here meant the other soldiers were dead as well. "You can patch me up when we reach Master Orin's." He nodded, but I could tell he didn't like the idea.

Carefully, Dav picked me up and carried me outside. I knew he was trying his best to be gentle, but I hurt everywhere and cried out, clutching his jacket and gritting my teeth. The moment he stepped out the door I heard Wera gasp.

"Is she alive?" Her voice caught as she spoke.

"Yes, I am," I replied and lifted my head off Dav's shoulder.

"Can she ride Diddles?" he asked.

"Yes, yes. Of course," Wera quickly answered then commanded the bug to lie down, so I could more easily climb on.

Otto approached Dav, apologizing for being unable to stop the soldiers. His cheek was bruised, and there was blood on his chin. Dav waved his hand at the man before he could finish, insisting that there was no need. He instructed Otto to gather a few things and come with us now that his home was no longer safe for him to stay.

While we waited for Otto, Dav helped me get situated on Diddles and cleaned some of the blood from my face. We still had another hour or so to Master Orin's and we'd have to make a run for it to cross the valley before sunrise.

Wera wrapped my cloak around me. I thanked her and noticed blood on her clothing, which she insisted wasn't hers. The other soldiers all lay dead on the ground, some near the barn, a couple by the house, and a few who apparently tried to flee before they were killed.

I looked around at our friends. Eamon was wrapping an injury on his hand and had a few scratches on his face. Halvor had a fresh bandage on his arm, and Fye'Gor had a few cuts and bruises on his hands.

He stood away from everyone with his head down, little Dung Heap by his side, almost hiding behind him.

"Fye'Gor, are you all right?" I asked, worried he was hurt and hadn't said anything.

"No," he grumbled, refusing to look at me. "'Tis all me fault. I knew I shouldn't 'ave brought 'im." He waved at Dungy.

"I can't blame him," I said. "He thought he was protecting us." Fye'Gor only grumbled more. "Besides, I owe him one. Dungy saved me in the Valley of the Giants when a Calvar jumped out of nowhere. I didn't know that beneath that fur of his there are quills as sharp as needles."

"Oye, yeah," Eamon stated. "Dey certainly made that bugger over dere 'owl when 'e stuck 'im." He pointed at the dead soldier lying closest to the barn door.

The others gawked for a moment about the look on the soldier's face when they all burst out of the barn, describing it as if he had seen a monster.

As soon as Otto returned from the house with his bag and a walking stick, we were off, moving at a near run. Dav took Otto's bag to help the old man move faster, but it was easy to see his legs weren't what they used to be. Otto used his tall walking stick to help him go as fast as he could.

We barely made it into the woods when the first rays of light peeked over the horizon and into the valley. My head pounded, and every part of my body throbbed, but we didn't slow down. Dav stopped and looked back at me.

"Keep moving. She's starting to look pale," Wera ordered. She patted my leg and snapped her fingers at me. "Semmi! Keep your eyes open, my dear."

"Okay," I replied, trying to stay focused on everything around me. Wera began asking me questions to keep me awake and talking.

Up ahead, Dav signaled for everyone to stop. When we were silent, he whistled and waited. Within seconds, three warriors dressed in the same plain black uniform stepped out from behind the trees and bushes. They waved to signal he was clear to proceed and we moved forward. One of them blew a low-sounding horn, which reminded me of the bellow of an elk.

Through the trees, I could see Master Orin's house and barn, and a wave of relief came over me.

"We made it," I whispered. Reaching out, I took Wera's hand and smiled as best I could.

***

Lath was outside carrying an armful of wood from the barn toward the house when he saw us hurrying in from the forest behind the house. Past him, running up the road were two other warriors, heading toward us.

The others looked to Dav for his reaction. "It's okay," he said to the Norranians. "They're on our side."

"Lord Dav," Lath blurted and dropped the wood to come meet him. "We were beginning to fear the worst had happened to you both."

"Lath, these are friends from Norranheim," Dav said and did a quick introduction as he lifted me off Diddles. He asked that accommodation be made for their stay. "What's the matter, Lath? Never seen a giant ant before?" Dav asked sarcastically when Lath didn't move and only stared at Diddles.

"N-Not recently, sir," he said, eyes wide.

Dav's comment and Lath's answer made me laugh, which in turn caused a flash of pain to shoot through my body. I nearly cried out but managed to clench my teeth and cringe. Dav hurried to the house with me in his arms.

"Can I help?" Wera shouted, following behind us.

"Bring Semmi's bag," he yelled back.

Master Orin opened the front door to come out, but as soon as he looked at me, he stepped back inside leaving the door open. He shouted orders to Ms. Button to bring water, towels, and a medicine box.

"Bring her in here," Orin said, leading Dav over to the dining table.

With one arm, Orin slid everything off the table and onto the floor so Dav could lay me down. Ms. Button hurried into the room carrying a bucket and an armful of towels as Dav removed my cloak and started unbuttoning my leather jacket.

Ms. Button set the bucket and towels down on a nearby chair and produced a large wooden box from a hutch on the other side of the room. Setting it on the table, she opened it for Master Orin. Inside were dozens of small bottles filled with powders like the smaller box we had carried with us.

Master Orin took one of the towels and dipped it in the water. He sprinkled a light blue powder over it then held it to my face.

"Breathe deep, my dear," he told me.

"Dav," I whispered and reached up for him.

Orin moved the towel away and Dav took my hand. He leaned down and lightly kissed my forehead then my lips. "Everything's going to be okay," he whispered. "I love you."

"I love you too." He nodded to Orin who held the towel near my nose and mouth again where I could smell the sweet medicine. "It smells like the ocea..." My voice trailed off and I drifted into darkness.

As I slept, images flashed through my mind of Orin and Dav cleaning and dressing my injuries. In one of the images, Dav was yelling and I could hear him calling my name. Eamon was holding on to him, and I didn't understand why he looked so upset. Next, I could hear Orin telling him I was breathing and Wera was standing over me. Before I opened my eyes, I heard Dav's voice asking me to wake up.

I lifted my head and looked around the room. It wasn't the same one I had stayed in the first time I came here. This room had one large bed against the wall adjacent to the door with a window on the opposite side. Two short tables were on either side of the bed with a wooden trunk at the foot.

Daylight shone through the window and I sat up to look outside. I still felt a little groggy and there was a twinge of pain in my ribs as I pushed myself up but nothing like before. My clothes had been changed and I was wearing a short nightgown. It fit better than the one I wore last time, although it was a little shorter than I would have liked, barely reaching midthigh.

The bracelet Dav gave me was still around my wrist and I wondered where he was. As I sat on the edge of the bed and set my feet on the floor, I looked out the window. Muffled voices filtered inside, but all I could see was the forest through the glass.

Slowly, I stood up. My legs were wobbly as though I hadn't walked in days. On the wall next to the door was a mirror and I made my way over to it using the edge of the bed for support. Looking at my reflection, I saw cuts that were healing along my cheek and across my lips. The bruises I'd anticipated had nearly faded away, and I wondered how long I had been asleep. I lifted my gown and found more scabbed-over cuts and fading bruises on my ribs and back.

On my left side, however, there was still a deep dark purple bruise with a wide scabbed-over gash. I touched my fingers to it and found it remained very tender. The rest of my legs and hips had only a couple of bruises that were still visible.

I let my gown drop back down and walked back to the bed. My boots were set next to the trunk and a stack of new leather clothes were on top. I laid them out to change into. They were similar to the clothes I had before with black pants and a coat, except instead of a blue coat, this one was dark purple with another short sleeveless shirt of the same color to wear underneath it.

I was about to get undressed when the door opened. The sound startled me, and I pushed the bottom of my gown down until I saw it was Dav. He was dressed in a new black uniform and his hair had been cut. As soon as he saw I was up, he immediately rushed over to me. He took my face in his hands and kissed me like he thought he would never see me again.

He took a couple of deep breaths and clenched his jaw. Still holding me to him with his forehead touching mine, his body seemed tense and his brows knit in concern.

"What's wrong?"

At first, he only shook his head and wouldn't answer until I asked him again. "I almost lost you," he said and explained that after Orin put me to sleep, they found that some of my ribs were out of place. When Orin tried to pop them back, I screamed and gasped for air, then dropped against the table with no signs of life. "I thought you were dead, but Wera saved you."

Now the sketchy images made sense. They weren't dreams at all. "I remember hearing you yell my name and you looked upset. I didn't know why. I thought it was a dream," I told him and asked what Wera did to save me.

Lightly touching my side where I had seen the big bruise and gash, he told me how Wera said I was bleeding on the inside and that she knew how to help drain the blood so I could breathe.

"As soon as she did, you came back to life," he explained. "I've lost many friends over the years, but when I thought I was going to lose you…" He paused, unable to explain further.

"I'm so sorry." Although I'd been in a lot of pain, I had no idea how badly I was injured. Knowing how scared I was when he got shot with the arrow, I was dismayed that he had to go through the same fear of nearly losing me.

I lay my head against his chest and closed my eyes. As we stood there, he rubbed the back of my neck and told me I didn't need to apologize, that he knew I was only trying to protect everyone and to at last bring the book there.

"I'm glad you're alive and awake."

"Lord Varick was one of the soldiers who took my dad," I told him. "As soon as he heard my voice, he knew I was lying. He told me that Master Orin had stopped him from interrogating my dad. He wanted to know where I was from."

"What did you say?"

"What you told me to."

He took a deep breath and hugged me a little tighter.

"How long have I been asleep?" I asked before he could try to lay the blame on himself for my injuries as I knew he would. We had limited options, and I'd made the choice I thought would ensure our success.

He hesitated before finally telling me it had been five days. I couldn't believe it. It seemed like I had only been asleep a few hours. "That explains why I feel so wobbly," I joked, trying to ease the worry in his eyes.

"Do you want to lie back down?"

"Please, no. I could use some fresh air and a walk."

Dav waited outside the door while I changed into my new clothes, then offered his arm for support on our walk. He led me through the house, which I learned was one of the guesthouses Master Orin had for the warriors who often stayed there.

He went on to tell me all that had happened while I was asleep. They were making copies of the book we brought back and delivering them to every town and village. Every day, more copies were going out.

He handed me a copy that was sitting on a table in the main living area of the guesthouse. Inside the front cover were sketches of a Hvaldi man and woman based on carvings we had seen on our journey. There were also drawings of our Norranian friends. One with Wera holding the reins of Diddles, with Eamon standing next to her. Another with Fye'Gor, Halvor, and Dung Heap sitting together on a fence.

The words on the pages were beautifully written and translated perfectly. I smiled when I reached the back page where Master Orin had made a dedication thanking everyone involved for their efforts. He wrote that someday he hoped to build a monument where the names of their heroes could be listed, stating that for now, they knew who they were.

Dav told me my father was doing well. As promised, Master Orin was able to keep him from going to the prison colony and he was assigned to Lord Atwood as a mason to work off the debt of his crime. It made me feel good to know he was fine. Dav let me know that Orin was also able to deliver a message to him that I was safe.

With the success of our mission, the Warriors of Baleloch had been working double time to prepare for the possibility of war with the Order of Calvar. Master Orin's place was one of many farms used as a command post for their warriors and to store weapons, but his was the largest.

Over the last five days, dozens of warriors had come to stock up and receive their orders. Even our new friends, the Norranians, had assisted by making weapons to help with the preparations. Wera could build and assemble arrows faster than anyone. To everyone's surprise, Halvor was a master blacksmith. Dav showed me the new sword he'd made especially for him. The craftsmanship was amazing.

Eamon and Fye'Gor built a new training area for the warriors. They were also providing some additional training for new members and those needing to brush up on their skills. Dav mentioned that everyone was enjoying their new friends and they had been warmly welcomed by all who'd had the chance to meet them.

"Master Orin and the others will be happy to see you," he said when we reached the door to go outside.

"I'll be happy to see them too. I can't believe how much has happened."

"With the books going out, it won't be long before we see how the people respond," he said. "If it opens their eyes to see that the Calvar have been lying to them, it could start a rebellion. We need to be ready."

"How can I help?"

"You already have." He smiled. "For now, I want you to finish healing. There will be plenty you can do later."

He opened the front door and led me out. The guesthouse was one in a line of small houses built behind the barn. Dav let me know our Norranian friends were right next door. A stone path took us around the barn to the open area between the barn and house, which Dav referred to as the Yard.

Dozens of warriors were moving about carrying weapons to carts or organizing them in storage sheds. A few were working on the construction of a new building Dav said was to be used for planning. He told me they were making copies of the book in the barn loft. Production had increased the last couple of days thanks to Otto. He had created a simple machine allowing them to make numerous copies of every page rather than having to handwrite each one.

"Semmi!" Wera shouted.

I looked around and saw her running out of the barn. She gave me a big hug saying how happy she was to see me up. I thanked her for everything she'd done to save me.

"Seeing the two of you together is all the thanks I need." She smiled and returned to her work but promised we would all have dinner together that evening if I was up to it.

Master Orin was in the center of the Yard by the stone well, leaning on his walking stick and giving orders to warriors who approached him. He looked over and waved for us to join him.

"Did you tell Master Orin about us?" I asked as we walked toward him, curious what Orin would think of our relationship.

"Not that I needed to. He's old, not blind. But yes, I did."

"And?"

"He told me, he was very pleased with my choice," Dav answered, "but said he knew the moment he met you that you were perfect for me. The bigger question is whether your father will approve."

"I know he will," I replied, but Dav wasn't so sure, rattling off that he was responsible for my dad's capture, dragging me across two realms for a cause not of my own, and nearly getting me killed. "Stop." I tugged on his arm. "I'm alive and I still love you. The cause you are fighting for is very noble. I believe in it and will help in any way I can. Your people deserve to be free."

"Thank you. I love you too."

"As for my dad," I added as we finished walking over to Orin, "he'll understand."

CHAPTER TWENTY-FOUR

Master Orin reached out and kissed both my cheeks, expressing his joy at seeing me up on my feet and praising the progress made since our return.

"All of this is possible because of you, Semmi," Orin said, waving his arm out at all the warriors and townspeople who had come to support their cause by helping to prepare. "We sent the first copies of the book to Sweetwater and the word spread like wildfire." I could hear the excitement in his voice. "Within days, the people united and ran the Calvar out. Those willing have joined us to fight for our freedom. I suspect we should start receiving word from other towns about the people's reactions."

I appreciated his comments but quickly corrected him that Dav and our Norranian friends deserved just as much recognition, if not more for the success of our mission. Dav gave my hand a squeeze and I could tell he was smiling in his own little way.

Orin walked with us as I was shown around and introduced to all the senior warriors on the farm. They tipped their heads and offered their thanks. They also saluted Master Orin and Dav by covering their chests with their fists and bowing their heads.

Dav had told me before he was a highly skilled warrior, which explained why he was a guard in the sacred lands, but I didn't realize that it also made him one of their top commanders. All the other warriors showed a high degree of respect for him. Even those who were obviously twice his age sought his approval and guidance.

During our walk, Dav was pulled away several times to answer questions or address issues. That was when Orin offered me his arm to continue the tour. He couldn't say enough about how amazed he was with our Norranian friends.

"They are a truly wonderful people," Master Orin stated. "I can see Dav and Eamon have become quite good friends, as have you and Wera I've heard."

"Yes, we have."

I got to listen to a few conversations between Orin and other officers as they approached him with maps and suggestions for troop movements. I had never witnessed the progression of a war firsthand and found the strategy involved interesting. It seemed in every society I researched, war was always a constant. The oppressed were forever seeking to overthrow their oppressors for the freedom they desired. Over and over.

"Master Orin"—I turned to him—"can I ask you a question?" He nodded. "If the Calvar claim themselves as the one true race, or superior race, how did they gain so many followers outside of their bloodline? After everything I've seen and heard, why would people blindly bow down and willingly be used because the Calvar claimed they were more high and mighty than anyone else?"

"Bribery," he answered.

"You can't be serious." Surprised by his response, I found it difficult to believe people would turn a blind eye for a price.

"You'd be amazed what I've seen people do for money, land, or titles," he said. "It would make you sick. I've seen a beggar become a lord for turning in people who opposed the Order of Calvar, and some of them were his friends. And I've seen the Calvar take it all away just as fast as they hand it out."

"And yet you are willing to fight for those who would turn you over to the enemy for a handful of money?" I stated, caught somewhere between surprise and a deep respect for the Warriors of Baleloch for the sacrifice they would not hesitate to make in exchange for freedom.

"They're not all that way." Orin chuckled. "I've also seen a boy who didn't have a coin to his name grow up to be the most talented and respected warrior among his brethren."

"Dav." I smiled.

"Mm-hmm. When I found him, he only had one sole possession on him." The old man reached over and touched the bracelet around my wrist. "You must have given him something awfully special for him to place this on your arm."

"My heart." Warmth flowed through me as I thought about how much he meant to me. I glanced across the Yard where Dav was talking with a bunch of his men, giving them instructions. "He means everything to me."

"As I believe you do to him," Orin added. "The two of you have grown so much in the short time you were gone. Your growing relationship has strengthened you both. I am thankful you came into our lives."

"Me too," I said. "I understand now why you fight." Orin raised his eyebrows and asked me why I thought they did. "Because out of everything I've seen and gone through, I'd go through it all again for him."

"Exactly." Orin patted my hand.

I asked him what else I could do to help, and like Dav, he encouraged me to focus on my recovery. He kindly mentioned I looked like I could use a few more days of rest but promised he had a job suited to my expertise in mind.

Orin was soon pulled away and I was left to wander around on my own. I quickly found Wera and she gave me a task that allowed me to stay seated. My legs were getting tired, but I didn't want to go back to the guesthouse. It was a beautiful day and I enjoyed watching and listening to the preparations being made.

My task was simple: filling vials with the various healing powders to be used in small med kits like the one Dav carried with us. I listened to Wera jabber on about how well received they had been. Fye'Gor, Lath, and Otto enjoyed chatting and picking on the younger warriors. Eamon and Dav talked every evening and took time to practice their skills in the afternoon whenever possible.

Wera told me Halvor was the busiest of all, spending all day and most of the night at the forges. I didn't know he was a blacksmith by trade and was known throughout Norranheim for making the highest-quality weapons. She said the forges here were of much higher quality, allowing Halvor to create the most beautiful swords and axes she had ever seen. Having recently seen Dav's sword, I already knew what an amazing talent he had.

The day was coming to an end when Dav found me. He tried to apologize for getting pulled away, but I knew as a commander he had responsibilities to his men. Wera left us to start dinner, allowing us some time together. The farm was calming down and the warriors not on watch were heading in for the night.

Master Orin stood by his open door as we were getting ready to meet up with the Norranians for dinner. He was waving good night to us and told me to come by in the morning. We were about to turn away when I saw movement through the trees.

"Dav," I said, pointing toward the road. "It's a rider."

"The way he's riding it can't be good news," Dav stated, seeing the horse moving at a full run.

Master Orin walked over to join us as the rider came to a stop. He didn't bother getting off his horse before handing a folded letter to Dav.

"That's Lord Atwood's seal," Orin said when Dav turned the letter over to look at the waxed stamp. "Open it quickly."

Dav read the letter aloud. Lord Atwood sent word that a large army of the Calvar was assembling in the capital of Yorkshire. His sources told him that they planned on attacking the village of Thornwood in two days' time. He requested that reinforcements be sent as soon as possible to defend the village. Without them, they would be outnumbered three to one.

"Isn't Lord Atwood in Yorkshire?" Dav asked.

"No," Orin answered. "It wasn't safe any longer. He managed to arrange for a temple to be built in Thornwood. He's there with your father," he explained, looking at me. "The remaining council members, besides me, who oppose the Calvar are there as well. They mean to take us out, so they can gain full control."

"Fiske!" Dav shouted, leaving me standing with Orin.

A tall blond-haired warrior came running out of the barn. Dav gave him orders to prepare a contingent of warriors, supplies, and extra weapons and to be ready to leave at dawn. When he looked back at me, his eyes told me what I feared. He would be going with them.

***

Dinner was quiet. Dav told the others what had happened and that he would be leaving in the morning to lead the warriors. Thornwood was a key village for his people. To lose it would be detrimental to their cause.

"Will you watch over Semmi while I'm away?" Dav asked our Norranian friends when he probably thought I wasn't listening.

"Like you need to ask," Fye'Gor replied. "You 'ave our word."

Not knowing what to say, I barely spoke the rest of the evening. What do you say to someone you care about when you know there's a chance they may not come back? That thought terrified me, but I couldn't ask him to stay. His people depended on him.

Not wanting to burst out crying in front of our friends, I retired for the night and returned to our room. I changed into my nightgown and stood by the window spinning Dav's bracelet around my wrist.

My eyes were red and my cheeks were wet from crying when a knock came at the door. I heard Dav ask if he could come in and I dried my face before answering.

"You're upset with me," he said. He stood by the door, a glimmer of hurt in his eyes, as if waiting for me to tell him to leave.

"No, I'm not." My lips quivered as I spoke. "Your people need you, and I knew at some point this might happen. I didn't expect it to be so soon. And, I'm"—my voice cracked as I tried to tell him how I felt—"I'm scared of losing you."

"Look at me." He lifted my chin until my eyes met his. "That's not going to happen, and when this is all over, I promise I'll build you the home you've always wanted."

"Promise me you'll come back," I begged. "A home is nothing to me if I don't have you. Please?"

"I promise."

Still holding my face, he leaned down and sealed his promise with a kiss. As his hands slid down my back, he pulled me to him. I reached up and ran my fingers over his neck, and as our lips parted, I rested my face against his. At that moment, the world around us seemed to disappear and all I could see was him.

Never in my life did I imagine I would find someone I could love so much. He had become a part of me. No longer was I whole without him and there were no words that could possibly describe what he meant to me.

For tonight, we left the impending war outside and spent what little time we had with each other. The hours flew by, and at last, I fell asleep wrapped in his arms until the morning light made its way through the window.

I opened my eyes and saw Dav sitting on the edge of the bed pulling on his boots. He leaned over and kissed me good morning and I climbed out of bed to get dressed. I caught him stealing a few glances at me as I picked out some clean leathers to change into.

"Why do you keep staring?" I smiled shyly and ran my fingers through my hair thinking maybe it was a mess.

He winked and stepped over to kiss me. "Because you are everything in this world to me," he said as he hugged me close.

He kissed me once more then stepped out of the room while I finished getting ready.

***

In the Yard, two carts were filled with supplies and weapons, and at least two hundred warriors stood ready to march out. Fiske, the blond warrior from last night, approached us as soon as he saw Dav.

"We're ready for your inspection, my lord," he said and saluted.

Dav returned his salute then told me he would be right back. Master Orin stood outside his house with Lath and Ms. Button. Looking around, I noticed everyone was up and had gathered to bid our departing champions good luck and pray for their safe return. Wera came and stood by my side as I waited to hear it was time.

"Everything is going to be okay," she whispered, taking my arm.

"I pray with all my heart it will be," I replied, doing my best to stay strong.

We walked over to Master Orin together and stood with them watching the final preparations. Dav checked the wagons and addressed every warrior. When he was satisfied, he gave Fiske a nod of approval then walked over to us.

"Be safe, my son," Master Orin said to him and promised that I would be well watched over. Dav shook his hand, thanked him, and stepped close to me.

"Remember…" I started to say, but my voice gave out and my eyes watered.

"I know," he replied, leaning his head against mine. "I promised I'd come back and I will."

I told him I loved him, and he said the same, giving me one last kiss goodbye. "Dav," I said, holding onto his hand as he tried to step away. "If you see my dad—"

"I'll find him," he answered before I could finish, squeezing my hand before letting go.

He turned to walk back to his men when Eamon walked up next to him. He was dressed in a Warriors of Baleloch uniform with a pack on his back and his spears in his hand.

231

"What do you think you're doing?" Dav asked, looking at his friend.

"What does it look like I'm doin'?" he grumbled. "Someone's gotta watch your back to make sure you return." Eamon kissed Wera and turned to face Dav.

"You don't have to do this," Dav told him.

"Yes, I do," Eamon replied. "Like it or not, you're my friend. You'd do dah same for me and don't say you wouldn't." He smacked Dav on the arm and Dav smiled slightly. "Don't worry. Dah old boys will be here to protect dah girls."

"And 'oo you callin' old?" Fye'Gor growled as he and Halvor walked over to bid them goodbye and good luck. "You bring yourselves back 'ere."

Everyone watched as our warriors marched out. Dav, Eamon, and the other commanding officers rode on horseback. Before they were out of sight, Dav stopped and looked back at me, raising his hand in the air. I waved and blew him a kiss.

"Please come back," I whispered in prayer for his safe return.

***

The first day was working out to be the longest day of my life. Still under strict orders to relax and regain my strength, there was little I was allowed to do. I helped Wera with various tasks I could complete while sitting down, but the monotonous work seemed to make the day drag on. I needed something that occupied my mind, not just my hands.

I remembered Master Orin had said he had a task that suited my talents, which I assumed would be to translate something, and I set off to find him after finishing my work. It was already late in the afternoon. The farm seemed so empty without as many soldiers around. Fye'Gor mentioned during our afternoon meal that over the last five days, more than a thousand soldiers had come in and out of the farm and he expected we would see more here soon.

"Semmi, my dear," Orin said when I found him over by one of the storage sheds receiving a report on their weapons stores. "How are you feeling?"

"Physically," I clarified, "better than yesterday." Mentally, I couldn't even begin to describe how I was feeling.

"I see," he said. "I know in times like this it's hard to say goodbye to those we love, not knowing if they will return, but have faith. Dav is the finest warrior I have ever seen. He'll come back."

"I know. Doesn't mean I don't worry."

"No, it doesn't" he agreed. "He's my son, you know. Nan may not have borne him, but I knew the moment I looked at him, cold and shivering, that he always would be. I worry every time he leaves my sight. Even though he's a grown man, when I look at him, I still see the baby I found." He told me all about Dav's childhood, making me laugh hysterically at the silly stories parents love to tell to embarrass their children.

I asked about Dav's stoic, emotionless nature and was told he had been that way since the day he found him. Rarely cried or laughed or even smiled. "Until I saw him with you," Orin said. "From the moment he brought you here, I could see a change in him. I remember thinking to myself, my prayers have finally been answered. He found someone who could touch his heart the way no one could."

I thanked him for his kind words. Orin told me how he was once a young warrior like Dav, dedicated to their cause with no plans to be a husband or a father, and then *there she was*, as he put it, and before he knew it, she'd stolen his heart.

Orin mentioned he named Dav after his grandfather, Davik, a man he admired and looked up to.

"I could jabber on all day if you don't stop me." He laughed. "Was there something you needed, my dear?"

"Actually, yes." I chuckled, remembering why I came to him. "Yesterday you said you had a task for me."

"Yes, yes. Come." He took my hand and led me over to a tent next to his home that they were using as their command area until the new building was finished.

Inside, he asked one of the commanders for some letters he explained were correspondences they had intercepted belonging to the Calvar. One glance at the writing and I knew what he wanted from me. They weren't written in their language, but in one I hadn't seen before.

"Dav told me you have been able to teach yourself several languages," Orin mentioned. "I was hoping, with a little luck, you might be able to figure these out."

"I'll do my best." I took the four letters and a stack of paper to write on and headed back to the barn where Wera was working. She was putting together fire-starting kits by mixing black and red powder together. The powder was then poured into vials and placed with a striker in leather pouches.

Glancing at the notes, Wera asked about them and I explained what they were. Her mouth dropped open when I told her how many languages I knew. Similar to Polarious, Norranheim had only one language that she knew of but over the centuries, it had changed a bit. Yet it wasn't enough to categorize the old language as a different one.

Wera asked how I learned so many, especially without the help of someone who already knew each language. I explained that in Balfjord there were thousands of languages. After I learned the first few, learning the others became much easier.

I told Wera that when trying to learn a new written language, I started by looking for similarities to other languages. Often, a number of languages could evolve from a single root language. Time and migration of societies could cause languages to change drastically.

"So, do you see any similarities in that one?" Wera asked, pointing at the letters.

"Actually, yes," I answered, taking a closer look. "It may be a different dialect of their written language."

Unfamiliar with their writing, I needed some samples for comparison. I remembered there were a few books in the guesthouse where Dav and I had stayed, and I hurried over to grab one.

Hours passed as I compared the two writings. Some letters were simply written upside down or backward, while others were very different, but I could still recognize the letter they were modified from. This led me to believe that the Calvar might have altered the common language to make it more difficult for others to decipher, but when I tried to match the letters, it didn't work.

They did more than modify the language; they completely reassigned each letter. The modified letter no longer represented the letter it was derived from. I had my work cut out for me if I was going to figure this out and soon.

This puzzle was exactly what I needed to keep my mind occupied in Dav's absence as I waited for word on their progress. That news came three days later. A rider carrying a letter arrived after midday.

I raced out of the barn where I sat each day with Wera working on my translation. Orin was already reading the letter when I reached him. He smiled and handed it to me.

"All good news," he said, "and I do believe Dav wrote a note for you in there."

They had arrived in Thornwood ahead of the Calvar attack, which began within hours. Dav wrote that it took little effort to fend off the attack, reporting no casualties and only minor injuries. The number of Calvar who'd invaded the village in Yorkshire was far less than estimated, leading him to believe there might be another attack coming. He added that he had sent out scouts to verify what soldiers remained in the city.

At the bottom of the letter were a few lines of Hvaldi text in Dav's handwriting where he expressed how much he loved and missed me and that he had found my dad. He was well and relieved to hear that I was safe.

"All good things I hope," Master Orin said.

"He found my dad," I replied happily, "and he's okay."

"Wonderful!" Orin replied. "And how are you progressing? I've hardly seen you the last couple days."

"Slow," I answered solemnly. I explained that the Calvar appeared to have used the common writing form to create their own language, but I was having difficulty cracking it. From one letter to another, the writing didn't seem consistent. "I feel like there's something I'm not seeing."

"I have faith in you, my dear. You'll figure it out."

CHAPTER TWENTY-FIVE

The next day was the most active I had seen since our arrival. Riders were coming in and out all day bringing the best news we could have hoped for. For the first time, we were hearing of the effect of the mass distribution of the Hvaldi's *Our Final Chapter* book. Hundreds of copies had gone out by now, but until today, we had yet to discover people's reactions to the truth.

Like the people of Sweetwater, villagers were rising up against the Calvar in their towns and pushing back. Many of the reports confirmed most villages were successful in driving the soldiers out or eliminating them completely. A few others were reaching out to the Warriors of Baleloch for help.

Orin and his commanders stood around a table with a map of the country. On it they had placed carved markers like a chessboard to identify the locations of their warriors and the Calvar. They added flags to cities requesting assistance and would decide on a plan of action to help them. I sat nearby writing messages for Orin and his commanders to be delivered to other camps, giving them orders on which villages needed their aid.

Two small groups were even dispatched from Orin's farm, dropping our numbers to less than a few dozen. It was a tough call to make. Orin and the other commanders debated back and forth on the subject, but in the end, they knew that we were the closest to these villages. At such a crucial time, they felt they had to go to their people's aid even if that meant leaving the farm poorly guarded.

One incoming rider carried two letters found on the bodies of a Calvar general killed during the uprising of a neighboring town. Orin handed them directly to me and asked again about my progress. I felt horrible admitting I still hadn't successfully deciphered any of the letters.

After I finished the last of the orders, he released me to get back to my work. I returned to the Norranians' guesthouse. Ever since Dav had left, I'd found myself spending most of my evenings there to avoid being alone in our room.

Wera was making dinner while Fye'Gor and Halvor talked at the dinner table. They were fascinated with the complexity of the letters I was working on, and I expressed my frustration with the correspondence, hoping they might have a suggestion. I was desperate for anything that could help.

"Maybe you're overthinkin' it," Fye'Gor said. "These letters seem awfully long to be delivering orders."

"Maybe," Wera cut in, picking up one of the letters, "the orders are 'idden in the letter."

"What do you mean, 'idden in dah letter?" Fye'Gor asked, looking at her like she was crazy.

"It's not as silly as you might think, old man," she snipped then clarified what she meant. "When Eamon and I first met, me dad didn't like 'im and wouldn't let 'im anywhere near me. So, 'e used to send letters." She described that his letters looked like a bunch of rubbish and her parents didn't think much of them, but she knew the secret to finding his note within it.

"Argh," Fye'Gor huffed. "I always knew you 'ad dat boy whooped."

Everyone had a good laugh and soon turned in after dinner. With little time to work on the letters today, I decided to stay up for a while. I looked back and forth between them and my notes. They looked like a language, but there were too many inconsistencies from one to the other. What wasn't I seeing?

I wondered if Fye'Gor was right. It made sense. Maybe I was overthinking the complexity of the letters. Creating an entire language to communicate seemed a bit like overkill. Yet a code hidden in a bunch of babble would be much easier to conceal and decode later. I needed to figure out the secret to finding the real message within the rubbish, as Wera put it.

Going through the Calvar correspondence once again, I looked carefully at each word. "Wera, you're a genius," I whispered as I saw that each word contained a single letter with only one modification: the letter was written upside down or backward while all the others were completely changed.

On a separate piece of paper, I wrote down each of the individual letters in order on the first correspondence. Seeing the letters by themselves, the messages were clear. It was a list of Calvar military locations and troop movements.

Remembering the map in the command tent, I recognized several of the village names located west of Yorkshire, some less than a day's travel from here.

I quickly went through the others, pulling out the letters so I could read them. The second correspondence contained more troop movements and a listing of the troop sizes. If the numbers were right, there were far more of them than us.

"That's why Dav said they needed the support of the people if we were to defeat them," I whispered.

The next two noted various locations where they believed the Warriors of Baleloch were stationed with estimates on our numbers. To my surprise, they had greatly overestimated us, something we could definitely use against them.

When I got to the two we'd received today, my mouth fell open. "Oh no," I gasped. There was no time to waste. I grabbed everything off the table and ran out the door to Master Orin's house.

"Master Orin!" I shouted as I beat on the door. "Master Orin!"

My shouting caught the attention of another commander named Colborn, who was making his rounds as well as my Norranian friends who must have heard me race out of their house. They hurried over to me as Lath opened the door with a lantern in his hand.

"What's all the ruckus?" Lath asked, looking as if he had been yanked out of bed.

"I need to speak to Master Orin immediately." Lath must have seen the seriousness in my face and left at once to get Master Orin. I handed my translations to Colborn who stood next to me. "The attack on Thornwood was only a ruse to draw warriors away from here. The Calvar are coming and we don't have much time."

Colborn read through the correspondences and Master Orin shouted from inside, wanting to know what all the yelling was about. Colborn requested Master Orin meet us in the command tent as soon as possible and asked Halvor to fetch Commander Torsten to join us.

It only took a few minutes for everyone to assemble around the map table. Colborn instructed me to explain the situation based on my translations. I told Wera her suggestion was right. The Calvar didn't create a new language; they only made it look that way to hide the real message within.

As I read them aloud, Colborn marked on the map the locations and troop movements. I then explained that the attack on Thornwood was set up as a distraction to draw our warriors away.

"That's why the Calvar organized so many soldiers in Yorkshire. So, we would think it would be a major assault," I said. "And why wouldn't we, given the number of high-ranking people who live there? But, according to this letter"—I handed it to Master Orin—"their real target is us. They know the book that's causing the uprising is coming from here and they want the distribution stopped."

"How long do we have?" Torsten asked. He was tall, standing a good head over Colborn, with salt-and-pepper hair.

"The day after tomorrow," Orin answered, passing the translations to him. "Thank you for waking us so quickly, my dear." He asked how many warriors we currently had on the farm.

"Luckily two groups returned today, so we have almost two hundred, but it's not nearly enough," Torsten replied. "If these numbers are correct, they have us by nearly six to one."

"Send your fastest rider to get Dav," Orin instructed but seemed like he was unsure of his decision.

"Sir, there's no way any rider could get to him and back before the attack begins," Colborn said. "We could send one west. He would be able to reach four outposts before morning if he leaves now."

"Even if they sent every warrior they had, we'd still be outnumbered," Orin commented.

"But at least we could put up a better fight," Torsten added. He also pointed out they had been victorious before in battles that were three to one in the Calvar's favor strictly because of the rigorous and extensive training their warriors went through.

Orin approved sending a rider west to round up as many warriors as possible to come to our aid. "There are more than four hundred of our warriors in Thornwood," Orin said, obviously frustrated. "If only we could get them here."

"I 'ave an idea," Fye'Gor said, stepping forward and whistling for Dung Heap. He explained that Dungy could run far faster than any horse and could easily reach Dav before morning.

"Do it," Orin ordered. "Semmi, write a message for Dav explaining our situation. If he can get it by morning, it's possible they could get here. Maybe a little late, but it'll be close."

Fye'Gor tied a leather strap around Dung Heap's neck and attached the message. "Find Dav and Eamon," he instructed the furry beast. He barked once and ran out of sight.

Not five minutes later, a rider was speeding out to head west as ordered. Another warrior was sent out on foot to scout the area and confirm if the Calvar were closing in on us. With our limited numbers,

Orin asked for other suggestions to help improve our chances of survival.

Halvor and Fye'Gor suggested that with some help, they could set up snares and traps in the forest. These could help slow down an assault and serve to warn us of when the Calvar were coming. Orin approved and Colborn grabbed four warriors to assist them.

"Semmi." Orin turned to me and Wera who had remained inside the tent with him. "In Balfjord, are there any weapons you know of that could help us?"

My first thought was a gun, but I didn't have the slightest idea of how to make one. They already fought with most of the weapons used during ancient times in Balfjord: swords, bows and arrows, and axes. I thought of a trebuchet, which I did know how to build, but there were too many trees around the farm. They were better suited for battles on open fields.

A painting I saw in a museum years ago popped into my mind. It depicted a battle between two ancient armies and was the first time I had ever seen a trebuchet. I was so amazed by the apparatus that I made my dad teach me to build one, so I could see how it worked. We made a miniature version of one and instead of burning pots of oil, we only flung rocks. The burning pots of oil stuck in my mind and I remembered the fire-starting kits Wera was working on.

"I may know of something," I said and asked Wera if we still had the black and red powders. She said there were plenty. "Master Orin, is there any way to ignite the powders without fire?"

"Yes." He explained that if we added orange powder to the mixture with a sprinkle of teal over the top, it would make a big poof of green fire with blue sparks when thrown or dropped. He chuckled, saying he used to make it during festivals to watch the kids giggle.

"Perfect!" I stated then grabbed Wera's hand and headed to the barn.

"What are we doing?" she asked.

"Hopefully, we are going to make a bomb you can throw," I told her.

CHAPTER TWENTY-SIX

Wera made a vial of the powder as Orin instructed. I took it and placed it in a leather pouch surrounded by bits of metal I'd scooped up off the floor by the forges. Tying the top closed, we decided it would be best to test one before making any more.

Colborn accompanied us into the forest to conduct our test. The moons were starting to set, but it would still be several hours before the sun came up. We picked a spot far enough away from buildings and living quarters in case it didn't go as planned. The area was fairly open, allowing the moonlight to shine down on us.

"Is this going to work?" Colborn asked, a little unimpressed with the small size of the pouch.

"I don't know," I replied, carefully holding it, unsure how much jostling it would take to trigger the reaction Orin described. "I've never made anything like this before."

"So, then where did you come up with the idea?" Wera asked.

I started to explain the painting of the trebuchet with the exploding pots of oil when Colborn grabbed the pouch from my hand and threw it out into the forest. It hit the trunk of a nearby tree and exploded in a beautiful, yet violent ball of green fire.

We all clamped our hands over our ears and dropped to the ground as it exploded. When I finally lifted my head to see how well the test went, smoke filled the entire area. The sound of wood cracking caught my attention, and the tree that the pouch hit fell over.

Wera and I both looked at the destruction with wide eyes, our mouths hanging open. I had hoped it would cause some damage, but this was more than I expected.

"Make more," Colborn said. The look on his face was similar to ours. "Lots more."

"Yeah," Wera agreed, still staring at the damage.

***

More pouches were made, arrows assembled, swords sharpened, and defense strategies planned. The entire farm was abuzz in preparation for an impending attack. The scout returned a few hours after sunrise only to confirm the validity of my translations.

I happened to be in the command tent, reporting on the progress of the assembly work in the barn, when the warrior arrived. He reported that the Calvar weren't yet in a position to attack but were moving quickly to set up in the forest on the north and east sides of the farm. From what he saw, the warrior believed we had until midday tomorrow to be ready.

Orin turned to me with a worried look. We had yet to have any reinforcements return to the city and it was clear he feared for all our lives. I tried to reassure him that it was still early in the day and to have faith as he had told me to do.

I returned to the barn where Wera was tying the last of the pouches closed. We had used all the powder in the barn and storage sheds. Next, we moved on to building more arrows. Ms. Button sat with us cutting and rolling strips of fabric to be used to treat injuries. We barely spoke a word except to pass the scissors or ask for another empty quiver. And when we ran out of quivers, we simply tied the arrows in bunches.

The sun was starting its descent when a warrior came for me. Colborn and Orin had requested me in the command tent. It had been hours since I had been out of the barn and was relieved to see a few groups of newly arrived warriors in the Yard. There were only a few dozen of them, but that was better than none.

The moment I ducked my head into the tent, Colborn handed me another correspondence. Orin was sitting at the map table looking at all the pieces. It was hard to read his expression. In part, he looked almost happy, while his face still reflected the concern from earlier. Two other warriors stood nearby giving a report of other battles progressing across the country.

I listened as I translated the new information. Like the reaction from the people of Sweetwater, other villages, towns, and cities all across the country were fighting back against the Calvar for their deceit. Even those who were longtime supporters were now seeing the truth and pushing back.

One of the warriors, named Keagan, claimed he worked as a stable boy in Yorkshire and overheard the Calvar council members speaking. The distribution of the book caught them off guard and they underestimated the effect it would have on the people, believing their followers would stay faithful. He said they were unprepared for the backlash and knew the odds of a victory in their favor were becoming slim. However, if they could take out the source of the book and kill Master Orin, it would leave the Warriors of Baleloch in disarray, giving them the opportunity to rebuild their order in a new light.

"Master Orin, we must move you to a safer location," Colborn immediately suggested.

"No, it's too late for that," Orin replied. "I wouldn't leave and abandon you anyways. I may be old, but I am one of you. We will make our stand here. We have done what we can to send word for reinforcements and prepare for battle."

"But Master," Keagan pleaded, "they are going to hit us with the bulk of their forces. We can't afford to lose you."

"I am an old man," Orin said sternly. "The Warriors of Baleloch will not fall apart without me. I have faith in our commanders that they will hold everyone together and continue on if I'm lost. And I trust that from them they will select a replacement that I would be proud of."

The commander and two warriors saluted Master Orin, and Keagan apologized for his weakness, but Orin told him his concern and desire to protect his fellow warriors was not a weakness. Keagan and his companion were dismissed and given orders to report to Torsten.

"What do you have for us, Semmi?" Orin asked. "Good or bad?"

"Both," I answered. "It corroborates what Keagan has told us. Calvar control has fallen in nearly every city and village across the country. They report they expect to lose their hold on Yorkshire within the coming days. They have requested all soldiers to fall back to Green Meadows and Sweetwater to assist in the attack here."

"Our survival is looking grim," Colborn commented.

"Yes, but our people will be free when this is over," Orin said almost proudly. "That's what's important. That's what we are fighting for." He stood and a peaceful smile slowly spread across his face. "Gather our warriors," he said to Colborn. "I would like to address them."

***

Fye'Gor and Halvor returned with their team before dusk in time to hear Master Orin's address. They came and stood next to Wera and me, letting us know they had set enough traps to definitely make a dent in the Calvar's numbers if they dared to approach the farm.

Wera was excited to tell them about the exploding pouches we created and Fye'Gor mentioned he'd like to see one in action. Our conversation was cut short when we saw Master Orin making his way to the center of the Yard. Those not on watch gathered to hear him speak.

Commander Torsten and Colborn helped Master Orin onto a large crate where he could look out over everyone. He waved his hands for us to quiet down.

"I'll try to keep this short as I know we still have responsibilities to attend to before tomorrow," he began. "As many of you know, not very long ago we received a gift of a book written by the Hvaldi"—Orin held one of the copies in the air—"telling us how we all came to be here in Polarious. That each of our ancestors was hand-selected to carry on the memory and existence of an amazing and intelligent race. This was their realm, their home, and they gave it to us. All of us.

"Those raised by the old beliefs have grown up hearing the stories of the Hvaldi," he continued. "Over time, they have become nothing more than fairy tales, replaced by the lies told by the Order of Calvar. But, thanks to the selfless efforts of Semmi, a traveler from Balfjord, and our new friends from Norranheim, we have been given the opportunity to free our people by delivering the truth to them.

"And it's working," Orin boasted. "Our people now see who we are and where we came from." He turned to me and the Norranians. "Thank you, all. We know that this is not your fight, but I believe I can speak for every one of the Warriors of Baleloch when I tell you how much it means to have you here."

Master Orin took a deep breath as he looked out at all his men, then smiled before going on. "I've known many of you since you were children, knew your parents, and now some of you have children of your own," he said. "The Warriors of Baleloch was created hundreds of years ago to accomplish exactly what we are doing here today. To give freedom back to our people."

He continued. "The Calvar have chosen to make their final battle here, and let's make sure it is," Orin told them. "I want all of you to remember, this is what you have trained for your entire lives. We are the Warriors of Baleloch, the army of the people, and whether we live or die tomorrow, know that we have already won. We are free!"

The men all cheered and raised their swords in the air. I wondered if they knew how historic this moment was…that hundreds of years from now people would learn about what they did here. I had spent all my life studying history through writings and relics left behind at ancient sites, but for the first time, I was now witnessing it firsthand.

***

Wera and I helped Ms. Button prepare a feast for everyone. The warriors were told to eat their fill and get plenty of rest for tomorrow, although I was sure sleep was the last thing on their minds. Like me, they were probably thinking of their loved ones and whether they would ever see them again.

As I thought of my dad and Dav, I was glad I had been able to tell them both how much I loved them when I saw them last. Closing my eyes and rubbing my bracelet, I quietly prayed that I'd see them again soon.

The farm was quiet as the moons shone down on us. *The calm before the storm* is what my dad would say if he were here. I could almost hear him in the silence. Not wanting to be alone, I joined the Norranians for the night.

They were all sitting around the fireplace discussing plans for tomorrow when I walked in. Wera brought me something to drink and I sat down with them. Fye'Gor and Halvor asked how I was holding up.

"I'd be lying if I said I was fine," I told them. "I'm…oh, I don't know what I am. Sad, scared, nervous, terrified, and everything in between. I don't know how I'm supposed to feel in this situation."

"I'd say you're feelin' about what you should," Fye'Gor said.

He told us a story of a battle between a neighboring clan in Norranheim when he was a young warrior. Halvor said he was only a boy and Wera wasn't even born yet. Fye'Gor described the last night of the battle and his team was pinned down. Outnumbered and low on supplies, they prevailed.

"It's amazin' 'ow much 'arder you are willin' to fight when dah cost is your 'ome or your freedom," Fye'Gor told us.

I know he was trying to boost our spirits, but given our numbers, it was difficult to stay positive. "Do you think Dungy made it?" I asked him, hoping that Dav would reach us in time.

"I know 'e did," Fye'Gor answered. "For all 'is faults, 'e's dah best companion to 'ave in a situation like dis, and 'e's saved me backside more dan once."

"Don't worry, love," Wera said, taking my hand and rubbing the top. "I know 'e'll make it. You know 'e will."

Before lying down to sleep, Fye'Gor told Wera and me to stay close to him and Halvor. "We gave Dav and Eamon our word to protect you both," he reminded us. "I've never broken me word and I ain't goin' to. Understand?" He pointed at each of us and we nodded.

"Good," Halvor said and handed us each a gift. For Wera, he had forged her a new set of throwing knives, and for me, a beautifully crafted sword. It fit perfectly in my hands.

"Thank you, Halvor."

CHAPTER TWENTY-SEVEN

When I woke, the sun had yet to rise and already I could hear warriors moving about outside. Wera was up making her morning tea, which definitely had more of a kick than her evening tea. She let me know Master Orin requested me in the command tent as soon as I was awake. I took a cup of tea along with a flat cake she had set out and headed out the door, but not before strapping on my new sword.

"Remember what Fye'Gor said," she shouted.

"I'll be back," I promised, knowing what she was referring to.

In the Yard, Ms. Button had a table with an assortment of muffins and cakes. Warriors stopped and grabbed a few then headed to their posts. Orin was with Torsten and Colborn in the command tent standing over the map table.

"You asked to see me, Master Orin."

"Semmi, my dear, please come in."

He gave me some good news. More warriors had come to our aid overnight. We were still nearly five to one in the Calvar's favor, but every additional warrior increased our odds. A rider had also come in early in the morning promising more warriors by the end of the day.

"Have we heard anything from Dav?" I asked, hoping that he was on his way with reinforcements.

"Not yet," Colborn answered, "but even if he was able to send a rider to alert us of his arrival, they wouldn't be able to get here until this evening at the earliest. Are you sure that furry thing made it?"

"Fye'Gor assured me Dungy would," I told him. "That *furry thing* is a very loyal creature, and trust me, he's more vicious than he looks."

"Well, we'll hope for the best," Orin cut in and instructed Torsten to go over our plans for the battle.

The last report they received was that the Calvar were spread out to the north and east of the farm. He pointed to where our guards were stationed outside the perimeter, which was nothing more than a short stone wall that surrounded the house, barn, and guest cottages. Orin also explained that once the attack began, the traps set out by the Norranians would allow time for the guards to fall back behind the wall. Archers were posted along rooftops and trees to provide additional cover, they were also armed with our pouches in the event the Calvar got close enough to use them.

"If they reach the interior, it will be hand-to-hand combat from there," Colborn added. He explained that Master Orin, Lath, and Ms. Button would be guarded in one of the guest cottages to the west of the farm.

"You and Wera should stay with us," Orin said. "Dav is my son and I'd never forgive myself if I let something happen to you."

"Fye'Gor and Halvor gave Dav and Eamon their word to protect us," I told him. "I promised them I would stay close. We have made plans to set up a triage area in the Yard for any wounded."

Our conversation was cut short by shouting coming from the forest. We all rushed out of the tent to see what was going on. From all around, we heard howling and yelling echoing through the trees.

"I thought they wouldn't be in position to attack until midday," I said.

"According to Keagan and another report, they shouldn't," Colborn answered. "Doesn't mean they wouldn't send a small troop in to distract us and try to create a panic. Our guards will notify us if they see anyone."

The commander shouted orders over the hoots and howls, instructing them to remain calm and watch for our guard's signal of enemy approach. Everyone moved to get into their positions. Two warriors came to escort Master Orin, Lath, and Ms. Button to the western guesthouse and I returned to mine.

I walked back to the bedroom and grabbed my bag, which I had prepared last night in the event we had to flee the farm. As I walked toward the door, I looked back at the bed and remembered the last night I spent with Dav. "I love you," I whispered aloud, hoping he could hear me somehow. "I wish you were here."

***

The howling in the forest continued for hours, getting louder as time passed. It was after midday when we heard the double blow of the guard's horns. Halvor explained two blows was to alert us that the Calvar had been sighted, three blows for incoming soldiers on foot, and four blows were for archers. Fye'Gor and Halvor carried their weapons and watched the forest beyond, ready to defend us at a moment's notice.

As promised, I was with the Norranians outside one of the storage sheds where we had set up an area to tend to any injured warriors. Piles of blankets were set next to a table filled with healing powders and clean linens for wrapping. On the other side of the table were several buckets of water and towels. We also moved the long workbenches from the barn out with us.

In an instant, the forest went silent. The eerie calm made my stomach twist and turn. The warriors around us gripped their weapons and listened for another signal. My heart was beating so hard, the *thump, thump, thump* in my head nearly drowned out all other sounds.

At once, guards began sounding the triple tone of incoming soldiers. The alarm seemed to be coming from all around us. It was soon followed by the snap of traps going off and the screams of those caught in them.

From what I could tell, the guards on the eastern side of the farm pulled back to the perimeter allowing the archers a clear shot. They were in the trees and at the back of Master Orin's house firing into the woods. Then there was the first boom, followed by another and another. They were throwing pouches, which meant the Calvar were going to reach our perimeter any second.

The north side of the farm was next to follow. Everywhere swords clashed and screams of the injured rang out. Through the trees, I could see our warriors fighting. Some were taking on two and three soldiers at a time. It was easy to see the Calvar didn't receive the extensive training that the Warriors of Baleloch did, but their numbers would be hard to compete with.

It didn't take long for the injured to start coming in. Fye'Gor and Halvor raced to help them as soon as they were in sight. Wera and I had to keep our heads on a swivel as we cleaned and dressed their wounds. As the number of wounded grew, it created gaps in our lines allowing some of the Calvar soldiers to gain access to the farm.

Fye'Gor made quick work of those who dared get too close, as did Halvor. Of the wounded, those who were able hurried back out to fight. From one to another, I moved as fast as possible. Everywhere I looked there was blood—all over the tables, the ground, and me.

"We're holding them back, but they keep coming," one of the warriors said to Commander Torsten as I stitched up a gash across his chest and covered it in healing powders. "I don't know how much longer we can keep the perimeter on the east side."

Torsten nodded. He was faced with difficult decisions. There was little room to pull back without opening up the Yard to attack. He gave orders to hold the line and moved warriors stationed to the west in to assist.

As the battle raged, every hour felt like days with no end in sight. More and more soldiers were breaching the perimeter and finding their way in. Fye'Gor, Halvor, and a few warriors worked to keep them at bay.

Out of the corner of my eye, I saw a group of soldiers racing up the road toward us. I looked over to Fye'Gor and the others, but they were dealing with another group that had slipped in from the north. There was no one to stop them. I grabbed a basket of pouches from a nearby shed and ran out to the center of the Yard. Putting the stone well between them and me, I started hurling the pouches one after another at the soldiers once they were within range.

When the smoke cleared, the soldiers lay on the ground. One was missing his leg, another an arm as he tried to crawl away but soon dropped to the ground with the others.

"Semmi!" Fye'Gor shouted and motioned for me to come back behind him.

I stood up to move and heard over the sounds of battle, four tones bellow out. I looked up to see a barrage of arrows flying through the trees toward our warriors along the perimeter. One of the archers in a tree by Master Orin's house was hit and fell.

Everything seemed to move in slow motion when I saw what he was holding in his arms. A basket filled with pouches. When he hit the house, the whole side exploded and burst into flames. I was thrown to the ground from the concussion of the blast.

The wind was knocked out of me and I was covered in nicks and cuts from fragments of wood and glass that splintered apart during the explosion. My ears rang, and everything went quiet.

"Semmi!" Halvor yelled, but his voice sounded muffled and far away. "Semmi! Come on!"

A hand grabbed my arm and pulled me to my feet. Halvor half dragged me over to Wera by one of the tables.

"Semmi!" she yelled, holding my face to look at me. "Can you hear me?"

"Barely." I heard her ask if I was hurt and I told her I didn't think so, at least not seriously.

She helped me to my feet and I looked over at the house. It was completely engulfed in flames and the fire was spreading quickly. It didn't take long for it to reach the barn. The heat was unbearable. Fye'Gor gave orders for us to start moving who we could farther west to get away from the fire.

More soldiers were moving in. Those who could still fight stepped up and everyone else helped the warriors who needed assistance to move. Wera flung a couple of her knives at incoming soldiers clearing a path for our wounded warriors to walk between the sheds and toward the guest cabins.

She led them through, and I stayed behind to make sure everyone made it out, while our other warriors fended off the encroaching Calvar. I looked over my shoulder as I helped the last of the wounded over to the path between the sheds and saw Halvor go down.

"No!" I screamed.

Pulling my sword, I raced over, blocking the soldier's sword as he attempted to deliver another deadly blow. The block caught the soldier by surprise and I was able to kick the man in the stomach knocking him to the ground. Halvor sat up and flung one of his axes at the downed soldier catching him in the side of the head.

"Are you hurt?" I asked him.

"I'll live," he growled, and he cringed from the wound in his leg.

Across the Yard, Colborn and Torsten yelled for the warriors to push forward, and I could almost see a smile on their faces. I waved at Fye'Gor and pointed to the commanders.

"Get 'im outta 'ere," Fye'Gor ordered, pulling his friend to his feet so I could grab him. "I'll check it out."

I nodded and with Halvor's arm over my shoulder followed the path between the sheds. Wera was running toward us and grabbed Halvor's other arm to help him move faster.

"Something's happening," I told her, explaining that the Calvar stopped advancing and the commanders were ordering the warriors to push forward.

We carried Halvor over to the new location for the wounded. Master Orin, Ms. Button, and Lath were helping to get everyone settled.

As I set Halvor down, blood poured from the wound on his leg. We needed to get it under control and fast. Ms. Button came over to help us. She ripped open his pants to get a better look.

"I can slow the bleeding," she said, "but we need the yellow healing powder and clean linens to get it completely stopped."

"We left them back by the shed," I said, worried for my friend's life. "I'll go back for them."

"I'm going with you," Wera quickly added.

"No!" Halvor snapped, trying to sit up to stop us. "You're not goin' by yourselves."

"Yes, we are, old man," Wera snapped back at him, "and it's not up for debate."

CHAPTER TWENTY-EIGHT

When we reached the center of the farm, the house and barn were ablaze and smoke filled the area. People ran through it, but with the smoke surrounding them, it was hard to tell if they were friend or foe.

The boxes of healing powders and rolls of linens were still sitting on the table where we'd left them. We grabbed everything we could carry and raced back. Ms. Button mixed together the needed powders, treated Halvor's wound, and wrapped it.

The smoke drifted through the trees and a few warriors yelled that someone was coming. It was Keagan, the rider I had seen the night before. He was yelling for Master Orin.

"Our reinforcements have arrived," he shouted in excitement. "We have the Calvar on the run!"

There was cheering all around. Some raised their hands hooting, others closed their eyes and smiled in prayer. Ms. Button was in tears, saying *thank you*, over and over. With the Calvar on the run, I figured the farm would be clear of danger and requested Master Orin's permission to take a couple of warriors with me to look for anyone who might be injured.

Keagan immediately volunteered to help, as did a few others who were able to walk. We set off, keeping to the perimeter to stay away from the still-burning structures at the center of the farm.

Smoke blanketed the area making it difficult to see anyone. I instructed them to spread out in a line but to stay close enough together so that we didn't accidentally walk past anyone who needed our help.

At an empty guard station, one of many that surrounded the farm, I found a couple of med packs. The wounded were carried away to be treated and the dead were marked so their bodies could be collected later.

To my surprise, when we came across any injured Calvar, the warriors didn't attempt to kill them. After they were disarmed, I was asked to treat their injuries, and they were carried away. One of the warriors explained to me that the battle was over and to kill them now would be considered dishonorable. Their fate would be decided later.

The sounds of battle faded and the flames from the fires died down. Other warriors joined in on our search for the injured. Hours passed and the moons were high above as I walked into the Yard to see if there was anything left we could use.

I walked out to the center and looked around at everything. Master Orin's home had burned down leaving only a few beams and the stone chimney standing. The barn wasn't much better off. The storage sheds were still standing and only the one on the end had been singed.

Near the well, a flicker caught my eye. Something shiny in the dirt was reflecting the light of the moons and I knelt to see what it was. There in the dirt was my bracelet from Dav. It must have fallen off when the house exploded. I picked it up and slipped it back over my wrist and held my hand to my chest.

The bodies of the dead littered the ground in all sorts of unnatural positions. Closing my eyes, I started to cry. Partly they were tears of joy but also those of sadness for the lives that had been lost. I pictured Dav's face and wished he was there.

"I need you," I whispered.

"Semmi!" Someone called my name from far away.

At first, I thought my mind was playing tricks on me, thinking that it sounded like Dav, until I heard it again. I stood trying to figure out where it was coming from.

"Dav!" I yelled back, praying I was right.

"Semmi!" came the shout again, a little louder.

This time I knew it was him. I shouted his name again and he ran out from between the sheds. He stopped for a moment as he stepped out of the shadows. I had never been so happy to see him. As soon as he spotted me near the well, he ran to me and lifted me off my feet, nearly tackling me to the ground.

Neither one of us could speak. He kissed me repeatedly and I ran my fingers over his face, feeling the dampness of tears on his cheeks.

"I'm okay," I finally whispered to him.

"I didn't think we were going to make it in time," he said. "When Dungy showed up with your note…"

"Shh," I stopped him and kissed him again. "I love you with all my heart."

"I love you too." He stood up and helped me to my feet. "You have no idea how much I missed you."

"Yes, I do." I smiled up at him and laid my head against his chest with my arms around him.

"I found someone for you."

"My dad?" I asked, and he nodded.

Dav took my hand and turned to lead me back toward where we were taking the wounded when my dad stepped out from between the sheds. He was thinner than the last time I'd seen him, and he had a bit of a beard growing. He still wore the same clothes he was in when we came here, but they were tattered and had patches sewn over the knees and elbows.

"Dad," I gasped.

"Hi sweetheart." I ran over to him and he hugged me to his chest. "Oh, I missed you." He squeezed me a little tighter. "Thank you." He turned to Dav, extending his hand to him.

The look in Dav's eyes and his hesitation to accept my dad's hand told me he didn't feel he'd done as well as he'd hoped, but my dad gripped his hand and nodded. After another squeeze, I let go and stepped back next to Dav, taking his hand.

My dad glanced down at our joined hands and over at Dav. Neither one said a thing. They stared at each other, and for a moment, I worried about what my dad thought. At last, he smiled and nodded his approval, shaking Dav's hand again.

"I'd, ah, say one of those sayings dads do when someone comes for their little girl," my dad said, looking at Dav and clearing his throat, "but, ah, I've seen you fight, so there's no point. Take good care of her. She's everything to me."

"As she is to me," Dav replied. "I give you my word."

"A little tip," my dad said, raising his eyebrows. "She's a lot like her mother"—he glanced at me then back to Dav—"and can be a little stubborn at times."

"Noticed," Dav replied with a crooked smile.

"Hey!" I snapped and tried to keep from laughing.

***

The attack on Master Orin's farm was the final battle in this short but monumental war. Dav's people had won their freedom and could now begin to rebuild their country in a way that would ensure no one like the Order of Calvar could take it away from them again.

Everywhere we went the Warriors of Baleloch were cheered and praised for their valiant efforts. They were heroes to everyone. When I went to town with Dav and my dad, people would smile and wave to us.

It was amazing to see the transformation of the villagers in such a short time: from quiet and cautious, never knowing when the Calvar would come demanding more taxes or stealing their goods, to people who were happy and in good spirits wherever you looked.

Our Norranian friends stayed to help rebuild Master Orin's home. My dad, Fye'Gor, and Halvor became good friends. Their favorite pastime was ordering around the *youngens*, as they liked to call Dav and Eamon.

I was happy to see how much my dad liked Dav, and it was no surprise when Dav came to my dad with the big question. The event was one of the happiest days of my life and Master Orin was deeply honored to be asked to preside over the ceremony.

Ms. Button and Wera decorated the farm with thousands of brightly colored flowers, lace, and ribbons. Dav looked more handsome than ever in a white version of his uniform and I never felt so beautiful in my lacy dress with a crown of white and blue flowers.

People traveled from all over to watch the event. The Warriors of Baleloch stood at attention during the ceremony and shouted in unison when we were presented for the first time as husband and wife. People whispered, "That's her" and "They're the ones who saved us" as we walked by, and the reception line was a mile long, filled with those who wanted to shake our hands.

"So, my husband," I said to Dav as we danced our first dance together, "about the house you promised to build." He raised an eyebrow as I continued my question. "Have you thought about where we should build it?"

"I was thinking next to a little pond," he answered, looking down at me from the corner of his eye.

"With a small tree in the middle?" I asked with a grin.

He smiled back and told me that the Norranians had asked us to go with them when they returned home. He knew it would make me happy. They had become such close friends that I couldn't imagine anywhere else I'd rather call home.

My dad and Lord Atwood had apparently become good friends while he served to build the new cathedral. They quickly joined together on a mission to rebuild the Hvaldi cities in the sacred lands that had been destroyed by the Calvar. Hundreds of people volunteered to assist, jumping at the opportunity to learn about the people who brought them here and rediscover their lost history.

To my surprise, dozens of scholars requested permission to join the Norranians and us when we returned to Norranheim, expressing their desire to study in the Hvaldi city. It took months to first teach them the basics of the Hvaldi language before we were able to start effectively researching all the information that had been left behind.

Slowly, we began uncovering the history of this forgotten race, a people dedicated to the study of other cultures in the pursuit of perfecting their own. They'd sought to find a harmonious balance within their society where all people had the ability to prosper through their own free will, while simultaneously benefiting society as a whole.

No longer would they be forgotten. Their knowledge would now be passed on to future generations to ensure their legacy would thrive and not perish.

With the creation of a new council by the people, a declaration was passed using the guidelines set forth by the Hvaldi, which would prevent control from ever being removed from the hands of the people. For the first time since the Calvar took control, the people were free—free to live their lives the way they saw fit. Their future was their own.

Years later, during one of my dad's frequent visits to our home, Dav asked him if he thought the people would ever have to fight for their freedom again. I waited to hear those ever-so-famous words he had said to me many times—*all great societies fall*—but to my surprise, they didn't come.

"Maybe," my dad said to Dav, patting him on the shoulder, "but not today and hopefully, not for a long time."